HIS

FATHER'S MISTRESS

His Father's Mistress

Ritu Lalit

LiFi Publications Pvt. Ltd.
New Delhi

Published by:
LiFi Publications Pvt. Ltd.
211, 2nd Floor, Gagandeep
12, Rajendra Place, New Delhi–110 008, India
Phone : (011) 2574 1000
E-mail : info@lifipublications.com
Web : www.lifipublications.com

ISBN 13: 978-93-82536-37-6 ISBN 10: 93-82536-37-X

First published in 2014

Cataloging in Publication Data—DK
[Courtesy: D.K. Agencies (P) Ltd. <docinfo@dkagencies.com>]

Lalit, Ritu, 1964–
His father's mistress / Ritu Lalit.
p. cm.
Novel.
ISBN 9789382536376

1. Indic fiction (English). I. Title.

DDC 823.92 23

Printed in India by D.K. Fine Art Press (P) Ltd., Delhi–52.

Contents

1

The Old Order Gives Way to the New

It was 6 a.m., and the haveli was just shaking off its slumber. The staff in the kitchen were getting tea and breakfast ready. The gardener was overseeing his boys who were watering the plants. The sprinklers were being set up to water the grass. The haveli was actually a group of interconnected buildings. The main building, where the old Rani of Nausar had her rooms, was the original palace of the *Maharao* of Nausar. It had once been the seat of the royal family of Nausar. When the present owner had inherited it, the haveli had been derelict. The royal family of this small province had not been able to afford its upkeep or even give it a fresh coat of paint. But the Maharao Digvijay Singh had made a series of well thought out decisions, which had led to a huge inflow of money. Neighboring homes and land had been bought and the family seat had been expanded.

The history of their family was not playing on the mind of twenty eight year old Mehak Rajoria, the youngest daughter of Maharao Digvijay Singh and the estranged wife of Somnath Rajoria. She walked down the stairs of the west wing, a comparatively recently constructed building with modern plumbing and electricity, wearing a tracksuit, hair tied up in a ponytail, and began jogging half-heartedly in the path cut through the well manicured lawn, appreciating the artistically placed flower beds. She had insisted on getting summer roses planted, she loved their fragrance, though her older sister Himani thought they lacked class. A smile lit up her impish face; she loved winning these pointless battles against her sourpuss sister. Mehak was a pretty sight, her fit body clad in a tracksuit, her hair bouncing from the ponytail, and her feet shod in a very expensive pair of jogging shoes as she turned the corner bringing her near the main gate made of heavy iron, manned by guards round the clock.

A police jeep was parked outside the gate and a couple of brown clothed policemen stood in the guard room talking to the night guard. Frowning slightly she walked towards them, raised her brow haughtily and asked, "Yes?"

The night guard quickly whispered, "Mehak Madam, his daughter."

The police officer folded his hands in a Namaste and said, "I am sorry to bring you a bad news, Madam. Maharao Digvijay Singh met with an accident."

She paled, and then said with composure, "Has he been taken to the hospital?"

"Madam, the body is being brought back to the haveli."

She stumbled as she took a step back, taking support of the wall of the guard room. Taking a deep breath, she nodded, turned and walked towards the haveli. Sitting down on the front stairs she dialed a number on her cellphone, "Adi, where are you?"

"I'm at Ma's home. What's wrong? You sound scared."

"There was an accident, daddy's dead."

"Holy shit!" was the reply. "Mehak, I am so sorry. I'll be over soon."

Daddy's dead. There she had said it, and somehow saying it made it more real. As it transpired, she did not have to do anything more. Wails started coming from inside. That must be her older sister, Himani and her mother. They loved to wail about nothing at all, most of the time. Now they had something real to wail about. She kept sitting on the stairs for a long time. Then Vishnu, her cousin came out and sat down next to her. Dull, stolid and pleasant Vishnu. His face showed nothing but concern. He was so unfailingly correct that it set her teeth on edge most of the time. Today she welcomed his concern and leaned against his shoulder.

"Are you okay?" he asked.

She nodded and smiled tiredly.

"Stay brave. He lived a good life," he added.

She made a face. A good life? An excellent life in fact! Maharao Digvijay Singh was one of the rare species of humanity, a predator. He had started his life as the twenty two year old improverished ruler of a small province called Nausar, Uttar Pradesh, in a newly independent India. India's political masters had been supported by the royalty, but that was not enough. First they had been persuaded to cede their provinces, merge into India. Privy Purses had been granted to them as compensation. But then, in one fell stroke privy purses were abolished, reducing many erstwhile nobles to utter penury, unused as they were, to work. But it did not destroy Digvijay Singh, or Devious Singh, as he was known to his friends and enemies. A man ahead of his times, he had made the most of the changing world, starting a small hotel when his fellow nobles found it demeaning to serve food and drinks to people of lower castes.

The hotel, cheekily called Royal One, had become a huge success. Then other hotels called Royal Two, Three etc. came up, arousing envy and hatred in most of his erstwhile cronies and friends. Not that he cared. In fact, he enjoyed flaunting his success and growing clout in their faces.

Mehak came to her feet as her uncle Girdhari, a slim man in his early fifties, came out still clad in his pajamas, his salt and pepper hair untidy. Unlike his brother, he was a gentle soul, a bookish man with a prominent hunch. "Uncle!" she said hugging him. He ruffled her hair, his light brown eyes filled with compassion and concern.

"Has Sumit been informed? I know he is in town."

She shook her head. She had rung up her older brother but reached his voice mail. "I tried his number, there was no reply. It was his birthday yesterday. He must have partied late into the night," she replied. "Don't worry Uncle, I will go to his apartment and wake him up."

He nodded distractedly; shoulders slumped as though the cares of the world had fallen on them. He said gently, "Eat before you do so. I have ordered Kishan to prepare breakfast before the body gets here."

She shuddered, but nodded and hugged him; he had been more of a father to her and her siblings than her own father had been. Then she walked up the marble steps. The heavy wooden doors had been flung open, and servants were moving the ornate couches and tables away to make space for the mourners. Someone was pulling away the brocade and velvet curtains. But Mehak stopped in her tracks, recoiling momentarily at the sight of her sister and mother sitting on the floor, still dressed in their nightclothes and wailing.

Her lips twitched with amusement and she fled to her room. They were really overdoing it. Her father had flaunted his mistress in his wife's face, and had ordered Himani to pack up and go back to her in-laws' home and open a *Jyotish* shop for her husband. Her brother, Sumit who shared her macabre sense of humor would have loved the scene.

She kicked off her shoes and sat down on the couch gazing at the plush room, with its walnut wood panelling and Queen Anne furniture.

Daddy's dead, and how does it affect me?

Well, no one could force her to go back to her husband for sure. No one, besides her father and Sumit, could make her do what she did not want to.

Sumit! She tried his number again, but reached his voice mail once again. It was just 7.30 a.m. She would have to go and drag him to their father's funeral. She did not relish the task. She rang up her close friend Aditya again. "Adi, I am getting dressed now. I'll drive down to Sumit's after breakfast. Meet me there in about two hours."

In a smaller haveli, which had seen better days a long time ago, Aditya Banasur put the phone down, and looked at his mother Sejal, who was sitting straight backed in her chair, staring blankly into space ever since he had broken the news to her. He paced around in the small living room, one of the four rooms that were kept open for the owner. The other rooms had been locked up two decades ago, since his father's death.

"Ma, are you okay?" Adi asked.

Sejal nodded with an effort. "I am fine."

He resumed his pacing on the worn carpet throwing an occasional glance at her. But Sejal was far away in the past, recalling her girlhood. She had been, like girls from the royal families of yore, married as a child and sent to her husband's estate on hitting puberty. Barely a week after she had arrived at her husband Paramjeet's home, he had taken her to his friend, Prince Digvijay's home. The entire province of Uttarakhand had been excited. Some traveling priest had uncovered a mammoth *shivling* 11 feet tall with the circumference of 50 feet near the River Nausar. Pammy had wanted to view it, so had Digvijay. That was the first time they had met. His hungry hawk-like eyes had rested on her for a long time, and she had recoiled whispering to Parminder, her husband, "Your friend scares me." Pammy had laughed at her girlish fear.

"I have to leave. I have to go with Mehak and get Sumit ready." Aditya gently broke his mother's reverie.

She got up with an effort and he realized with a pang that she had aged. "Adi, tell the driver to get the car ready. I would like to go to the haveli."

"Are you sure?"

"Yes," she said firmly. Digvijay was dead, but she had been a part of his life. She had hated him at first but had grown to understand and like him...maybe even love him.

After her son left she sighed, recalling the time of utter ruin. Her own husband Parminder had been brought up as a prince; he did not know how to adapt to the new India. After the privy purses were abolished, some of the royals had tried to retain their relevance in the changing country by entering politics. Sadly many were ill-prepared and had lost their deposits. Parminder had been one of them. He had taken the coward's way out, and shot himself in the head. The estates had been mortgaged to the hilt and she was left with three children and a pile of debt.

Digvijay had stepped into the breach. For that she was always grateful.

Sejal stepped into the bathroom and turned on the shower, and the scalding hot water mingled with her tears, as her memories surfaced.

Parminder shouting at Digvijay, "You are just an oily business man; you have no right to call yourself a royal! You demean us all by serving tea and food to low caste people."

After his death, she had accused Digvijay, "You killed him. You should have stopped him from fighting those elections. Everyone knew that Shastri would win. You wanted my husband to lose. I have seen the way you look at me. You wanted him dead!"

She shook her head to clear the unwelcome memories. The fact was that he had paid off Parminder's debts, married off her daughters and raised her son along with his, educated him well.

Becoming his 'second wife' was a small price to pay for all that.

✦ ✦ ✦

2

The Heir

Blissfully unaware of the fact that his fortune had changed, the only son of Digvijay Singh was deep in slumber in Flat No. 301, Royal Apartments, Nausar. He had celebrated his thirtieth birthday in the company of friends and lovely lady escorts, reaching his small apartment at four in the morning and passed out in a drunken stupor.

At eleven in the morning, the doorbell of his apartment echoed shrilly and a servant hastened to open the door. Mehak ignored the courteous greeting of the servant and marched in, her impatient heels tapping on the marbled floor. Aditya was already there, sitting on the living room couch. Waving him a sketchy greeting she asked loudly, "Has my brother woken up? I know he is here. His Cayenne is parked outside."

The servant abandoned the desire to lie to his Sahib's sister and scuttled away, sure that the Sahib would be very angry. She flung the bedroom door wide open and said loudly, "Sumit wake up. Sit up now. Adi, help me!"

Aditya, who had followed her to the door, looked around. Clothes were strewn on the floor, a chair which had probably been in the way had been kicked to one side and the owner of the flat was sprawled on the bed, mouth open, snoring heavily. He said mildly, "He looks completely out of it, Mehak. He must have come home late last night. Be gentle."

She shrugged and threw the blanket off the prone figure.

Sumit groaned and blearily opened one bloodshot eye, staring at his sister, "You were always a pest. Marriage has not improved you one bit!"

She gave an impatient sigh and stared back at him, a tall man with curly hair and gray eyes framed with ridiculously long eyelashes. He had their mother's elegant looks. Women had always fallen in love with him, but she was immune to his charms. She turned off the air conditioner and pulled open the blinds. He put a pillow on his head to block out the harsh sunlight, and mumbled, "Why are you doing this? Go find someone else to trouble."

"Wake up Sumit, daddy is dead."

That woke him up. He sat up and blinked at her, confusedly. Then he laughed loudly and fell back on his pillows. She stared at him silently.

"What killed him, apoplexy?" he asked.

"Sumit," she said reproachfully.

"Oh spare me Mehak. I haven't met him for the last couple of years. And the last time we met, we were not on good terms." That was a mild way to put it; he had nearly punched the old tyrant.

"That was seven years ago," informed his sister.

"Really? Time sure flies when daddy dearest is not around to make life hell for me."

Mehak ignored him and asked coldly, "Do you have a white kurta pajama? You have to be seen in the haveli, in mourning clothes," she asked throwing open the wardrobe. "Who does your clothes? Someone has to get you dressed. Anyway, I got you whites. Get them ironed and get dressed."

He lay there, making no effort to get up. "Cluck, cluck, cluck. Go cluck somewhere else. I can't mourn him, not in the mood."

"Not funny Sumit. Get up and be there in time." Then she sighed, and addressed Aditya, "Adi, can you please help? He has three hours."

Aditya Banasur was a sober, mild mannered person, unlike Mehak and Sumit who were bold and impetuous. He said in his soft voice, "It is okay Mehak. You go on, ahead to the haveli. I'll bring him with me."

Mehak left, admonishing them to not be late. Sumit sat up, his head swam. He shook it to clear it and asked, "How and when?"

"Early morning. He was going to the club. A truck rammed into the car, the driver fled."

"Pity, I would have rewarded the man."

Aditya looked at his foster brother thoughtfully and asked, "Did you have anything to do with that?"

"What? Don't be silly! Did you?"

Aditya looked at him shocked. Sumit persisted, "He would never have allowed Mehak to divorce that douche bag Somnath you know."

"He was good to me, Sumit. I cannot forget that when he brought me to the haveli, I was just a penniless orphan with a pile of debts."

Sumit had the grace to look ashamed, "Sorry." Then he shrugged and said in his usual sarcastic manner, "Well then, we better get to the haveli so that others don't think we killed the old coot!"

He got up, staggered a bit, but made it to the bathroom without falling. Then he threw up into the pot. Aditya turned on the television to drown out the sound. A badly made simulation of the truck accident was being aired, with the ticker tape running at the base of the screen, "Digvijay Singh prominent hotelier, owner of the Royal Hotels lost his life in a tragic road accident. He is survived by his wife, Devika Singh, son Sumit Singh and two daughters."

He shook his head as he took out his mobile. This would not do, the ladies would not like it. He rang up the news channel that was airing this news, "No, madam. The late Digvijay Singh was not a plain mister. He was of royal blood. Please use the correct form of address. He was Maharao Digvijay Singh, and is survived by Rani Devika Singh and *Yuvraj* Sumit Singh. His daughters are *Yuvrani* Himani and Yuvrani Mehak. Note it down please."

"Yes Sir. May I know who is calling?" they asked.

"Aditya Singh Banasur, Director Purchase, Royal Hotels and Resorts," he replied and disconnected the call.

He started pacing around the room, his face thoughtful. He was hungry. He went into the tiny living room, which looked as though it had been furnished with the haveli discards. A huge Regency style dining table with overstuffed chairs took over most of the space, leaving very little space for the couch and armchairs. There was hardly any space to walk around in. He opened a door that led into the kitchen.

"We need lunch for two people," he said and walked into an adjoining room, which was simply furnished with cane back chairs and a wall mirror. It probably served as a guest room. He turned away on catching sight of his own reflection in a mirror; he looked younger than his thirty years, had average height, and was willowy slender. He looked very much like his mother, who was considered a beauty; some old royals even thought that she was more beautiful than than the late Maharani Gayatri Devi. His strong jaw line and height rescued him from what might have been his 'effeminate charms'.

Actually he was not admiring himself, he was reflecting on the unexpected events of the morning. No one expected Maharao Digvijay Singh to die so soon. In his lifetime he had made a huge impact on not only the limited world of the royals, but also on the hotel industry of India. He had been a rigid, intolerant and proud man, even his enemies (and he had plenty of those) had to admit that he was one of the few royals who had made it so big in the new India. He never forgave nor forgot an insult, but he was said to be fair. A shadow crossed the young royal's pleasant face. Even his mother Sejal had said that Digvijay was fair, but had no soft feelings whatsoever. He shook his head, he did not resent their relationship, but...

He brought back himself to the present, recalling a recent incident. A man who made furniture for the hotels had fought with him, openly declaring to the whole of Nausar that he was a poisonous cobra.

He walked back to the bedroom and knocked on the bathroom door and asked, "What was that furniture man's name, the one who called Devious Singh a snake?" he yelled.

Sumit opened the door a scratch and said, "Huh?"

Adi repeated the question.

"Some Singhania or something. It was all over town. Brave man. He should have been given a *Param Veer Chakra*," replied Sumit.

Aditya shrugged. "Not brave, foolish perhaps. He did not last long."

"Yes. I would have called Devious Singh a viper, not a cobra, or maybe a python. He crushed that poor man like an insect, forcing him to retire from active business. His son took over and agreed to Devious' terms."

Yes, old Digvijay Singh had been like that, a very good friend, but an implacable enemy. He often drove the people who annoyed him, to death. He did not inspire love, but one could admire him from a distance, like a magnificent hooded cobra.

Sumit came out dressed in the newly bought white kurta pajama, his hair still wet from the shower.

"You are the Maharao now, Sumit," he said solemnly.

"God help us all then," said Sumit bitterly. "I have it from everyone I have met that I am not half the man Devious Singh was."

"You are different, definitely different. Maybe we should thank God for that."

"God does not run this place, Devious Singh used to. Now I wonder who will," said Sumit. He took a deep breath, slipped his feet into the white leather slippers the servant was holding reverentially and said, "Well what are we waiting for? Let us find out shall we?"

"Have you had breakfast?" asked Aditya.

"No."

"Let us eat first. I can't face him dead on an empty stomach," Aditya shuddered.

Sumit threw his head up and laughed, "Speak for yourself. I can't face him dead or alive, on an empty stomach. Come on, let's eat."

They sat down to eat. Aditya piled his plate up with mutton curry and rice, and Sumit averted his eyes, shuddering slightly. He served himself some porridge and spooned it without any appetite, reflecting on the last time he had met his father.

He had not thought about it for a long time. He had been young, innocent and in love. He wanted to marry her. Funny, he remembered the woman's name, her milky white breasts and those large dark eyes. But he could not remember her face. Sandhya, the up and coming actress he had met in Mumbai. He had been twenty, naive, and besotted with Sandhya of the hot kisses on sticky passionate nights, Sandhya of the huge tits, Sandhya who had a husband she had conveniently forgotten to mention.

Was it just seven years ago? It seemed like eons had passed, so much had happened. He had declared his intentions publicly. A huge mistake. Almost overnight, a sleazy tabloid found out about her, the husband had also clicked compromising photos of Sumit and her on her bed. His father had summoned him and deliberately spread the photos on the table. The man had ice in his blood. He had coldly said, "I suppose I should be happy that you like women, not men."

Sumit had stared everywhere but at the pictures, feeling betrayed. "I wanted to marry her. She never told me about a husband," he had mumbled.

Then his father had pronounced his judgment, "The woman will get what she deserves. You will go abroad for your MBA. It will be settled by the time you come back."

He had tried to argue, plead for Sandhya. He loved her. The old man had said, "She duped you. It affects me. She lied to the Maharao's son. This cannot be allowed, Sumit. The servants are packing your things and Aditya's too. Forget her."

He should have, but he had been twenty and in love. With some romantic notion in his head to take her away with him, he had flown to Mumbai to meet her. She had been destroyed by his father's goons, raped and threatened. Her producers had been forced to back off. Her husband had nearly beaten him up. He should have not gone to Mumbai. Ignorance sometimes is bliss. His father was one mean old coot.

Fuming, he had flown back home and gone straight to the old man's office, raged, called him names, feudal and monstrous being the mildest of them. His father had coldly had him thrown out of the office.

At home, his mother had blamed him instead of giving him sympathy. Angry and hurt, he had accused her of being cold-hearted. She had said coldly, "No ruler behaves like a lovesick puppy. You have shamed the family. How dare you give the press an opportunity to gossip about us?"

Himani had been quietly jubilant, revelling in his fall from grace. Mehak had sat holding his hand trying to console him. "Sumit what did you say to him? He is freaking out; he says you are not his son anymore."

"The old man has lost it," he had said, mutinously.

At a loss, he had gone to Banasur to appeal to Aditya's mother. Only Sejal Auntie could appeal to his father's softer side.

"Has everyone gone insane? You are just a boy, and you were duped," she had said. She had tried to make the old man see sense; he had to give her that! Naturally she had failed. Devious Singh listened to no one.

He had been sent to UK ostensibly for his MBA, but in truth he had been exiled, not even invited for Himani or Mehak's weddings! After he and Adi had completed their studies and returned, Aditya had been inducted into the hotels and given a set of rooms in the haveli. Sumit had been escorted to Flat No. 301, Royal Apartments, one of the flats in a modest high rise built in the town of Nausar for employees of Royal One by his father's lawyers. The lawyers informed him that he would be given an allowance and could live in the apartment, but was not welcome at the haveli. He had gone to meet his father at the Royal One office, but the old man had been implacable. He had lost it and nearly strangled him. The security had thrown him out. No one came to meet him, except Mehak. Mehak never cared about consequences.

Those who insulted his father were dealt with violently at his behest.... In that sense, Sumit was very fortunate to have stayed alive during his father's 'reign'. Now that the great Devious Singh was dead, he had left behind a huge empire, and also a lot of enemies, waiting to avenge themselves. He looked at Aditya eating while watching TV and said softly, "God help us all."

Aditya smiled, "There, they have changed the ticker tape. They finally got it right."

The ticker tape now said: 'Maharao Digvijay Singh of Nausar, the founder and owner of Royal Hotels and Luxury Resorts lost his life in a tragic road accident. He is survived by his wife, Maharani Devika Singh, son Yuvraj Sumit Singh and Yuvrani Himani and Yuvrani Mehak, his two daughters. The truck driver is still absconding.'

"Good work, buddy," said the Yuvraj, dryly. "Let us go and face the world. Your car or mine?"

"Your Cayenne. It's famous as the spoilt prince's chariot."

"Yeah, whatever."

✦ ✦ ✦

3

Waves and Ripples

It was around 8 a.m., the children of the ashram were playing a noisy game of football. Chandan asked them, "Where is the Sant?"

"At the river," said four year old Tarun. "I told him I would get the river water, but he insisted on going himself."

Chandan nodded and walked quickly towards the river ghat, his tall and muscular frame making him stand out, even though he wore the customary saffron wrap or lungi on his lower body, and his hair was cropped short, leaving a long strand called the bodi on the crown. He wore a long string of *rudraksha* beads, commonly used as a rosary around his neck, which fell on his muscular chest.

"The Maharao is dead," Chandan said to the old priest Anirudh who was on the lowest step of the ghat, filling water into his *kamandala*, a brass pot used for the rituals.

Sant Anirudh sat impassively watching the river flow by, as he evaluated the information. He filled up the vessel and stood up, "Waves and ripples. When anything huge falls into the water that is what happens. The trick is to float and not sink and drown."

Chandan ground his teeth in impatience, but did not respond, he was used to the old man talking obscurely. Anirudh straightened his shoulders and tightened his lungi and picked up the kamandala. "Has the Rani contacted us?"

"No Sant ji," replied Chandan curtly, his dislike for the widow of the dead Maharao palpable.

Anirudh smiled, "Tolerance, Chandan. She is not a thinker, that one. Besides she has had a hard life."

Chandan took away the kamandala from the old man's hand and helped him climb the stairs, "No wonder they call you Sant, Saint. You can see good in even the most obnoxious people."

The old man smiled, "Get the things ready for the final rites of the Maharao. And yes, tell Pritam to be ready. As the oldest of my disciples, you both will accompany me to the haveli."

✦

In a small office, which smelt strongly of timber wood, four men of varying ages sat in cane couches, or lounged on desks, glued to a wall mounted television. Though the office had been swept and dusted in the morning, wood shavings still lurked in forgotten corners, and sawdust, which had been dusted away slowly settling back on the two filing cabinets and the desks. The typist and peon had been told to go out and enjoy. They were smoking at the nearby cigarette kiosk while their bosses were partying inside the office. Though it was barely ten, a bottle of whisky, a plate full of fried cashew nuts and a box of sweets lay open in front of Chanchal Shastri, the General

Secretary of Loshar Samaj Party; a stout round faced bald man in his early fifties and his small group of men.

Chanchal stuffed another betel leaf into his mouth and said, with great jubilation, "Devious Singh is dead." His companions gave polite smiles as they exchanged glances, he had been repeating that for the past one hour.

Unlike his father, Kewal Shastri, the MP of Nausar, who respected the dead Maharao, Chanchal knew what the man was, a rapacious poisonous snake.

A long time back, when Kewal Shastri had embarked on his political career, he had found an influential backer in Digvijay Singh who had funded him and encouraged him to fight the elections against the prince of the neighboring state, Paramjeet Singh Banasur. Kewal Shastri had been very grateful, and had, in turn, bent rules ensuring that the state machinery deferred their working to Digvijay's ambitions. Chanchal, not moved by any finer feeling of gratefulness was always wary of the old man. Who knew? Some day, the snake would set up another person to destroy them.

"Poisoned?" asked Vikas, a party worker of Nausar Samaj Party, who had just walked in with another bottle of whisky asked.

"No, apparently it was a road accident," Chanchal said glued to the TV.

"Yeah that would work. One can't poison a snake," Vikas nodded.

They laughed as Chanchal said, "Send the peon to get chicken tikka. It's party time!"

Resham, Chanchal's twenty seven year old son, pushed his wavy hair away from his forehead as he swung his jeans clad legs, and grinned as the woman on TV had repeated for the umpteenth time that the truck driver was absconding. His close friend and aide Amol clapped a hand on his shoulder and they shared a pleased smile.

All talk stopped as old Kewal Shastri, in his late seventies walked into the room, dressed in his customary woollen kurta and pajama, with a shawl wrapped around his once strong and powerful body. He paused at the doorway and took in the scene, banged his walking stick on the wooden floor of the office and looked at his son, Chanchal with barely concealed dislike, "Why are you here, watching this on TV? Maharao Digvijay Singh was a friend of ours. You should be at the haveli." He turned his eyes away as Chanchal spat out some betel juice, his son lacked class. He turned to his grandson Resham and asked, "Resham, do you know anything about his son? Will he be a problem for us?"

Resham glanced at Amol who answered for him, "They say he does not even work with the old man. For all you know he maybe a bastard. He is quite a playboy. He comes to town, with lots of friends and girls. They stay at his apartment, have noisy parties and then leave."

Kewal snorted. He would believe that when he came to know the heir better. "Have you made friends with the heir's sisters?"

"Yes, I am friendly with both the sons-in-law. Even his older sister likes me. Why?" Chanchal said.

"Do not underestimate Royal. It has put our state on the map. Call my driver. I have to go pay my respects. And one more thing, do not celebrate; it is not the time for such things."

"What about the mistress?" Chanchal asked in a sulky tone. His father always ignored him.

Kewal said softly, "Please do not be so crude, Chanchal. She is the Rani of Banasur, not a slut. What about her?"

"Some one should, you know, befriend her. She's suffered a loss," he said with a smile.

Kewal smiled with barely veiled contempt. "Wonderful! Why don't you visit her after the cremation and console her for her loss?"

The old man left, and Chanchal stared after his father in resentment. The old man was so out of touch. He was allowing his fear and awe of the late Maharao to cloud his judgement. The late Maharao had left behind two accountants; Girdhari and Vishnu were just that! And one debauch son. Yes, he would meet the mistress. She was a beauty.

He got up from the couch, drained his glass and said, "Come; let us go to the cremation ground. My father's orders."

There was a murmur of approval from his sycophants.

✦

It was two days since the Superintendent of Police of Nausar, Altaf Malik a slim man with salt and pepper hair, had joined office. He was sitting at home today, watching television. His pleasant face, and non-threatening demeanor was misleading, something many criminals now cooling their heels in various jails of the country would vouch for. This was his third posting this year. Politicians did not like policemen like him who actually enjoyed doing their job. They found them inconvenient and sent them away to forgotten corners of the country. Like Nausar...

He watched the news unfold on the state sponsored television channel, perched on an iron box. The entire government allotted bungalow was a mess, as things were being unpacked. He had often told his wife that it was a waste of time and effort to unpack their luggage, when they would have to leave within a few months, but she never listened.

"He looks stuck up. Did he know you were coming into his town and decided he'd rather die than meet you?" Nafisa said in a sweetly sarcastic tone as she unlocked an almirah and started arranging linen in it neatly. What was with women and linen?

He polished his glasses and got off the trunk he was perched on and asked, "Do you want any help?"

She answered but his attention was drawn back to the television as images of people from different nationalities driving up the imposing driveway and disappearing inside the building, was telecast. Then there was some commotion as a burly guard caught a photographer who had crept past the guards into the haveli and shot a few photos. The photographer was evicted, but the portrait of the Maharao in his youth, surrounded by his children that he had managed to capture was aired.

"I thought the old Maharao had just one son," he wondered aloud.

Nafisa replied, "You know nothing, S.P. Sahib, the other boy is the Maharao's second wife's son. They are very close, the Yuvraj and Aditya Banasur."

"How do you know?" he asked.

She smiled naughtily and threw a pile of pillowcases at him.

He caught them and smiled back, "How?"

"If you must know, the maid I hired today was full of stories about the haveli. The old man, his stuck up wife who dabbles in black magic, their older daughter, just like the mother, the younger daughter who is wild and the debauch son. Oh yes, the second wife, and her son, too. The old king's death is the biggest news in Nausar."

"Wow! I am impressed. Thanks my love. You are the best wife I could have."

"Huh, I am the only wife you'll ever have. Who else would be able to handle your constant transfers? Now, why don't you go to work and let me sort out the linen?"

"Yeah, I guess I better go to the haveli. After all the Maharao was royalty." He started tucking his khaki shirt into his regulation trousers, and hunting for his belt.

"Nah! He was Money! Wonder who inherits? The son was estranged."

Malik looked at his wife with a frown on his face.

"Altaf, no. Stop looking for crime where there is none," she admonished him.

✦

It was 3 p.m. when Sumit and Aditya stepped out of their car and were ushered in to the haveli by the guards. Sumit looked back, it seemed as though the whole state had gathered outside the haveli.

"Well blow me down! One could easily be fooled into thinking that the old man was loved," the Yuvraj quipped.

"The princely states and privy purses were abolished, but he was still our king, Sumit," said Aditya solemnly.

"What utter rubbish! I hope for your own sake you don't believe your own tales. They have all come here to make sure we burn him down, properly."

Aditya opened his mouth to remonstrate, but Sumit had already entered the haveli. The furniture of the huge hall had been removed and the floor was covered with durries. The room smelt of havan *samagri* (a mixture of various dried herbal medicines roots and leaves) used in sacred *homa*, and incense sticks. The hall was packed with mourners who parted to allow the heir to come to the centre where his father's body, covered with white sheets lay. The family priest, Sant Anirudh, looked at Sumit and pointed at a spot next to the dead man's head, indicating that he sit down. But Sumit stopped near Chandan who was a boyhood playmate and whispered, "You look like a wrestler Chandan!"

Chandan flushed and smiled. Then Sumit caught sight of his sisters standing next to their mother. It was a long time since he had met Himani and his mother. He nodded formally at them, and looked away, the memory of the last time they had met fresh on his mind.

Aditya stepped away and went to his mother who was sitting at the back. Sejal, dressed in a white sari looked elegant and aloof. She inclined her head to acknowledge both Aditya and Sumit. Sumit gave her a small smile. Sant Anirudh cleared his throat noisily, and Sumit quickly sat down where the priest indicated, with a solemn expression on his face. While the Sant chanted mantras, he stared at the lifeless form of his father, surrounded by floral wreathes and incense sticks, looking so puny and harmless. It was hard to believe that this man had created an empire out of nothing and also caused so much havoc in their lives. Then he glanced at the photo kept next to the body. Devious Singh had grown old since their stormy last meeting. His hair was sparser and his face more lean and wrinkled. But the eyes were still the same, cold gray and menacing. They looked down that thin nose and stared at him, much like the time when he had called him a heartless and ego maniacal monster.

He turned away and caught sight of his uncle, Girdhari who was staring at the body fixedly, his face stony and eyes distant. For the first time he wondered what his uncle felt. Surely no one who lived and worked closely with Devious Singh could harbor any soft feelings for the man, but old Girdhari was devoted to the hotels. He was flanked by his sons, Vishnu and Shivam. He remembered Vishnu, a year younger than him, a solemn boy with a stolid disposition. He had been a level-headed and extremely boring boy, who had never been involved in any of the pranks Sumit routinely got Mehak and Aditya into.

He did not remember Shivam at all. What he did recall was that the boy had been sickly, subject to febrile convulsions and in and out of hospitals and sick rooms. He was tall, painfully thin with the sallow complexion of an invalid and a sulky look on his face. The prayers were coming to an end. Sant Anirudh said, "Maharao ji, please stand up and hand me the *gangajal* and the sacred ash."

Sumit suppressed a small start of surprise and complied. He watched the priest put drops of the water in his father's mouth and smear his forehead with sacred ash. Yes he was now Maharao and the fortunes and well being of the clan rested on his shoulder. A heavy burden, he reflected, flexing his shoulders as though subconsciously preparing himself for the role.

"*Ram Naam Satya Hai*!" chanted every one in the hall as the body was shifted to a palanquin specially brought for the occasion, the traditional chant which implies that the dead body no longer contains the truth (breath) which is God's name. The body bedecked with flowers, would be paraded through the town, and then taken to the cremation grounds. Keeping his eyes focused at a speck in the distance, Sumit quietly followed the body, along with his uncle and cousins. The ladies would stay back; cremations were no place for women.

His uncle came and stood next to him, "Come back to the haveli, we are having a meeting after the cremation and bath," he whispered.

Damn it, can't it wait? But he remained solemn outwardly and nodded, noticing the glances of relief his uncle and cousin exchanged. He was an adult now; he would not create difficulties for others just because he could!

After the cremation when people were dispersing, Sumit heard someone laugh coarsely and say, "He did not look so impressive. Neither does his son. Did you see him?" He turned and noted the rough looking men standing near the Nausar Samaj Party car. Party workers? Or local louts?

"I hear the new Maharao is a great fucker but not much more," said one of them, his coarse language making Sumit and Aditya wince.

There was a crude laugh as the other man said, "Show me a cunt and I'll fuck it too. What's so great about that?"

Sumit grit his teeth and got into his car. Aditya scowled. The former Maharao would have annihilated the person, but the Yuvraj had swallowed the insult. "You should have reacted. One can't go around being nice, Sumit. It shows weakness," he advised.

Sumit smiled, "And what would that achieve apart from entertaining the masses? Let's go, Aditya."

They got into Aditya's modest car and drove away from the cremation grounds, with Aditya casting sidelong glances at his companion. They had drifted apart and lost touch. Sumit's father had disapproved of anyone meeting his estranged son, and Sumit and he had agreed to stay away. There was too much at stake.

Still, the older Sumit would have fought, he had changed a lot. "That was a local boy, Amol. He is Resham Shastri's aide, and he has a bunch of shady friends." he informed Sumit. Sumit nodded silently, still lost in thought as they drove in silence. Then he broke the silence with an observation, "Did you notice Chandan, he looks like a boxer, not a priest."

"Yes. He goes on long walks and even wrestles with the Sant Anirudh's protégés. Remember Pratham and Arun?"

"Yes."

"Arun took off to the Himalayas, seems he had visions and stuff."

Sumit snorted, "He was a half wit. Visions would not have been hard to achieve."

Memories of their boyhood came to his mind. His mother would spend long boring hours in the temple conducting yagnas and he along with Adi and Mehak played volleyball and cricket with the three ashram boys. Aditiya added, "There are whispers that Chandan is not a brahman but of a lower caste."

"How the fuck does that matter?" Sumit snorted. "He was brought up as a brahman, knows the job and if he does it well, its fine."

Aditya shook his head, "That's not how it works. You've been away too long."

Outside Royal Apartments, Adi stopped the car and admonished him, "Don't be late for the family meeting, Sumit. I'll arrange to get the Cayenne driven back to you in time."

He nodded and went up to his apartment. His father's death should have thrilled him. Instead of being elated, he felt...nothing. In his lifetime, Digvijay had expected complete and unquestioning obedience, something Sumit had rebelled against. He should have been dancing with joy.

And his mother...how could someone so cold and unmaternal have given birth to three children?

The phone rang; it was his close friend and partner, Brian Underwood. "Yes Brian?" He said.

"How did it go mate?" Brian asked Sumit.

Sumit shrugged. "Well he is dead for sure."

"Oh c'mon Sumit, stop being so defensive. It is okay to be sad, he was your father."

Sumit winced, "Shit, I think I am still hungover from the party yesterday. Brian, I am considering a merger with Royal, some sort of agreement. But it will have to wait until I know what the will says. Last I knew my father and uncle were equal partners."

"Good idea!" Brian said.

"Can you get the paper work in order?" inquired Sumit.

"Sure Sumit. I am scouting for land. Now that your old man won't make trouble, we can consider India. Property is cheap in this country."

By the time he got off the phone, it was late. Consequently, he was the last to reach the haveli. An unexpected wave of nostalgia hit him as he entered the old hall, which they called the *baithak*. This was where his father conducted his business. It was unchanged, old ornate chairs were neatly arranged around the huge conference table. The ornate wooden *jhoola* still swung from its heavily carved wooden stand. Its cushioned seat was empty. Huge man-sized chessmen were lined up against the wall. Mehak, Adi and he had played hide and seek here during the summers when his father had been out of town.

He took a deep breath and glanced at the assembled family members. He had to take charge and the time was now. With assumed confidence, he strode up to the jhoola, his father's seat and sat down. Then he gazed poker faced at the assembled people.

Both his sisters were seated along with their husbands, so was his mother and aunt. His mouth twitched, *Women attending family meetings?* My father would not have liked that!

Vishnu and Girdhari were seated to his right, with Shivam standing behind him, looking wary. He smiled, "I wish we had met in better circumstances, but such is life."

Shivam whispered into Vishnu's ear, "This is a family meeting. Why is Adityaji here? *Tayiji* says his mother..." and then he realized that his voice had carried to everyone assembled in the room and subsided, flushing painfully.

Girdhari said angrily, "Shut up, boy!"

"Aditya is family!" said Mehak and Sumit simultaneously. Then they looked at each other and Mehak sat down. Sumit continued, "In the past few years, he has been more of a son to the Maharao than I have been. He has as much of a right as any of us to be here."

Vishnu remarked, "I wish you had been inducted into the business in his lifetime...."

Girdhari said, "The bankers have asked us to ratify your position in the board at the earliest. We need to have an Extraordinary General Meeting of the Board. It is not the best time for business. The economic slump has hit the hotels badly. There are other issues too. The environmental lobby is pressing hard against our resort in the hills; they are not letting construction take place. The Maharao was in discussions with the minister. There are a few pending cases, the trade union...."

Sumit stared at his uncle impassively. He knew everything. After all, his father was the founder of the hotels, they were his. So, his uncle and cousins were anxious. This was good, anxiety kept people on their toes.

"I have certain personal affairs to settle before I join the group formally. Since when have the bankers been calling the shots? It is our business, not theirs!" Sumit said.

Himani said, her voice rising dramatically. "Are you meaning to imply that my brother is not capable of filling the Maharao's shoes?"

Sumit clenched his teeth. "I wish you had left that unsaid, sister. They are worried, and rightly so. Uncle, I know that I am young, and the Maharao kept me away from the running of the hotels. But I can assure you...."

Himani's husband Rohtash Singh Puri said in sharp, doleful tones, "There could only be one Maharao. We have been orphaned."

Aditya's mouth twitched in amusement and Sumit's eyes twinkled. Mehak sniffed in disapproval. Their father had married his daughters off to further his ambitions. It was said that he had wanted a small but effective political leader elected in Halar, to perfect his plans for acquiring some land, which came under the forest belt. Rohtash's father, a local politician with some royal blood, had fit the bill. Himani was the gift bestowed on the Puri family. A bitter gift, thought Sumit. His older sister had resented the fact that she had been consigned to the backwaters of Halar, and made a nagging querulous wife. As soon as she could, she had prevailed upon Rohtash and brought him to Nausar. Their first child had been born here. Rohtash, unable to control his wife, or make an impression on his in-laws, had escaped into his obscure books of astrology and *vaastu shastra*.

Rohtash was not done as yet. "I also think that Sumit is too young and too irresponsible to take Maharao's place. Perhaps our mother, Maharani Devika should stand in his stead."

Somnath, Mehak's husband laughed openly. "Now women are going to run businesses and families, are they?" he sneered.

Maharani Devika said, her voice dripping with displeasure and pride, "I was wife to one of the strongest men in the state. I gave him a son, strong and capable. Why should I dabble in unwomanly things? He is the Maharao's son, and heir. It was his wish that his son takes his place. May I remind you that we were almost beggars when my husband founded this empire?"

"No one is questioning anything but Sumit's capability to head the business and the family, Tayiji," intervened Vishnu smoothly. "He is inexperienced, and his past history has been unstable."

Maharani Devika looked at all of them sternly and said, "My husband died this morning. You all seem to be in a great hurry to settle things immediately. He would have cut all of you into a million pieces for such effrontery." Her voice broke, but she controlled it and added, "It was the Maharao's wish that his son take his place. Nothing has changed."

There was a murmur and nervous clearing of throats at her reaction. Shivam said snidely, "But Sumit *bhaiya* has such a fast lifestyle. And that scandal..." shuddering theatrically.

Mehak snapped, "Why is this pest here? Who brought this disaster to a meeting of adults?" She looked at her aunt accusingly, "How does a child know such old tales? Listen brat, little boys like you should not be present. If they are, they should just listen and keep shut."

Shivam reddened and his lower lip trembled. Mehak stared at him glacially, noticing his discomfort with satisfaction. Girdhari tried to pacify them, "Ah, Sumit was slightly older than young Shivam at that time. Now he is a grown man. I think Sumit should get married as soon as customs allow. It will sober him down. As a matter of fact I know of a really suitable bride. She comes from the royal family of Jodhpur."

The room erupted in a babble of everyone trying to speak all at the same time. Sumit's eyes flashed with anger, the last thing he wanted was to get married, that too to some spy his family foisted on him. He sprang to his feet, wanting to protest. Aditya, who was standing by his side, pushed him down and muttered, "Don't react. Just keep shut!"

Girdhari looked at his nephew and said gently, "Don't get on your high horses, Sumit. It was your father's wish, it is in the will. He felt you were leading an irresponsible lifestyle which could ruin the hotels if you wished to join the business. He wanted you to sober down, son."

Sumit shrugged off Aditya's restraining hand and stood up. "Thank you, beloved family members. I deeply value your suggestions, but I am already engaged."

There was a startled gasp; he noted with satisfaction that his mother was too stunned to react. Then she asked, "Is she of royal blood? We have not heard of her, why?"

Sumit said coldly, "Madam, your concern is surprising. After all, you never checked on me for the last so many years. Besides, I do not believe in this royal blood business. She is from a good family, is educated and will make a good wife."

Rohtash began, "But the Maharao used to say..."

"This is 2013, not 1930. Girdhari uncle, you used to tell us that when the Maharao and you started these hotels, people laughed at you for serving low caste people. The hotels are what sustain us. She is a simple girl, and very suitable."

Aditya stood up, preempting any other comment, "Oh this is wonderful, Sumit. Congratulations! When is the party? We'd like to meet the girl."

And may I kill you, please? thought Sumit but shook hands with good grace, hugged him and whispered, "We need to get out as soon as possible."

Girdhari sighed, "Sometimes I don't understand this modern world. Where did you meet her? That Book your face, that something on the internet?"

"Daddy, it's Facebook," Shivam muttered.

"Oh yes, whatever. Sumit, this is not at all acceptable. We will see the bride, meet her family. The horoscopes have to be matched; the family has to be approved of."

"How can you talk about weddings? Your brother, my husband died today." Devika said.

"Yes. Sorry," said Girdhari. "But if Santji finds her suitable and we approve, there can be a formal engagement ceremony, and we can carry out some rituals."

Sumit shrugged, "But of course." He got up and started walking to the door.

"Sumit," called Girdhari.

"Yes uncle?" He stopped but did not turn to face them.

"Son, inform your fiancé and her family that we shall meet her after the thirteen day period. And we need to have the Extra Ordinary General Meeting within twenty eight days, it's the norm."

He nodded quietly, and clenched his jaws as he turned and left the room.

✦ ✦ ✦

4

Desperate Game Play

Sumit strode out, without a backward glance. He was in a funk. He stopped for a moment, when his glance fell on a portrait of the late Maharao. A grim smile came on his face as it occurred to him that no one had shed a single tear for the man. His smile left as soon as he caught sight of Adi and Mehak running after him. He did not need to rehash what had occurred in the baithak, especially with Mehak. He lengthened his stride, rushed out into the driveway, jumped into his car and drove away. His cell phone rang and Mehak's name flashed on the screen. Not now!

The phone buzzed, a SMS. He switched the phone off.

"No, I won't allow them to take it away from me, Royal is mine!" he said aloud.

He walked into his apartment and flung himself on a couch, his face stern. His servants were well trained and knew better than to disturb him in this mood. A servant placed a bottle, ice and soda in front of him, and vanished into the kitchen. Sumit started drinking steadily. He had polished half the whisky bottle when Aditya and Mehak landed at the apartment.

Mehak said acidly, "Well, well! The great Maharao of Nausar, the heir of Royal Hotels and Resorts is just a scared rat, hiding behind a bottle rather than facing his family."

"Get out!" he snapped.

"So Shivam, for once in his stupid life spoke the truth. There is no girl," she said, looking around. "I meant to tell you in the morning, you have horrible taste in furniture, brother dearest."

He looked at Aditya, "Why did you bring her here, Aditya?"

"You are not half the man daddy was. I think I would have made a better heir than you." Mehak said, ignoring the jibe.

"So have you come here to castrate me?" Sumit retorted.

Mehak made a disgusted sound.

He laughed coarsely and said, "You know little sister, I have always wondered why you kept on dropping in here, even when Devious Singh had forbidden everyone from keeping in touch."

"Why don't you call him daddy?"

"And what do I call you? Daddy's little spy?"

She slapped him hard on his face. He grabbed her hand and twisted it viciously, "Don't ever do this again."

She angrily hissed at him, "Okay, let's talk business. Girdhari Chacha is a fifty percent partner, and Vishnu is already securely in charge of the hotels. The way we see it, Himani and I, they own a huge slice of the property, our property. If Vishnu becomes Chairman, all is lost Sumit. In fact, Himani thinks that soon they will have the controlling shares, not us."

He stared at her with narrowed eyes, "Why did you leave your husband, Mehak?"

"We're incompatible. That is not what we are discussing." Mehak pulled her hand away.

"Really? I have reason to believe that Devious Singh was considering reducing your stake in the company if you did not make your marriage work." In fact, he had informants in the hotel staff. A paper to that effect had been drafted quite recently.

She flushed and said, "That's a lie. I was his favorite."

"Little liar! And why is Himani sucking up to me?"

Mehak smirked, "You noticed that too? She wants Rohtash to be the sole supplier of food and grains for Royal Hotels."

"No way. He'd make a hash of it," said Sumit immediately.

"Your father thought so too. She is trying to flatter you, soften you," said Aditya, who had just entered from the kitchen. "If you don't mind, I have asked your servants to serve us some dinner. It's been a long day."

"Uh huh. You both go ahead, I'm not hungry," he said, draining his glass and pouring another stiff drink.

Aditya and Mehak exchanged glances. "I think we need a bride for Sumit." Aditya said thoughtfully, "but there is so little time. Let me think if I can arrange someone."

"Sumit has a lot of women, so I think he must be spoiled for choice! Why not select one?" enquired Mehak.

Both the men looked at her scornfully.

"Alright, alright! I can see that was a bad idea," she said with a shrug.

"You're screwed," said Aditya.

"I know," he said, gulping some more whisky.

Mehak grumbled, "Daddy would have never done such a silly thing. You'll ruin everything that daddy built for us."

"Daddy built this huge pile not for us Mehak, but for his own ego. But don't worry, I have no intention of letting Girdhari Chacha and his precious sons corner more of it than they have already," Sumit snapped.

"You are a disaster, Sumit!" she persisted.

He stared at her, his eyes cold and Aditya intervened, "People, calm down. We have to think. There should be some girl who is suitable and willing to marry you."

Mehak said, "Why is it that you always get into trouble? I know no other person who is out to destroy himself like you. Such a loser!"

"Why, you bitch!" Sumit shot back.

"Coming from a debauch like you that is rich," she snapped. "What have you done for yourself? You're living off Royal Hotels. At your age, daddy was building this empire."

"You don't know anything about me and what I do. By the way, at your age, Mother was building a family." he snarled.

They glared at each other.

"People!" Aditya sighed. "Alright, it's been a long day. We all need food and drink. I am going to the kitchen to hurry the servants up. Try not to kill each other while I am away."

They glared at each other. She was biting the inside of her cheek, like she always did as a little girl. His face softened and he smiled. She had always been a headstrong brat. "Scared now that daddy's dead, brat?"

Her face crumpled. "Everyone hates us Sumit. Daddy always knew what to do. He was harsh, but he would never let anyone harm us."

He sighed. Thankfully, he had learnt to live without the old man. "Don't be so scared. Find me a girl and I will marry her within a week, customs can take a hike."

She smiled weakly. "I wish it was that simple."

"It is. And, Mehak, I am not living off Royal Hotels, and I'm not such a debauch either."

Aditya was back with two servants carrying trays with food and a decanter of whisky, ice and glasses. "You are wonderful, Adi," said Sumit. "I don't know what I would do without you."

"Oh you would manage," he said airily. "You have done so for the last decade. If nothing else works, poof! You vanish for months at a stretch!"

Sumit smiled enigmatically. The first time he had left Nausar was just after Aditya had been inducted into the hotels. Smarting with anger and resentment, he had gone back to the UK and then France. Together with a college friend, Brian Underwood, he had bought a vineyard. They had then traveled all over Europe selling their wine to cafes and taverns. Those five years had been exciting and eventful, traveling across the length and breadth of Europe, creating a market for his brand, Coronet Wines.

Then he came back to Nausar, just to needle the old man, party, create a huge noise. To his extreme frustration, the old Maharao never reacted. He carried on as if his son was dead. Sumit left and swore that he would never come back, but he returned, always. Nausar was in his blood. So was Royal, his heritage.

"Are you going to run away again?" Mehak asked.

"He is dead now; there is no one to run away from anymore," replied Sumit.

"I am glad," she said tiredly. They quietly sat down at the dining table, and ate. They had not finished the meal when Aditya's cell phone rang.

"Good Evening, Mr. Bhatia. Thank you for your condolences. I will convey it to the family. Mr. Bhatia, can you meet me at office around 11 a.m.? It is something personal."

When he got off the phone, he announced with a huge grin, "Children, problem solved."

"What do you mean?" Sumit asked.

"That was Shankar Bhatia, a vendor. He supplies all our soft furnishings. Mr. Bhatia has a young daughter, unmarried and very beautiful. She is going to marry the heir of Royal Hotels. I am going to give him the good news tomorrow."

Mehak said scornfully, "But he is just a cloth merchant."

Aditya said, "Sumit, thank God you did not say that your bride was of royal blood."

"I don't like stuffy women," Sumit said.

"Whatever. A royal bride would be hard to manage at such a short notice. This man owns six cloth mills. If the Maharao is pleased, the man will own six more. It is not often that luck smiles on a man who has marriageable daughters."

"What if he refuses?" asked Sumit.

Mehak looked at him shocked. "Refuse the Yuvraj's proposal? A mere cloth merchant? He would not dare!"

Sumit shrugged. Sometimes he felt as though his family lived in a time warp. "If it works..." he said.

Shankar Bhatia was dazzled by the proposal; refusing such a wonderful offer did not occur to him. He even dared to dream of a brilliant future for his younger daughter and son. All he managed to say was, "Please request the Maharao to do us the honor of visiting our home in the evening to meet the family."

"Meet him, Sumit and be nice," Adi told him on the phone later.

"I can't do it alone. Why don't you come with me?"

Adi said, "I would, but Ma wants me at home. That politician Chanchal Shastri is visiting her. Ma finds him uncomfortable."

"Is Sejal Auntie joining politics?" Sumit laughed.

"Very funny, Sumit. Take Mehak with you. They would appreciate it."

The next evening, Sumit drove down to the haveli to pick up Mehak. Vishnu was pacing around in the lobby. He looked up as the front door opened, quickly disconnecting the call and putting a file down. "Hi Sumit, it's really good to see you," he said with a pleased smile. "You really should think about moving back here."

Sumit smiled formally and looked around. The furniture of the lobby had changed. It was not the Empire furniture his mother favored. Someone had replaced it with Swiss style armchairs in walnut wood, with small tables. It made this small room look spacious. "I'll think about it," he said with a formal smile, shaking his hand.

"No, I mean it, seriously. It would be like old times again, the entire family together."

Sumit studied his face, pleasant and open. His eyes were sincere and frankly welcoming. "Yes, it would be," he said softly, his own smile more open and genuine.

Vishnu glanced at someone behind Sumit's shoulder, a slight frown marring his pleasant expression, "Please excuse me," he said abruptly and walked off.

Sumit turned and came face to face with Devika and Himani. "What did he want?" asked Himani.

"To say hello," Sumit replied, "Something you don't think necessary."

"Whatever," she said with a shrug, sitting down on an armchair. "Really Sumit, you should have considered your status and family background before getting engaged to a commoner. Mother is so upset."

Himani resembled their father the most; she was tall, slim with thin lips that barely covered her wide teeth. In Digvijay they gave the appearance of a hunter, but in Himani, they gave the impression of rampant discontent and greed, something that her beady black eyes accentuated.

He drew a deep breath, forcing himself to be calm, "Himani, my status is that of an outcast, so I am marrying above myself."

Himani snorted, "Don't be stupid! You are the Maharao. Rohtash is consulting the leading astrologers for the correct date of your coronation."

"Really? I thought he would be consulting these astrologers on how and when to get our mother coronated."

"Sumit!" said their mother glacially. "Really, this is so dreadfully common! Rohtash has immense affection for me."

"How lucky for you, Madam," murmured Sumit. Mehak dressed sedately in a sari joined them and said, "Hello, Sumit. Let's go, we're getting late."

He turned and walked out, angrily, followed by Mehak. "You should have been ready. I don't want to interact with those two any more than I have to."

"Get used to it. As Maharao, you will interact with them on a daily basis." She got into the car and gave the driver the address of the Bhatia residence.

"Not if I can help it," he said slamming the car door.

"Stop being childish, Sumit. Make this work, for all our sakes. As it is Shivam is going around saying that there is no girl. He is his mother's mouthpiece. We do not need such gossip."

"I am not a child Mehak," he said. "Why are all the women in my family such nags?"

"And what do you know about women? I mean normal women, not the Page 3 types you sleep with!"

Angry, he turned his face away and looked out of the window.

She continued, "I have made some discrete enquiries. The girl is lovely, but dumb. She will definitely make a long suffering wife. God knows, you need one!"

"Sounds boring," he said, trying to be polite.

"I know, but then the exciting types may have husbands and infants tucked away somewhere. We may end up having smutty photos and MMSs of yours circulating all around," she said waspishly. "Behave, Sumit. Don't ruin this like the rest of your life."

Sumit gritted his teeth and maintained a cold silence. He was still fuming when they reached the Bhatia house. He stayed for precisely fifteen minutes, formally proposed and once the proposal was formally accepted, he got up to leave. It never occurred to him to meet the girl he had proposed to. His behavior was very proper, aloof and cold. Mehak smiled and tried to strike up a polite conversation with their host and hostess, but he cast an awful chill on the visit. She rose with him and left.

✦ ✦ ✦

5

The Proposal

An hour before Sumit Singh Nausar's visit, Vaishali the seventeen year old younger daughter of Shankar Bhatia climbed into the house from the living room window, hoping to avoid her mother and sister, who, in her opinion were horribly shrieky, something she did not need at the current moment. Her small perfectly angular face had a huge bruise on one side, and her eye was swollen shut. She also had the beginning of a huge headache. What started off as a simple game of hockey had turned disastrous. Her younger brother Sidharth or Sid, as he was called, had swung his hockey stick wildly and taken a swipe at her face. It was a hockey stick, not a damn cricket bat!

All she needed was a bit of luck. She would creep into her room, and hopefully not meet her mother till the next day, when the swelling would have subsided.

Sadly, her luck was out. The formal living room, which was normally unused, had occupants. Her mother, Shrishti was supervising two maids who were cleaning it up. The Persian carpet had been taken out of storage and was being laid on the marble floor. The couches were being vaccummed and the entire place was being dusted. Shrishti took one look at her daughter and shrieked, "Just look at this girl. How many times have I told you not to play with those horrible boys?"

She winced. Ma screeched again, "Go wash your face, and clean up. There are guests coming over."

Vaishali meekly trotted up to her bathroom with her mother following her. She caught sight of her face in the mirror and grimaced painfully, stifling a groan. She looked horrible. She rinsed her face, staring at the muddy water streaked with blood fearfully. In a show of bravado, she attempted a smile and said, "Its okay Ma, it looks worse than it feels."

She caught sight of the expression on her mother's face in the bathroom mirror and ducked but could not avoid the smack her irate parent landed on her bony back.

"Ow Ma, that hurt," she complained.

Sidharth, her fourteen year old brother, stood at the bathroom door, a cheeky grin on his face. He closely resembled Vaishali, had similar wavy hair cropped short and had sharp features. His jeans was torn in two places and stained with grass and sweat. They looked like their mother, but were skinny and dark skinned. Right now, he was grinning goofily, relieved that his sister was okay. Shrishti turned, saw him at the door and remarked coldly "What are you standing here grinning like an oaf for? Shoo!"

He shooed and Vaishali tried to follow suit. The inevitable comparisons started "Why can't you be like Pallavi? You are a disaster, Vaishali. I did my best, but you are so difficult. She would have never..."

Vaishali brushed past her, opened the window of her bedroom, jumped from the balcony onto the ledge and into the lawn. Shrishti looked for something to vent her temper on, and caught sight of the hapless maid and snapped, "What are you doing? Go get the special tea set out, the one Sahib got from England recently."

Out in the lawn, Vaishali heaved a sigh of relief and then muttered to herself, "Pallavi this, Pallavi that! That stupid cow can never do anything in life but sit and giggle with her silly friends and watch horrible TV soaps. I am so glad I did not go to a stupid girls' school like her."

"Vaish!" Sid called from his balcony.

"Damn you Sid!" she said squinting up at her brother, "Don't you know the difference between a ball and a head? It hurts! And it has set Ma off again."

"Forget that. You know who the guests are? They're coming to 'see' Pallavi di. She's getting married," he said climbing on to the window ledge.

"No! Papa agreed to get her married to that stupid Raman."

"Swear! *Ma Kasam*! I heard Papa tell Ma that it is a brilliant match."

"Come down and tell me more!" Vaish said. He hesitated. She grabbed the ledge and hauled herself up, and then pushed him down.

She jumped down after him and observed, "It's not that high, you scaredy poke. You are the world's most horrible hockey player, and a wuss!"

"Am not!"

"Are too!" She shook her head, it hurt and one eye was swollen shut, "You are sure that is what you heard?"

"Yeah! The parents are getting her married off. Then they'll get rid of you. I will be the lord and master of this house!" he said grinning evilly.

Vaish snorted in disbelief, "They can't get her married off, not if she refuses. And I am not getting married just yet."

"Ma says you're so dark and skinny, she will have problems getting you married."

Vaish was just going to say something rude when they heard a shriek, "Oh my God, Vaishali! What happened to your face?"

Vaish grinned and turned her swollen side towards her older sister, "My new make up, like it?"

"You are sixteen years old, and you behave like one of those hooligans playing cricket on the road."

"I am seventeen, and it was hockey," Vaish said and stuck out her tongue.

"How rude! Learn some manners. Nice girls don't behave like this."

"Nice! I am not nice!" snarled Vaishali. "You and your girl friends are nice. Did they put something into the water cooler of your stuck up school to make you all this giggly, shrieky excuse for a human being? Nice, huh!"

Pallavi opened her mouth to say something scathing, when Sid said sweetly, "You're getting married. Your husband and in-laws are coming to see you."

Pallavi stared at them shocked. They giggled and started singing, "You're getting married, you're getting married."

She turned and ran into the house.

"Thanks Sid," said Vaish as they high fived in triumph.

"Forgiven for your face?"

"You're forgiven," she said happily. "Come, let's go in and watch the cat freak out."

They giggled and crept in.

"No Papa," Pallavi was pleading.

Shankar was in no mood to listen, "I will not have such disobedience. They proposed and I accepted. Go and get dressed."

"Papa but Raman..."

He shouted angrily, "If I hear that boy's name once more from your mouth..." and raised his hand to slap her. She broke into tears and fled to her room.

He turned to Vaishali and said, "You! Go help your sister dress up."

Surprised, Vaishali opened her mouth to reply, but changed her mind as she saw the grim expression on his face. She quietly nodded and made her way to her sister's room. It seemed like a tsunami had struck it. Pallavi had opened her wardrobe and was throwing out all her clothes. Pallavi hurled a chiffon sari (still on its hanger) at her and she ducked. "Cool down Pallavi Di."

Pallavi burst into sobs as she sat down on the dresser with her back to the mirror.

The sisters had never been close, but Vaish experienced a pang of sympathy. She shifted a green silk dress on the bed and sat down, saying softly, "They'll be here soon, Pallavi Di."

Pallavi raised her face, her lovely eyes welling up with tears. She shrugged and said with a strained smile, "You're right. Which dress should I wear?"

"I don't know. What about your new orange salwar kameez? It will go so well with your fair skin."

"Okay," she said indifferently, fishing it out of the pile of clothes on the bed and marched into the bathroom to change.

Vaishali stood there for a while. The room was normally very girly, neat and clean, with its chintzy curtains and teddy bears and cutesy cushions. Carefully avoiding the clothes strewn on the floor, she switched on her MP3 player, and walked into the living room while inserting earphones into an ear. Her mother said abruptly, "Don't come out while we have company, understand?"

She stopped in surprise and then paled as she understood. Nodding, she turned away and walked into her room, slamming the door shut. "As if I can compete with Pallavi Di," she thought acidly. The door opened after a few minutes. Pallavi came in hesitantly, all dressed up. Vaishali removed the earphones in surprise. Her older sister never sought out her company.

"Vaish, I don't want to marry this man."

"So refuse."

"How can I? I am not brave like you. Raman is so heartbroken."

"Why?"

Then she launched into praises for her boyfriend. Vaishali tuned off after a while, she thought Raman was boring, and easily bullied by her sister. After an hour or so, Sid came into the room wolfing down a cutlet and informed them, "You know, two people came, a man and a woman, they talked with the parents for some time and left, they did not even have the cutlets. Want one? They're tasty."

Pallavi looked shocked. "I don't believe this! Just who does he think he is?"

Affronted, she stomped into the living room followed by her interested siblings, "Papa, I will not marry this man. If you force me, I'll kill myself."

Shrishti said, "Hush girl! He is a prince, the owner of Royal Hotels. You will be a princess, a queen!"

"I don't care; he did not even meet me. Mama, Please," she wailed.

"Maybe he is traditional, Pallavi. In our times too many couples never met before the wedding. Parents approved of the match. We had no say," her mother pleaded.

"You always said Raman was the best for me. He understands and loves me, Papa."

"The yuvraj must have been busy," said Shankar, lamely.

"Too busy to meet the bride he wants to marry?" she asked.

"He maybe shy," suggested Sid.

"Oh shut up pest!" Pallavi hissed.

"What kind of man does that, you know, in this day and age? What kind of man does not meet his bride?" she asked.

Their mother tried to reason with her, "Pallavi, listen to me. I know we agreed to your match with Raman. But consider this, you are so beautiful. You were born to be a Princess. This prince will fall in love with you as soon as he sees you."

"He is rich and royal," observed Vaishali. "Your poor Raman never stood a chance. His father died yesterday, it was on TV."

"Whose father, Raman's?" Pallavi sniffled.

"No, bimbo! Not your precious Raman's. This Royal, this prince what'shisname's!" she said scornfully, her mind racing. Why did this prince have to marry in a tearing hurry? His father had died just yesterday. And why Pallavi? That man could get any girl he wanted....

"How did he hear about our Pallavi?" she asked.

"Aditya Singh Banasur, Director Purchase of Royal brought this proposal. He saw Pallavi at the Diwali function at Royal."

"Oh I see." That made sense.

"I think I will drink poison. I'd rather be dead," said Pallavi in between sobs.

"And where will you get poison?" asked Sid interestedly.

"I hate you brat!" she said and threw herself on the couch, crying in real earnest.

Overwhelmed by all the histrionics, Shankar Bhatia turned to his wife and said, "Shrishti, tell your daughter that she has to behave herself. Our business depends on Royal Hotels. I cannot refuse the proposal."

Then, like other men subjected to feminine tears, he beat a hasty retreat. They heard the revving of the car engine and concluded that Shankar Bhatia had fled the scene.

"I will kill myself," repeated Pallavi as sobs shook her prone figure. Her siblings and mother did not react.

"I'll elope with Raman," she said.

That got their attention.

"Wow!" said Vaishali, impressed. "I did not know you had it in you!"

"I am twenty years old and I can!"

"Where will you go?" asked Sid.

"Don't you dare!" threatened their mother.

Vaishali handed her some tissue to wipe her face.

"It did not even occur to him to see me. Why doesn't he marry Vaishali?"

"Oh rubbish! Who will even notice her after seeing you?" The unconsciously scornful note in Shrishti's voice stung Vaish, who winced. Her sister and mother were beauties. They were about 5'3", fair, with lovely regular features, huge eyes and long silky hair. Vaishali was impossibly tall, 5'8" in her socks, heavily tanned and skinny. Full of nervous energy, she would be out playing games which she excelled at while her mother and sister were gentler and very feminine. She had never paid much attention to her appearance, had cut her hair so short once that her mother had threatened to kill her. Now it was around shoulder length gathered together in an untidy ponytail.

"I will graduate, travel abroad and have adventures while you have babies," she declared, "My future, dear sister, does not depend upon my looks."

Pallavi got up, walked to her room and locked it. The entire drama had given her a huge appetite so Vaishali went to the kitchen, piled a plate with cutlets, which she took to her room, ate as she watched some television and then slept.

✦ ✦ ✦

6

Blunder

Away from the world of proposals and battles for control, a scrawny young man named Yashpal jumped out of the truck he had hitched a ride on. He was about nineteen years old, wore a pair of cheap denims and a fake Lacoste tee shirt. His short cropped hair smelt strongly of *Jabakusum* oil. He carried a heavy bag on his shoulder, which he clung on to as though his life depended on it. He had traveled an entire day and night to reach his village, using less frequented and deserted paths. It was a journey of just five hours by road, but he had been warned about getting caught. Already, a smile of anticipation grew on his face. It was an hour before dawn, and she would come to the village hand pump to take her bath. He hoped she wouldn't be late. If he was caught talking to her, her brothers would kill them both.

She was already there, a young girl scarcely fifteen, his Bala. He did not care what the Sarpanch said. So what if they belonged to the same village? That did not make them brother and sister. He smiled as he watched her fill her bucket, keeping a wary eye for predators, beast and human. Then his smile broadened as she poured cold water over herself, her nipples stiffening under the thin shirt she was wearing. He watched her for a while and then crept behind her and whispered softly, "Bala."

She gasped and whirled around. Smiling coyly as she donned a dry shirt, fastened her lehnga shivering slightly. "Yashpal, what are you doing here? If anyone sees you, they will beat you up, or worse!"

"Shhh! Don't make a sound," he said dragging her behind the banyan tree. "Come with me. We can go to town, and get married. In the towns, no one cares about stupid things like caste and gotra."

"The Sarpanch says that since we have the same gotra, we are brother and sister. This cannot be," she said resignedly.

"Do you still love me or are you lusting after that idiot sarpanch?" he taunted.

"Of course not! I love and trust you," she whispered back indignantly.

"What that pompous bastard says does not matter anymore. See, I have money, lots of money. We will go far away and no one will find us there."

He opened his bag and took out a polybag full of currency notes.

Bala stared at them, and then backed away, "Have you robbed your Sahib? Are the police after you?"

"Don't ask stupid questions. A man has to take some risks. I did some work for my Sahib, dangerous work. He will protect me. Are you coming with me?"

She stared at the money fearfully. The pink thousand rupee notes looked like as though they were smeared with blood. "Leave this here, hide it," she ordered.

"Why?" he asked.

"It is scary. Hide the money!"

"Stupid girl! The train leaves in 20 minutes."

"So let us hurry and hide the money," she insisted.

They quietly crept into an abandoned field and dug a deep hole. He took out some money, and wrapped the rest in the polybag which she tied with a strip of cloth. Then both of them buried it. Yashpal kept grumbling, "I never want to come back to this village. I only came for you. Now I will have to return for the money." She kept her head down and silently worked. Once the money was hidden, she covered the freshly dug earth with some stones.

They heard the train chugging to a stop. "Stop that, you silly woman. Are you coming?" he said getting up impatiently. She nodded.

He faced her solemnly and added, "You can never meet your family if you come with me."

She shivered partly in fear and partly in excitement; she knew that, they both would be killed if they went against their community and their village. She nodded. He grinned, his good humor restored. They ran through the fields as the train slowly left the station, and jumped in before it sped up. Once they were far away from the village, he grew bolder. "My sahib is a big man. He trusts me, and will pay well and even give us a good place to live in. Just you wait and see," he bragged.

They reached the town in a few hours, where he took her to the temple where they exchanged garlands. After that, he took his bride to the garage where he worked. There they met another man, much older.

"Namaste, Bikram bhaiya," said Yashpal.

The man looked at him and frowned, "Why have you come back, Yashpal? Sahib told you not to come here at least for a year or two."

"I got married. I came for Sahib's blessings. This is my bride." Yashpal said. She executed a shy namaste.

The older man did not even look at her. He spat in disgust and grumbled, "You fool. Go back where you came from."

Yashpal insisted, "I have to meet Sahib. He said he would give me more money once the job was done."

"Does Sahib know you are here?" asked the man.

"I called him," said Yashpal.

The man stared at him horrified. Then he shook his head sadly, "You bloody fool! You idiot!" and went into the office and picked up the receiver of the telephone. They watched him dial a number. Bala asked Yashpal, "What has happened? Have you done something wrong?"

Yashpal pouted like a little boy. "This is not fair. The sahib said he would give me the balance money after the job."

Bikram returned in ten minutes looking grim, "I talked to Sahib. He is busy right now, but says you have to send the girl back to the village by the next bus or train and come to the cremation grounds near the Shiv temple in the evening. Sahib will meet you there."

Yashpal smiled, satisfied. He assured the other man, "Bhaiya I will go immediately after meeting Sahib. Come Bala."

"Where will I go?" she asked angrily, once they were out of earshot. "I can't go back."

"Oh come on, we have to celebrate. We just got married! We'll go to my room, after all it is our wedding day," he smiled naughtily. "Then we will go to the cremation grounds. You hide until I meet Sahib and get more money. Then we will go far away, to Kashmir. Have you ever seen snow?"

"Like in the movies?" she asked, delighted.

"Yes."

They consummated their marriage with gusto. In the evening they took a rickshaw to the cremation ground. The cremation ground was located outside the town of Nausar, on the banks of the river. A long time ago, Sant Anirudh had discovered a mammoth shivling at the banks of the river. Over the years, a grand temple had been built for the shivling. An ashram had also been built for orphan boys. Slightly away from these two, a small temple to *Yama*, the God of Death had been built. It was normally deserted; living people desire to have no truck with death. Today there was a group of people outside who had come to cremate a relative. Yashpal stopped the rickshaw under a peepul tree and said, "Stay with those people. I will come for you after I meet Sahib."

She nodded and dogged those people, hanging around them while they performed the last rites. Soon they started giving her curious glances, so she found a rudhraksha tree and sat down under it. It seemed to her that she waited for a long time. Darkness fell and bells tolled in the nearby Shiv temple, the evening prayers were conducted. She curled into a ball and dozed off, waking up with a start to the sounds of running feet. She came to her feet as she heard Yashpal's cry of fear, "Sahib, please. Please, Sahib, mercy. I have just got married."

"I told you to disappear, Yashpal." The voice was high pitched and cold.

"Mercy Sahib," he pleaded. "I'll leave. I'll never ask for money, I won't come back, I promise." She peered from behind the tree and caught sight of him, running, and the front of his shirt dark with blood. She bit back a scream as a man said coldly, "The son of a whore, fucking blackmailer, finish him!"

She took a step forward, her heart pounding a crazy beat. She opened her mouth to scream but no sound came out. Yashpal looked towards her and flung a hand out as though warning her to stay away, screaming "No!"

There was a metallic sound of a pistol shot and he stumbled forward and fell down in a crumpled heap.

"Throw him into the pyre," said the Sahib. She stared at him dazed. He looked so pleasant, so decent that it surprised her. "Pay the caretaker to forget what he just saw," he ordered.

Bala fell down to her knees, dazed as she realized that she was alone and friendless. Then her instinct to survive kicked in. She quickly crawled farther into the trees, hoping to escape notice, stopping as she stumbled against a leg of someone who had been urinating.

The man stared at her, and she shrank back. He put his finger to his mouth. She nodded. He indicated that she keep hiding there and walked back at a slow pace. She stared after him, shivering and in no condition to flee further.

The voices of the men faded and she heard a car start. She breathed a shuddering sigh of relief and gave in to tears. He came back and asked, "Who are you?"

"His wife Sahib," she said. "I won't say anything, I don't know anything. It was too dark to see. Let me go."

The man cursed fluently and said, "He had been told to send you home!"

She just shook her head gibbering with fright, her small body trembling. He scratched his head and then said, "His wife, you said? So your brothers will come to take you?"

"No Sahib, we got married today. No one knows about our marriage."

He thought for a while and then nodded, arriving at a decision, "Come with me."

She hesitated, but could not think of anything better to do. She stumbled after him, sobbing softly. He took her to a small shack at the end of the cremation ground, opened the door and said, "Stay here." In the dim light of the bulb in the shack she could make out that he was one of the men from the garage.

She stepped into the small dingy room lit up by a naked bulb hanging from a cobweb encrusted wire. It was dirty, its floor unswept. A wooden cot lay in the centre and a small kerosene stove with a blackened pan sat in one corner. She was still looking around when he locked the door behind her and walked away. Alone, she sat down on the floor dazed, reliving the horror she had witnessed. She lost track of time. After what seemed to her like a long time later, she shook her head, Yashpal gave his life trying to hide her. She had to survive. There were some lumpy smelly mattresses piled up on the floor against the wall. She chose a thick one, spread it on the floor and lay down.

Sleep was impossible but she kept lying there, Yashpal's last moments playing and replaying in her mind. The door opened sometime in the night, a man entered silently. She lay there quietly. His breath smelt of cheap alcohol, he pulled up her lehenga and tore off her underwear and blouse, and pushed himself inside her without any tenderness. She lay there still like a corpse. It gave her some sort of comfort, anything was better than being alone to relive the events of the night. He got up after he was done with her, cursing coarsely. "It's like taking a dead body." He kicked her in disgust and went out. She lay there, tears oozing out of the corners of her eyes. Another man came in and started unzipping his trousers. That galvanized her into action. She ran past him to the door, before he could grab her, straight towards the river. Others joined him, predators all. She made for the river, if she did not escape, she could just jump in.

A huge man dressed in the saffron robes of a priest pulled her into the shadows and put a finger to his lips. She fell to her knees. He pulled her behind a rudraksha tree. She backed away in fright, her arms going up to cover her nakedness. He took off the shawl that covered his upper body and dropped it on her, concealing her completely. He sat down next to her, crosslegged, with his rudraksha string in his hand as though in prayer. The men came towards him, hesitated and then left, perhaps intimidated by his size or his priest's garb. After a long time, he tapped her. She sat up and covered her nakedness with his shawl. They were near the ghat. To her left was an imposing Shiv temple. He nodded to her and got up, walking away. She quickly came to her feet and followed him. He went past the temple to a small building built on its side and knocked at a door. An old withered man opened the door, stared at her taking in her really battered appearance, and then said, "Come in, daughter. You are safe here."

✦ ✦ ✦

7

The Counter Proposal

"Vaishali! Vaishali! Wake up girl!" Her mother's panicky voice seemed to come from very far away.

"Huh! What happened?" she mumbled blearily, opening her good eye and shut it again.

Her mother shook her sharply and said, "Wake up, now!"

She checked the time on her alarm clock. It was about seven in the morning. "What happened?" She caught sight of her father standing anxiously at her door, staring at her. She sat up in alarm. "Is everything alright?"

"Did Pallavi say anything last night? Do you know where she is?" Shrishti asked.

Vaishali shook her head, her injured eye opened slightly. She squinted at her mother, and shook her head. "She went into her room and locked it. But you were there."

Her parents exchanged looks. She looked at them, dimly feeling that they really looked pale and old, their faces lined with furrows. She threw off her blanket and swung her feet off the bed.

"What happened to Pallavi di, Ma? Papa?" she asked. They did not reply, just exchanged fearful glances.

Her mother said softly, "If it was any other family – any other. Why did you accept the proposal?" Tears were running down her face unchecked.

"How could I have refused?" whispered her father, looking old and defeated.

She jumped out of bed and ran barefooted into Pallavi's room. Her bed was not slept in and clothes she had thrown around last night were still strewn all over it. Sid was standing by the window, looking towards their driveway. He whispered to her, "She ran away. Ma rang up Raman's house. He is not there either. Papa is furious."

Vaishali giggled, "I never knew she was that brave. That Raman is a pushover. Pallavi di must have bullied him." She inspected the strewn clothes and added, "She took all her new clothes."

Her mother called, "Vaishali, go take a bath, beta. We have to go out."

"Ma, I have college," she yelled back.

"No college today. Get dressed," returned the firm reply.

She washed, slipped into her jeans and sweatshirt and came down to the dining table. The air was thick with tension. She slipped into a chair next to Sid and waggled an eyebrow enquiringly. Sid looked down at his breakfast, avoiding her. She poured some cornflakes into her bowl.

Shankar cleared his throat and asked, "Vaishali, do you love your family?"

"Of course Papa," she poured some milk into her bowl.

"Would you like to see Sidharth live, be successful? Would you like your father to live long?"

She stopped and eyed him apprehensively, her appetite gone.

"Then you will get married to Sumit Singh, instead of your sister."

Cornered, she turned to her mother, to appeal, "You can't do this to me. I want to study," she blurted. "I am too young for marriage."

"Shrishti, get her ready. We have just about ten days," he said, ignoring her.

She pleaded, "Get Pallavi di back. Papa, you said we have ten days. Get her back."

When there was no response, she tried again, "Can't we ring them up and say she has gone? They can look for another bride."

He did not reply. She stared at her cereal, then jumped up and made for the door. She had to flee. She had to get in touch with relatives. Maybe they would be able to make her parents see sense.

Her father grabbed her before she could reach the door and hauled her by her sweatshirt to the nearest room, which was Pallavi's and made her sit on the bed, and shut the door.

"Papa, please. No Papa!"

"Listen to me carefully Vaishali. These people are proud, very proud. And they are powerful and dangerous. If they find out that your silly sister ran away, they will consider it an insult. They will destroy me. And I won't be the first person they would have destroyed. They have money and power. I am just a simple cloth manufacturer."

"You should not have said yes!" she accused him.

He snorted derisively. "You are just a kid, you will not understand."

"Yes, I am a kid, I am not ready for marriage," she pleaded, grasping at straws. "Papa, I don't want to marry, not just now. I want to study."

"Vaishali!" he replied as though goaded. "I wish you did not have to. When they find out, they'll hunt your silly sister out from any corner of this earth and kill her. You have heard about honor killing haven't you? They may kill us all. They can."

All the fight went out of her. She looked resentfully at her father suddenly seeing him for a weak man, who would use her sister and her to further his own success.

"Think about Sid and us, Vaishali."

She sat there quietly feeling like a trapped animal. The door opened and her mother came in, a huge smile plastered on her face, "We have to first fix your face and get you pretty things. Your bridegroom will love you."

"Close the door, Shrishti. The servants..."

She shut the door and sat down next to Vaishali and ran her fingers through her curls, "I wish you had not cut them so short."

Her father said, "Maybe we can say Pallavi has some serious disease. That is why you are to marry him in her place."

She looked around the extremely feminine room, shimmery clothes strewn all over, and soft toys on every surface, the chintzy curtains and soft pastel furnishings. She threw a pink sari blouse, embellished with crystals on the floor and kicked it. "Damn the bitch! I hate her," she sobbed bitterly.

A sullen faced Vaishali accompanied by her mother to a doctor, for treatment of her bruise. As soon as that was done, Shrishti whisked to a beauty parlor for tan removal. "I feel like an animal, getting fattened for slaughter," she complained bitterly, when she came home in the evening.

"You smell girly," Sid informed her.

She looked around her room, a stark contrast to her sister's room. It had a huge desk with a desktop computer. A dart board hung on a wall. A mirror with a functional dresser graced the other wall. An excercise ball and a beanbag served as chairs. She sat down on the excercise ball and Sid sat down on the beanbag. "Vaish what are you going to do?"

"Get married I guess," she said in a defeated tone. "The bitch cooked my goose."

"I went to the ashram after school. Sejal Auntie was there," he remarked.

"So?" she demanded.

"Her son is the prince's best friend. She sent her good wishes to Pallavi Di," replied Sid.

Vaishali shrugged her shoulders, a bitter expression on her face. Then she looked hopeful, "You think she could get the prince to back off?" Picking up a dart, she aimed at the board, wishing it was Pallavi's face.

Sid said, "Don't know why you are so bummed. He's rich and young. He travels and stuff, so he won't be poking his nose all the time in your life. The parents would never have let you travel alone or study far away. You'll be richer and more important than Pallavi di all your life."

She grabbed a bunch of darts and started flinging them at him. He fled.

✦

Sumit was busy with the rituals that Hindus believe essential for the welfare of a dead man's soul. He was at Haridwar, the place where the river Ganges descends into the plains for the first time, flowing down from its source, the Gangotri Glacier. As per Hindu belief, Haridwar is where drops of Amrit, elixir of immortality fell during the time of the churning of the ocean, *Samudra Manthan*, accidentally spilling over from the pitcher while being carried by the celestial bird Garuda. About three kilometers away from the main ghats of Haridwar, Sumit was at Kankhal, where he had to immerse the mortal remains of his father.

The local priest his uncle had employed for this ritual explained that Sati Ghat at Kankhal was the best place to be conducted, as the third Sikh Guru, Guru Amar Das had sanctified it.

Yeah, yeah whatever! The priests were smart, if a devout taking his holy dip at Har-ki-Pauri stumbled on bones, the priests would not be paid.

Thinking dark irreligious thoughts he stood on the third step at Kankhal, holding on to the iron chains watching the swiftly moving waters of the river swallowing the ashes of his father. For a moment he cynically hoped that Ganges would refuse to accept them. Then he shook his head: Who am I kidding? I learnt about life from Devious Singh and he taught me that there is no God, there is no good or bad, there is just hunter and prey.

Aditya put his hand on his arm, "Penny for your thoughts."

"They will cause you acidity."

He patted Sumit's back and lowered his voice, "I wish I had better news. Let's move away a bit."

Smiling politely at Vishnu and the other family members and key staff members of the hotels who had accompanied him to Haridwar, Sumit let go of the iron chain and climbed up the steps and they moved away, out of earshot. Aditya whispered, "I hear that your bride to be has fled."

"What?" said Sumit shocked.

"The family denies it of course, but my mother heard this from a friend who is their neighbor."

Sumit's eyes turned as flinty as his father's, and he said coldly, "Time to meet my future father-in-law."

"You remind me of your father when you stare at me like that. Stop talking like him." Aditya shuddered.

Sumit smiled icily and Aditya added hastily, "Dude! You better watch it. Next you know you will turn into him. Let us get away from here. His soul may just have floated out of that river and possessed you."

Sumit took a deep breath and said, "We better leave for town now. That bitch has put us in one hell of a fix!"

"We don't know for sure. We need to confirm this first," Aditya muttered worriedly.

"And keep it quiet." Sumit nodded.

✦

It was seven the next morning. Vaishali was sitting on the porch, contemplating her future bitterly, when a car parked in front of their gate. Two men, desperately in need of a change and a shave stepped out. She walked to the gate before they could ring the bell. "Yes?"

"I would like to meet Miss Bhatia please," said Sumit formally. Aditya supplied the name, "Pallavi Bhatia."

She flinched and asked warily, "Who are you?"

"Sumit Singh Nausar."

She looked him up and down, and then started shaking her head. "Oh my God! No! You're too old."

"What?" he exclaimed taken aback, his mind still not alert. He was not a morning person. "Who are you?" he countered.

"Vaishali Bhatia," she said still looking him dismayed.

"Wait a minute. Wasn't the name Pooja or something?" he asked.

Aditya smacked his head, and said, "Pallavi."

She opened her mouth to reply, but then caught sight of some very interested neighbor overhearing their conversation. "Can we discuss this inside please?" she said. She had planned this the whole week and practiced her lines. But his unexpected arrival at her doorstep made her nervous.

"Alright, where?" Sumit asked in a bemused tone. He had come geared up for a showdown and was unprepared for this.

She led them to the porch and waited until they sat down on the cane chairs, "The parents are asleep and so are the servants."

"And your sister?" he said, leaning back on his chair and staring at her, a tall girl, her sleep tousled curls giving her the appearance of a naughty school kid.

She drew patterns on the floor with her bare toes, biting her lip.

"Well?" he prompted.

She said in an incoherent rush, "You proposed to marry Pallavi, my older sister. She is the beautiful one. But she loves Raman and she refused. You want a bride, and so, m-m-maybe you can marry me."

He asked, "She refused?"

She studied her toes as she nodded.

"You mean this Pooja refused me for some insignificant ordinary man? Is she mad?" he asked haughtily.

"Why do you care? You don't even remember her name. It's Pallavi."

"Look my answer is no, I can't marry you," said Sumit.

"Why?" she asked.

"You're just a school girl. So she has run off with some idiot hasn't she?" he asked coldly. "Just go and call your father, and we grown ups can settle this among ourselves." He looked murderous.

"No you listen to me, Mr. Singh or Yuvraj or whatever you call yourself. Stop being so bloody patronising! You had no right to come into our lives, dish out that stupid proposal and cause us all tension," she shot back.

"Your father...now! End of discussion," he retorted.

She shook her head. This was going all wrong. He had to say yes, her mother had made her see that. For Sid's sake, for her family's sake.

Cornered, she felt tears fill up her eyes, but controlled them. This was not the time for tears. She shot back, "And what will you tell your cousins and relatives, the ones you told that you already had a fiancé?"

Both Aditya and he exchanged glances. He looked at her face, taking in the strong jaw, wide forehead and rather mobile mouth, "Not such a kid after all! How do you know?" asked Sumit.

"Gossip. Your family is the most talked about in this town. Even kids in my college know about your mysterious fiancé. By the way, I am eighteen and in college."

He looked at her slender athletic frame clad in a pair of shorts and tee shirt and said, "Bullshit! You look fifteen. Okay talk, I am listening."

"Okay, fine, I am seventeen. Here is my plan. You told your family you were in a relationship with a nice girl from a good family. I fit the bill."

"What's in it for you?"

"My father gets to save the family honor and my sister gets to marry the boy she loves."

He laughed cynically, "And you are the sacrificial goat."

Her eyes filled up. "Please Mr. Singh. Pallavi di has disappeared; no one knows where she is. Papa is going to tell you that she has some serious disease, so maybe you can marry me."

"What a pathetic lie."

"I know. He wants me to marry you. He hopes you will agree. He hopes..." she let that trail as it occurred to her that her father was not a very smart man.

"And what do you want?" he asked thoughtfully.

"To finish my studies, work, have a career. I don't want to be a boring tame wife, with babies and card parties and kirtans." Her voice dripped with disgust.

He laughed unpleasantly, "Grow up kid. If I agree, you will have to be a proper wife. Your studies are over. And we shall have sex, you will have babies. I am no self sacrificing fairy tale hero. If that is acceptable, fine. If not..." he let the words hang.

Aditya spluttered out his indignation, but Vaishali looked down at her toes for a few moments, her brain working furiously, evaluating this. Then she raised her eyes and met his, saying firmly, "I would like to work."

"Only in our own hotels," he said.

"It's a deal, Mr. Singh." This was more than she had hoped.

"Good. My name is Sumit. Go and inform your father that I will pay him a visit in two hours."

"Are you out of your mind? She's just a kid!" said Aditya once she had run inside.

Sumit put his arm around Aditya's shoulder and led him out of the gate, "Can you imagine what the world would say if they came to know that a girl ran away rather than marry me? This one is young, agreed. That makes her adaptable."

Aditya said, "You're mad."

"Let's go, have breakfast, clean up and then meet the man. Oh yes, meet the girl too. My ego can't handle another bride running away," he replied gently scratching the stubble on his chin.

They sat down in the car. Sumit checked his reflection in the rear view mirror and said, "Adi, can I ask you a question? Will you reply honestly?"

"Of course."

"Do I really look that old?"

Aditya dissolved into laughter.

It was half an hour's journey over potholed roads to Banasur. They parked the car outside the small haveli and rang the bell. Sejal Banasur answered the door.

"Ma, congratulate Sumit. He's getting married." Aditya informed his mother.

"Yes I know. Pallavi is a beauty. Congratulations Sumit."

"Thank you, Sejal Auntie. You look well. Did we wake you up?"

She laughed, and he smiled back, charmed as everyone was, with her elegant beauty. "Not at all. I went to the ashram this morning. Chandan's boys are enacting a small play on Krishna. They've enlisted me as the director. Have you met Pallavi?"

"Auntie, why are you pulling my leg? You know that girl ran away. Actually I am marrying Vaishali."

"My God! I mean, congratulations!"

"Oh come on, Ma! She is not that young. You were a child when you got married. In fact she is older than my sisters were when you married them off," Aditya protested. "Come Sumit, you take the bathroom in my sisters' room. We have to get ready soon."

✦ ✦ ✦

8

The Priest

Eid Mubarak, Mian.

Chandan woke up with a start, he could smell kebabs frying; even taste them in his mouth. He groaned and sat up in his rope cot and looked around his small room with its small stool and the wall on which a calendar depicting Kailash Parbat was hung on a nail. The events of past few days had brought back the past he wanted to forget. He sat and stared at his palms the way Sant Anirudh had taught him, chanting softly, *Karagre Vasti Laxmi, Kar Madhye Saraswati, Kar Mule Tu Govindam, Prabhate Kar Darshanam.*

The past was done, over...but was it?

He rarely thought of the past, tried to block it off. His desire to eat kebabs had saved him and his baby sister. Ammi had given him some money and told him to take Azra with him to the fair grounds and eat kebabs. She and the other women had been cooking the Eid feast.

The fair ground was right next to their home.

"Eid Mubarak, Mian," the boy frying the kebabs had grinned, handing him a serving of piping hot kebabs.

Buying Azra a duck shaped balloon which made a sound when she waved it, he had wandered around the fair grounds, watching kids ride the giant wheel. Someone had screamed, "Fire". Their little colony had been gutted, and riots had broken out. Grabbing Azra, he tried to run back home. There was no home to run back to.

He hated fire. He hated the thoughts that had resurfaced, the questions that tormented him. Did his mother, his young aunts survive? If so, what had they seen? How had they fared? Did they experience what the girl he had rescued did? He hoped not.

Carrying Azra who was clinging on to her stupid duck, waving it in the air, he ran around trying to find shelter, finally hiding in a disused pipe. Arun was already hiding there, his back badly burnt and front teeth broken. Preet joined them later, along with his baby brother Jassi.

Sant Anirudh had found them, late in the night, hungry, ill and scared. During the course of the day and night they had bonded, becoming fast friends, fiercely protective about the two infants, Azra and Jassi. He never talked about the past, neither did Arun. In fact Arun did not speak much, just cried bitterly in his sleep. As they grew older the tears stopped and he devoted himself completely to God Shiva. Pratham still talked about the old days, when he was Preet. He also visited Jassi and went to the far-away town where Azra now lived with her husband and babies. Chandan had not even attended her wedding.

Rescuing that girl had triggered the memories. He sighed and wondered what the last moments of his mother, his cousin sisters had been like. Had it been as nightmarish as the girl's? He walked out of his room. It was early morning. He picked up his kamandala and walked to the bank of River Nausar. Unlike the fateful day when he had helped dig out the huge shivling, the river bank was now a proper ghat, with steps made of Dhaulpur stone. On holidays families came to the ghat and had picnics. Children clamored for boat rides. The stone ghat was dotted with neem, rudraksha and *safeda* trees. He washed his face, filled up his kamandala with water from the river and sat down under a rudraksha tree, deep in reverie.

The past had to be faced. Someone had gone to Azra's village, enquiring about her past. Jassi had angrily chased them away. The whispers and insinuations had started, about Muslims defiling the Shiv Mandir.

He had offered to go away, perhaps to the towns far away. But Sant Anirudh refused to consider it; he kept saying obscure things like, "There is a shift in the energy patterns. Soon this will blow away."

"How do you know?" Pratham had asked.

"It comes in my dreams," Santji had replied. Santji had blind faith in his dreams; after all, years ago, he had led five orphans away from their home town to Nausar, to safety on the strength of a dream. He had dreamt of a shivling buried under a rudraksha tree which would give them shelter. Preet who was now Pratham, his baby brother Jassi, Chand and Azra and Arun had followed him here. Arun had been the oldest, just seven years old.

Too young to doubt their savior, they had followed him, even helped the priest dig the place he thought the shivling was buried. With childish faith they had laughed and clapped when they had uncovered the shivling lying in the sandy river bank. Too traumatized by the past they welcomed the Sant's actions when he burnt their clothes right near the submerged shivling, and shaved off their heads, leaving a tuft of hair back like a brahman. None of them refused to wear the sacred thread or questioned the name giving ceremony he conducted at dawn. He had given them life, so the life was his to direct.

By the time the curious villagers came to the rudraksha tree, they were dressed in brahman garb, and named Chandan and Pratham. Arun still answered to his old name.

The babies were given away to a kindly and childless landowner who wanted to adopt them.

Pratham came and sat down next to him staring at the girl sitting alone on the ghat, "Has she spoken?"

Chandan glanced towards the solitary figure and said, "No. Santji says she has seen too much so she will take time."

"Did we?"

"I don't remember. We must have."

"I am getting married," Pratham said abruptly. Chandan did not reply. "You are supposed to congratulate me, you know," Pratham said with a loud laugh.

Chandan gave an awkward smile, "Oh, sorry. Congratulations."

"Her name is Kamli; she lives in Jassi's village. Chandan, have you told Santji about Amol's threat?"

Chandan sighed. The problem with the old Sant was that he was impractical. He was so detached that it was difficult to make him see reality. "I did and as expected, he spouted obscure stuff at me about energies shifting and all that."

Pratham grimaced and then stood up, his shoulders drooping just a little; he took a few hesitant steps and raised his head shaking it wearily, "Humanity and its follies..."

Chandan grinned, Pratham was a wonderful mimic. "Is that what he said when you told him about your marriage?"

Pratham took a few more shuffling steps like the old Sant, "Marriage? Are you sure that is what you want? I suppose I must congratulate you. Go son, but remember marriage is a two-edged sword."

The mimicry was so powerful that Chandan let out a shout of laughter, clapping his hands. Pratham chuckled and said, "It made me wonder if I should take his blessings or run away."

Bala glanced at them fearfully as their laughter carried through in the quiet morning and then fled into the kitchen. She knew she was safe here for now, but sooner or later she would have to face the world outside. The ashram housed boys, not girls. Soon the lady who cooked would be here, to prepare breakfast. She quickly took a bath and went to help the cook.

She was serving breakfast when she heard a childish voice, "Santji, good morning. Are you feeling well?" It was ten year old Sudhakar.

"Yes, I am fine," Old Anirudh said with a smile. "I heard some voices, do we have a visitor?"

"Tuhin says it's the queen. I laughed at him. We don't have queens in India, only England has a queen," the boy said with a grin. "Then I hid and watched. It was only a woman."

This brought a genuine smile to the old Sant's face. "Yes, I see. Eat your breakfast before the kitchen people scold you. And learn your verses well. I will listen to them in the afternoon."

The boy nodded and started spooning his breakfast and the old man went to his private courtyard. Bala hid behind a door to look at the queen.

It was an open courtyard. The morning sunrays fell on the basil plant that was in the centre. Santji was watering it, chanting prayers under his breath. Four plastic chairs were kept in one side, for special devotees to whom the Sant granted audience. There was one huge wooden door, which was normally kept locked. Santji set down this kamandala and lit an incence stick and stuck it in the mud near the basil plant's roots. An imperious looking and wrinkled old lady in an ivory colored silk sari swept into the private courtyard. Her hair was tied in a small bun. It seemed as though she had not paid much attention to her grooming in the past few weeks, whites showed in her carefully dyed hair. She wore a heavy rope like gold chain in her neck and quantities of gold bangles and rings that jangled when she made any gesture. Diamonds glittered in her ears. She drew a chair and sat down opposite Sant Anirudh.

She spoke in a nasal querulous voice, "Santji, when you desired to set up the Ayurvedic dispensary and start this small ashram, we, the royalty of Nausar granted you this land."

"Yes I remember," he said.

"Whenever you have asked us for donations, we have been more than generous," reminded the woman.

"The ashram thanks you for the support, Rani," replied Sant Anirudh.

"I came to you time and again with my problem, a very old problem. On your advice performed many rituals, fed countless cows and brahmans, but the problem still remained," said the woman.

"Yes?" enquired Anirudh.

"I wanted revenge; I wanted the end of my humiliation, but not like this," she said. It was just a whisper.

His aged eyes were thoughtful as he recalled her as a young woman, soft, self-absorbed and slightly foolish. Now underneath the pride and the stiff regal deportment, she was hard and bitter. "I warned you. I said it time and again. I repeat it again, Rani, be careful what you wish for. God can grant our wishes in ways that may not be...nice."

She got up and walked out abruptly. The old man looked towards Bala and said, "She is just an angry and bitter woman, child. Look at her carefully and do not let your life and experiences turn you into someone so bitter."

Bala jumped. She had been unaware that he had seen her. She scurried back into the kitchen.

✦ ✦ ✦

9

The Foster Brother

In the dining room at the Bhatia residence, Shrishti Bhatia, dressed in a crumpled blue nightgown, with hair hanging down untidily on her back asked her younger daughter in a scandalized tone, "And you said what?"

"I told him that Pallavi di had run off and I would marry him instead, that is all. He agreed." Vaishali said with a shrug. Then she made a face and declared, "He is old!"

Her parents gazed at each other shocked, and quickly got into action. Vaishali was shooed into her room, "Take a bath, shampoo your hair with the special shampoo the beautician has given you. What are you going to wear? I can't believe he saw you in that horrible pair of shorts!" Shrishti said, wringing her hands.

Shrishti rushed to the kitchen still talking, "Never have I felt so deeply embarrassed. I hope he is not amusing himself at our expense." She shrieked at the maid, "Not here you stupid woman. Get out, go to the living room. Did I not tell you that first the living room has to be cleaned? Why do I get such idiots to work for me?" She yelled at the cook, "Make something fancy for breakfast. Soak some *urad dal*; we need *dahi bhalle* for the visitors! What else do we serve?"

Sid woke up to find the household in a tizzy and did what any sensible fourteen year old does in such a situation. He did not venture out of his room until he was sure that the school bus had left. Shrishti walked into Vaishali's room with a sari and Pallavi's make up, saw him sitting on her bed and threw her hands up. He was sent to his room to bathe and get into his best clothes for the occasion.

Unaware and completely unappreciative of the fact that their visit had created a crisis of sorts in the Bhatia household, a couple of hours later, both Sumit and Aditya, bathed, shaved and wearing freshly ironed suits arrived. They were being ushered into the living room with grave formality when they heard a whispered boyish comment, "Which one's your husband? Oh c'mon Vaish, they don't look that old."

That was followed by a desperate reply, "Shush Sid! I hope he didn't hear you!"

The Yuvraj tried to keep a serious expression on his face but his lips twitched and eyes twinkled as he spotted the siblings peering from behind the curtain. Aditya caught sight of them and winked. They sat down and while Aditya exchanged pleasantries with Shankar Bhatia, Sumit sat observing the couple. Mr. Bhatia was tall, with an athletic frame of someone who had been an outdoor person in his youth. However age and business pressures had caught up with him, adding fat to his frame. His sparse gray hair revealed bald patches on his head. Unlike him, his wife showed very few signs of aging. She was of medium height, fair and had large eyes rimmed with kohl. Her long and lustrous hair was clasped at the nape of her neck, with curls cascading down her back. Both of them watched him warily as they sat opposite him. Aditya kept up polite conversation, complimenting Mrs. Bhatia on her tasteful living room and the deliciously soft dahi bhalle.

Aditya frowned slightly at Sumit, who smiled and recalled his social obligation, "I apologize for coming here at such a short notice. It is highly irregular, but looking at the situation..."

Shankar shifted uncomfortably, "Maharao, I thank you for giving my daughter a patient hearing. She is rather impulsive."

Sumit did not know what to say, so he asked, "Where is your daughter?"

Shankar and Shrishti misinterpreted the question and exchanged alarmed glances. Aditya stepped into the breach, "Yes, where is Vaishali?"

Shrishti quickly jumped up and said, "I'll call her."

As though waiting for this, Vaishali preempted her by walking into the room, holding Sid's hand tightly. Her appearance ruffled Sumit, and his lips twitched with amusement. Dressed in a light pink sari, obviously bought for a much fairer complexioned girl, she looked like an awkward child in a masquerade. He kept a straight face and courteously got up and greeted her and Sid. Once they sat down, he took his seat.

After breakfast, Shankar got up, "I think we should leave the couple alone."

He and Shrishti got up and left, expecting Aditya and Sid to follow but Vaish clutched her brother's hand and looked at the visitors imploringly.

Sumit said softly, "What is biting you? You were fine this morning!"

"Ma scolded her for proposing to you," Sid whispered. "She has been ordered to behave properly."

"Would you like to join us for lunch at the Royal, just Vaishali and you?" he asked, trying to put the girl at ease.

"Cool!" said Sid with a grin and then looked at his sister. "Vaish, can you walk in that thing?"

"Why don't you change into jeans or something comfortable, Vaishali? We'll wait." Sumit said.

It was a small gesture but earned her everlasting gratitude. A huge smile lit her face, transforming it completely. Sumit took in a sharp intake of breath as she said shyly, "I'll just change and be back. Come, Sid."

"Damn! The child is a beauty," commented Aditya as soon as they left the room. "Trust you to have all the luck in women."

"Come on! She's just a kid," Sumit shrugged.

"A kid you're going to marry," pointed out Aditya with amusement. Sumit grimaced.

The Bhatias entered the room. Shankar Bhatia asked the customary question any father of the bride asks, "Sumit ji, do you have any special demands?"

"What? No Mr. Bhatia. No dowry is expected. My wife is my responsibility. From now on, I will take care of her."

"No! My daughter is not yours yet, you are not even engaged to her!" Shankar said firmly.

"I am not a conventional man, Mr. Bhatia. But I am a proud man, and my wife to be is my responsibility."

Aditya intervened smoothly, "I am sure all this can be discussed at the time of the engagement, the formal engagement." He nudged Sumit, who shut up.

Sumit said, "Sir, we would like to take Vaishali and Sid out for lunch with your permission."

Shankar nodded and said, "Let me inform her mother."

Once Shankar left the room, Aditya said, "Whoa tiger, stop that caveman act. Your uncle can have this talk with them."

Sumit took a deep breath, smiling ruefully, "I missed you, Adi."

Aditya smiled back. Then he said, "Are you sure about the wedding and dowry? Your mother won't like it." His lip twisted bitterly. The Rani had poisoned his childhood. At times, he had felt she grudged every grain he ate. Sumit and Mehak had accepted him completely, and given him so much love that it had overshadowed Devika's hostility.

"She is welcome not to. The girl is doing me a huge favor, it is enough," Sumit replied. Vaishali and Sid came into the room dressed in jeans and sweat shirts. He muttered, "Damn, I feel like a baby sitter!"

Aditya broke into laughter.

Sumit ran his fingers through his hair and looked at all three of them, and broke into a smile, feeling relaxed after a long time. Sid asked Aditya, "So you are Sumit *Jeej*'s friend?"

Sumit said, "No, he is my brother."

Aditya lowered his eyes, to hide his emotions. For a long time, Sumit had distanced himself from his family and companions of his childhood. He even refused to address his parents as Mother and Father. His father's death seemed to have thawed him.

Lunch was a pleasant affair. Away from the watchful eyes of her anxious parents, Vaishali displayed a cheeky and irreverent sense of humor. She had a good grasp on politics and general knowledge. "Naturally. I am in first year LLB," she informed them.

"No, not a lawyer, I hate them," complained Sumit.

"No, you don't. You employ them. Eighty percent of all law graduates join Royal. The rest go out of state." She shrugged, "I wanted to go into private practice. I wanted to take cases to do with women's rights."

"I wonder, will you regret this marriage?" Sumit asked.

She gave it serious thought. Then she grinned, "As Rani, I can work for women's rights. I can employ lawyers to work for me. Can't I?"

"Easy, tigress. The Rani still lives," Sumit laughed. "But as the Maharao's wife you can do it, too."

"You don't mind?" she asked.

"Not at all," he smiled. Her eyes lit up.

Sid said, "God! You're going to spoil her silly and she is going to be intolerable."

"Isn't this your fifth ice cream?" she asked sweetly.

"Wasn't counting," he said stuffing a heaped spoonful into his mouth.

After lunch, Aditya accompanied Sumit to his flat where they sat discussing the Bhatias and Vaishali. Aditya complained, "Damn you Sumit, you are devilishly lucky. You are the only person I know who can make a mess with your life and then come out a winner! The girl is a beauty and unspoilt."

"Mehak giving you trouble?" Sumit asked, the old sarcasm back.

Aditya turned beetroot red. Sumit relented and thumped him on the back, "I am not blind. I've known about you both since we were in school. There was no hope; Devious Singh would not consider it ever."

Aditya cleared his throat uncomfortably, "I, yes, no, she... not what you think...no I mean."

"Brilliant!" Sumit applauded, "Absolutely clear and lucid."

Aditya took a shaky breath and asked, "You don't mind?"

"Hardly. You have awful taste though. She is a hell cat. Adi, just be careful, she is still married to that scumbag Somnath."

Aditya smiled, as he reflected that Vaishali was equally high spirited, if not more. He would love to see her making Sumit dance to her tunes. And his wish came true immediately. Sumit said, "Oh damn! I forgot, I have to go away for some days. I have to tell her. I hate it when women start whining."

He quickly dialed Vaishali, putting the call on speaker winking at Aditya, "Hey Vaish, I have to go away, some work. I won't be here for four days. I just thought I'd inform you," and he grimaced, bracing himself for feminine complaints.

Instead Vaishali said cheerfully, "Okay. This is great! Do you mind very much if I go hiking up the hills? It's something we planned a long time ago. Ma wants me to cancel now that I am getting married."

That knocked him off balance. The look on his face was so comical that Aditya snorted in amusement. Then Sumit said, "What trek? Where?"

"Oh it's just something we do, I am the secretary of the Nausar Nature Trail Club. We are forty or so people and we go trekking."

"Really? Tell me more."

"Ummm, it's for young people, you know, college and school kids, so maybe you'll find it boring. We just walk the whole day, go to the Pracheen Mandir, right up the hill, and then we walk back. We carry cameras and take pictures, and stuff..."

Sumit let the oblique reference to his age pass. The conversation was then about wildlife and a day long hike uphill, and not about how neglected Sumit's fiancé would feel.

"What business, Sumit?" Aditya asked as Sumit disconnected the phone.

"Remember Brian Underwood?"

"Yes, I do." Aditya said with a smile. Brian was an Irish student they had met in college, hot tempered and quick with his fists. The very first day in college, they had bumped into a hot-headed Brian looking for someone to pick on. Something had led to angry words being exchanged, and he had punched Sumit, calling him a wog and offering to wipe the floor with him. Sumit, already on a short fuse at the way he had been shipped off to England lunged at him. The fight had been intense, and both men had been equally matched. Aditya had brokered truce, and bought a round of drinks for them. Over drinks, both Brian and Sumit realized that they were quite similar and it was the beginning of an enduring friendship. Sumit had then started distancing himself from Aditya, who was at first confused and then relieved at this heaven sent opportunity to lead his own life.

"Brian and I bought a vineyard in Hampshire years ago," recalled Sumit.

Aditya looked at him surprised. "I see. You kept it pretty quiet."

"That was easy. I was in disgrace, no one wanted to know what I was doing. Surprisingly, the first vineyard was profitable. Then we bought more, mostly in Italy and France. Now we are looking for land in India." Both men shared the same thought that they left unspoken, now that Digvijay Singh was dead, there was nothing to fear...

Aditya sifted this information and then asked him thoughtfully, and then asked, "Where did you get the money to buy a vineyard?"

"Devious Singh gave you digs at the haveli and a job. He gave me a small allowance and this apartment. Someone, maybe the staff from the haveli furnished it with old stuff, things the haveli did not need. At first I was furious, there was no place to stand and the furniture was ghastly, smelly and ancient."

Aditya shook his head, "I am sure there is a point to this tale."

"Yes, bear with me. It's funny, in retrospect. I brought a girl home one night and she lost interest in me once she recognized a portrait in my bedroom done by Giuseppe Arcimboldo."

"A who?" Aditya asked.

"Some 15th century Italian painter. She mooned over this Giuseppe guy while I got bored and drank myself silly. The next morning I got rid of her, and got in touch with evaluators. They were very happy to inform me that the clutter I was living with was actually a pile of very valuable antiques. I sold most of it, and Brian helped raise us a loan from the Bank of England, and we were in business."

Aditya smiled, "The luck of the devil! But why are you telling me all this?"

"You are on the Board of Directors of Royal. You know Brian. I have plans, maybe a merger." Aditya raised his brow enquiringly, but Sumit just smiled. Knowing how reticent Sumit was, Aditya just let it pass. He would quiz Brian later.

They sat drinking, their camaraderie of the past making it very easy and pleasant. "Adi, have you ever been hiking in these hills?" Sumit asked.

"Once, years back." Aditya said looking out of the window, to hide a smile.

"Maybe we should join the trekking expedition. It should be fun."

Aditya finished his drink, a smile playing on his mouth. "Why not?"

✦ ✦ ✦

10

Narrow Escape

Sumit, Mehak and Aditya fell into an easy routine of meeting at Royal One for lunch, since Sumit hated the haveli and Mehak turned her nose up at the furnishing in Sumit's flat. "As it is we have enough of fossil furniture from the Raj Era at the haveli."

Mehak and Aditya spent the ensuing couple of days priming Sumit up for the day long trek. Aditya informed him, "Most nature trails begin at the bus stop at Shiv temple and then one walks uphill, along the Nausar River. I went on one a long time ago. We had lunch at Nausar River, roughly twelve kilometers inside the jungle, and then we had to climb ten kilometers uphill to the Pracheen Mandir or ancient temple. There is a spring there, which empties into Nausar River. Then we walk downhill, back to the temple. It is going to be strenuous, are you up to it?"

"I will pack enough mosquito repellant, Iodex sprays etc. You need shoes, sturdy ones, strong socks. Have you had your malaria shots?" Mehak asked.

"Malaria shots?" Sumit expressed surprise.

"Go visit the hospital, Sumit. One can't take chances," advised Aditya.

"I'll call the doctor, he'll send someone here," Mehak said, dialing a number.

"What was I thinking when I planned this trip," wondered Sumit aloud, throwing his hands up as he left for the washroom.

"Does he really think he planned this trip?" Mehak laughed. "Something tells me the minx is going to lead him by the nose."

"She confuses our great Maharao," Aditya said with a grin. "I am enjoying it!"

"I am really eager to meet her," Mehak replied. "Your mother says she is going to turn the haveli upside down. Does she know we are also joining the trek?"

He grinned naughtily, "It's a surprise."

The town of Nausar bordered vast tracts of jungles and gentle hills. Vaishali, a naturally athletic and outdoor person was a keen trekker. Sumit, on the other hand, had not woken up at dawn for a long time.

On the appointed day, at dawn, Sumit along with Aditya and Mehak drove up Shiv Mandir. Yawning heavily, Sumit accepted the backpack as he stepped out of the car and looked around. A cool breeze was playing. In the gray light a group of people were gathered together. Vaishali glanced their way and stopped in surprise, but Sid more than made up for her lack of reaction.

"Jeej!" he yelled as he ran up to Sumit, "I did not know you like to go climb hills."

"Easy champ!" he said, as he thumped him on the back. "I did not know you liked this."

"I am a trekker since I was ten. Tell me, was this place named after you or were you named after the town? I keep telling Vaish that her name will have a zip code now!"

Vaishali walked up to them and smiled politely, greeting Mehak and Aditya.

She whispered, "That is so lame."

Then she said in a polite tone, "I did not know you would be joining us." She beckoned the organizer and trek leader and introduced him first, "This is Saksham Sir. He is a wildlife photographer and conservationist. Meet the Maharao, his sister and Aditya Banasur."

Aditya smiled, "I know Saksham, and so does Mehak. How are you Saksham?"

"Prettily behaved," Mehak said to her, taking her away from the men.

She blushed, "Thank you. You are so elegant, so graceful. I know only one lady like this, Madam Sejal."

"Thank you. Sejal Banasur is Aditya's mother. She loves your energy. She will be visiting you one of these days," replied Mehak.

"She is his mother? Wow! I meet her at the ashram twice a week, she teaches the boys there, and so do I. She is so beautiful; I wish I looked like that."

Sid, full of energy and excitement, ran up ahead saying, "Hurry up oldies, you'll be the last to start off!"

Vaish followed him. "So what do you think?" Sumit asked Mehak.

"Charming. But if you marry her, the brother comes along," she pointed out.

"I know, and I don't mind. He is fun!" Sumit said, and then sighed, "I will have to walk with her. Can't have her thinking I'm old!" He lengthened his stride to catch up with Vaishali.

Aditya and Mehak trailed behind. Vaishali was naturally athletic, and it took all of Sumit's efforts to keep in pace with her. Vaishali knew a lot about the flora and fauna of the hills. She pointed out the pine and coniferous woodlands of the area. Nausar homed temperate forests unlike the alpine flora of the snow peaks in the distance. She pointed the chir pine, oak, maple and ash that grew abundantly. Sumit tried to concentrate but was tiring fast. He was privately relieved when they reached the bend in the rivers and the leader of the trek announced lunch. The river was narrow at this point, and fishermen and boats found it easy to cross here. A few enterprising people had erected shacks under the shady mulberry trees. Saksham pointed at a tree and said, "We have trained the villagers to make tussar silk from the worms. It is one of many such projects that have been set up. I hope you will lend your support."

While others were at the counter, getting lunch packets, Sumit walked to a wooden bench and sat down wearily, wiping his face.

"So, do you still think I am too old?" He asked Vaishali.

He was rewarded by the most unaffected shout of laughter, "No, you're not that old."

"Thank you for your approval," he said straight-faced. "I am so relieved."

She thawed completely. "Such drama!" she teased as she sat down on the table in front of him. Mehak and Aditya joined them and ordered cold drinks.

"Hey Vaish, let's go get lunch!" Sid said, tugging at her arm.

She jumped up to her feet with litheness that left the older people looking at her enviously. "You all keep sitting, I will fetch lunch."

Sumit's eyes followed her, with gentle amusement. Mehak watched Vaishali keenly. The girl was in her opinion, either a natural flirt or the most unselfconscious girl she had ever met. And Sumit seemed to indulge her horribly. Aditya whispered into her ear, "So what do you think?"

"Most unusual," she whispered back, her eye on Sumit whose eyes followed Vaishali as she walked to the small counter where lunch packets were being distributed, and brought them to their table, "I think brother dearest is smitten!"

They were eating lunch when Sid pointed at a man sitting slightly upstream washing his face, "Vaish look, its Chandan Pandit." Both of them quickly got to their feet and ran up to meet him.

Sumit got up and followed them, wanting to renew his acquaintance with the priest he had played with as a boy.

Chandan smiled as he saw him and folded his hands into a formal namaste, "Maharao ji, what a pleasant surprise!"

Sumit hugged him and said, "Please call me Sumit. You are far away from the ashram."

"Not really. This path leads to the ashram, it is just an hour away," he said pointing at a dirt track.

"Panditji, do you also go on treks?" Sid asked.

"No Sidharth, I don't. I had to meet someone."

"In the jungle?" he asked, surprised.

The priest smiled, "So you are on the nature trail?"

They nodded.

"On your way back, why don't you stop by at the ashram?" he asked them.

"We will," said Sid enthusiastically for all of them. "Won't we?" he asked Vaish and Sumit.

"Yes, we will," Sumit assured him.

They watched the priest walk away and resumed their trek. Vaishali said, "Sid loves playing cricket with those ashram kids."

"We did that too. Our game was volleyball. Chandan would be alone on one side of the net, and we all ganged up against him. We still lost," remembered Sumit.

"Vaish teaches the kids yoga and martial arts," Sid explained.

"Times have changed! Fighting in the ashram!" Sumit said with mock horror.

"Santji says it is a Shiv Mandir. Shiv ji was a warrior. Vaish is a good fighter. She taught me great moves," said a supportive Sid.

"Oh, I am scared," responded Sumit with a smile.

She ran up ahead, turned to face him, assuming the dancing pose of Goddess Kali and intoned solemnly, "You should be!"

He gave a shout of laughter, bringing a smile on the faces of Aditya and Mehak who were following them a few steps behind. "I think brother dearest is going to be too involved in his bride to pay much attention to what we are up to, what say?" Mehak murmured.

Aditya just grinned.

Aditya had brought a video camera and they spent a pleasant time recording the sights, wild fowl at the river, ducks swimming near the bank. By the time they reached the ancient temple, they were exhausted and sat on the grassy slopes, chatting. Vaishali shook Sid who was lying on his back on the grass, eyes closed. "Hey, let's go to the spring," she suggested.

"Go away," Sid said, not moving.

She sighed and stood up, stretched and walked up the mossy track to the spring. Once there, she sat down on a weathered rock, removed her shoes and dipped her feet in the chilly water, closing her eyes in relief.

Sumit, who had followed her, sat down next to her, "Nice place."

She smiled and said, "It is one of my favorites, ever since I saw it on my first trek. I was younger than Sid."

He said, "I never knew there was such scenic beauty in Nausar. I have seen very nice places in Ireland."

She turned towards him to reply but screamed, "Run!"

He said, "Huh?"

She sprang to her feet and gave him a huge push and jumped away from the path of a huge moss covered boulder that came crashing down at the very spot they were sitting moments ago. She stared wordlessly as the boulder hurtled downhill harmlessly. She glanced at Sumit who was frozen in an unnatural stance. He groaned in pain. She rushed to his side, "What is the matter? Did you get hurt?"

"My back!" he moaned. "Damn it, I am too unfit. Mehak packed some Iodex spray, can you get it?"

Saksham and a couple of trekkers came rushing up to them, "Thank heavens you are safe! That was a huge rock!"

"Are you okay? What is the matter with you?" Adi asked.

"My back!" groaned Sumit.

Mehak said haughtily, "Serves you right, trying to compete with someone who is not out of her teens."

Vaishali tried hard to hide her smile as she whistled loudly.

"What?" Sid shouted.

"Get some spray!" commanded Vaishali.

Mehak said, "I have some in my backpack." Still chuckling she fished it out and sprayed it on Sumit's back generously.

Sid said, "My father gets a catch in his back and the people in the ashram set it right for him."

"Sumit, can you walk? Shut up Mehak. Be nice," Aditya said.

"I don't think so," he groaned.

Saksham said, "There is a village closeby. We'll go there and send help. But someone will have to stay with the Maharao."

Some of the trekkers stayed back and the rest went to the village. Sumit tottered to the grassy slope with the help of Mehak and Vaishali, and lay down, his eyes closed. After an hour, Sid and Aditya shook him awake and helped him into a bullock cart. "You ride, we'll walk alongside," Adi advised Sumit.

Sumit lay in the bullock cart as it creaked forward, gritting his teeth. This was going to be bumpy ride. He noticed after a while that Aditya was having a whispered conversation with Mehak and Vaishali as Sid listened intently. He asked, "What's the problem?"

"You," Adi said. "Do you have enemies? You know the kind that would attack you?"

"No, not at all," he replied.

"Someone used an iron rod as a lever to dislodge the rock. That person pushed it downhill deliberately towards you," said Adi.

Sumit breathed softly, "No!"

✦

It was evening when Chandan reached Sant Anirudh's private courtyard. "What does the villager want?" Anirudh asked Chandan.

Chandan shrugged, "He threatens us."

"Do not allow yourself to get blackmailed Chandan. Call his bluff. We can face it all," the old Sant admonished him.

Chandan shook his head. "Sant ji, you have to understand, this can be dangerous." He changed the subject, "I met the trekkers on my way back. The young Maharao was walking with the Bhatia children."

Anirudh considered this, "There must be a purpose, there always is a purpose."

Chandan looked at the older man as he rambled, and then said gently, "It is almost time for the evening prayers, Rani Devika will be here Sant ji."

Ever since her husband had died, Devika came every evening for prayers. Perhaps she wanted some relief from the guilt for all her prayers for vengeance and death.

Sant Anirudh straightened his shoulders wearily and took a step towards the temple. He watched as Devika, accompanied as usual by her daughter Himani and her sons in law, Rohtash and Somnath entered the temple. Then he stopped and looked again towards the jungles. Something was happening, energies were shifting.

✦ ✦ ✦

11

War of Words

The bullock cart reached the ashram after sunset. Sumit, his back racked with pain, which was further aggravated by the bumpy bullock ride hobbled into the courtyard supported by Aditya, and collapsed on the stone bench. Sid ran to the small Ayurvedic dispensary that was located near the gate. Many ailing patients waited there patiently for their turn and Chandan was busy attending to them. He ran past them to Chandan.

To the far end of the courtyard, stood the main temple with the huge shivling, which dominated the entire complex. Evening *aarti*, prayers had just finished and people were stepping out of the main temple into the outer courtyard.

Devika, accompanied by Himani, Rohtash and Somnath, stopped in the well tended grounds near the gate and stared in surprise at her son who was lying on the stone bench, groaning, while a young girl in a sweaty tee shirt and muddy jeans rolled up a jacket into a makeshift pillow and slipped it under his head.

Somnath glared at his wife. Mehak tossed her head in defiance and ignored him, "Fancy seeing you here, Himani Di! But then I should not be surprised. You do pray a lot don't you?"

Once Vaishali was sure that Sumit was comfortable, she rushed past Himani and Devika, ran to the Sant, grabbed him by the arm and dragged him to Sumit. He chuckled indulgently and said, "*Arre* Vaishali, slow down girl, I am not so young. You are always in such a tearing hurry."

"My fiancé is in pain, Santji. Please help!" she said.

"Okay. It is so dark, I will need some light!" said Sant Anirudh.

"Hoy Sid!" Vaishali screamed. When there was no response she put two fingers in her mouth and let out a piercing whistle. Her brother screamed from somewhere inside the ashram, "What?"

"Lights!" she yelled.

"Coming!" was the response.

Soon Sid, accompanied by the ashram boys surrounded the prone figure carrying torches and petromax lamps. A folding cot was spread in the courtyard. Santji said, "Now shift to the cot and lie down on your stomach." Sumit tried to get up, but he was too stiff.

Never one to hesitate or think of appearances, Vaishali put an arm around his waist and helped him up, clicking her tongue impatiently, "Oh come on, and don't be such a gooby. He won't hurt you."

He groaned as he took a couple of steps and collapsed on the cot, and smiled through his pain, "What on earth is a gooby?"

"Shut up and let Santji help you," she said primly. Sid answered the question, "Huh, don't mind her Jeej. She just made up that word."

"Mehak, a word please," said Himani.

Mehak raised her brow. Himani whispered, "Is that untidy brat the woman Sumit plans to marry?"

Mehak nodded as she glanced at Vaishali. She had to admit that Vaishali looked really messy, her jeans stained with grass and mud, her sweaty tee shirt encrusted with mud, her hair tucked under a sweaty bandanna, with curls escaping out of it. Her jacket lay under Sumit's head.

"Well!" said Devika frostily, "This urchin, the Rani of Nausar? I have never been more humiliated in my life."

Aditya tapped Vaishali's shoulder and said, "Sumit's family is here." She turned to the spot he indicated, got up and folded her hands in a greeting. Devika ignored her, turned and walked out of the ashram followed by Himani, Rohtash and Somnath. Tears of shock filled Vaishali's eyes. Aditya pursed his lips and exchanged a glance with Mehak, and then murmured, "It is okay, girl. There is enough time to get to know them."

Mehak frowned after them and then said, "Hey Vaish!"

"What?" she asked, defensively.

"I think you are a minx, but I like you," Mehak said with a smile.

She grinned and brushed the tears away, saying gruffly, "I must be tired, otherwise this would not have bothered me."

"You've missed the bus back to town." said Aditya, "Should we send a car to drop you?"

"Papa will pick us up," she said politely.

"No, ring him up and tell him not to bother. Adi, send my driver to drop them home." Sumit said, his tone rough with pain as a young priest punched and pummelled his muscles to loosen them.

Once Vaishali and Sid left, Sumit said to Aditya, "Can you call my father's lawyer. I want to meet him tonight before I sleep. I don't have his number."

"You're not well, maybe tomorrow."

"No, tonight!" he said roughly. "I can't allow this behavior to continue. I need to know what the old man wrote in his will."

Adi nodded, it was about time.

An hour later, Mehak and Aditya helped Sumit back to his apartment. He wanted to go straight to bed or lie down on the couch, but his mother was seated in his tiny living room along with his uncle. He grimaced, but then realized it was just as well that they had come.

The wait had aggravated Devika's temper. The thought that an ill-bred urchin would usurp her place hurt her vanity. Just as he started lowering himself painfully in a couch, she came straight to the point, "Sumit I do not approve of your woman friend."

Sumit's eyes flashed with anger as he took his time adjusting his back, and then he said tersely, "I see."

"I will not allow this marriage to take place," she raged.

Sumit said, "Thank you for making your opinions clear. But the decision is mine to make."

She flushed at the coldly voiced jibe. "I will not allow a dirty ill-brought up commoner take my place as Rani."

"We are extremely fortunate that such things are beyond our power, Madam. For your information, I do not intend to bring my bride into that awful mausoleum."

Girdhari intervened, protesting, "*Bhabhi*, Sumit, please."

"Uncle, please explain certain things to the Rani of Nausar. I am getting married, and I expect my wife to be treated with respect. The ceremony can be held anywhere. In fact, I think Royal One is a good place, I hear that the arrangements the staff makes are excellent. I wonder if Vaishali would prefer the pool side or the roof top."

Himani said, "This is so common. It must be that girl's influence."

"Enough!" he said with icy rage. "Allow me to point out that she greeted you with grace and dignity, more royal than your behavior. I expect, no I demand that my fiancé be treated with respect by my family. If you find it difficult..."

Devika said coldly, "As the Maharao and my son, Sumit, I cannot allow you to demean yourself like this."

"Really? Such maternal feelings, Madam! Isn't it strange that my fiancée was more concerned about my back than you?"

She flushed and turned to Himani for help. Girdhari got up, wanting to withdraw from what was turning out to be a domestic squabble. Sumit forestalled him by saying, "Sit down Uncle. I have called the family lawyer to explain the late Maharao's will to me. I think Madam and my sisters need to understand it too."

Vishnu stared at him as though he was a strange animal. "Why the hurry?"

"You called a meeting the same day he died," reminded Sumit.

Vishnu acknowledged this with a nod and subsided. Girdhari sat down and said, "We have the best legal brains in our employment, and the will was made after extensive consultation with them and with me. You already have thirty percent stocks. The option is yours, to sell or to accept."

Just then, the door bell rang, and the servant ushered a thin bespectacled tall man, the family lawyer, Mr. Vimal Jain. Jain took one look at the assembled people and fussily spread the legal documents on the centre table and started, "The last will and testament of Maharao Digvijay Singh Nausar, hereinforth referred to as the deceased..."

"It's been a long day, come to the point, Mr. Jain. Just tell me how it affects me," demanded Sumit.

Mr. Jain cleared his throat and looked at the others for support. No one spoke. "Suraj, drinks, now," yelled Sumit. The decanter came and he pulled off the stopper and took a huge swig. The servant rushed to get ice and glasses.

"Proceed," ordered Sumit.

"As you are aware, the haveli is a family holding. As such, no divisions are to be made of it. The hotels were founded by your deceased father and his brother. As such, they both have stock of equal value, which is then further..." Jain said in a stilted tone, cheated of his moment of glory.

Sumit's eyes followed the servant who was serving the assembled people their drinks. He just waved to the lawyer silently to proceed.

"After your uncle's death, his stock gets divided between his two sons Vishnu and Shivam," Jain said.

"Damn it, man. That does not concern me. Tell me what concerns me." Sumit snapped.

"Sir, as such Yuvrani Himani and her husband hold five percent together, Yuvrani Mehak and her husband hold five percent. Thirty per cent is yours, as such...however..." and the man's glance wandered towards Sumit who was pouring another stiff drink from the decanter, "...However should you wish to not shoulder responsibility, there is a provision in the will. The Royal Group will be happy to buy you out, as such, at the market value prevailing at the time of purchase."

"You begin to interest me extremely," Sumit drawled, putting ice cubes into the glass. His eyes glittered dangerously as he said, "Did he specify what he wanted me to do to 'prove responsible?' Explain it clearly without any legal bullshit and any more 'as such'es."

The man flinched. "Within a period of six months after his death, you have to get married. The bride..." He cleared his throat and resumed, "The bride has to be deemed suitable in every respect by your uncle. You have to show active interest in the performance of the hotels. After six months your performance will be reviewed by the board."

Sumit smiled sweetly, "What Madam, your opinion regarding my bride does not matter? What a low blow!"

Ashen faced, Devika stood up, and wordlessly stormed out of the flat. His eyes alight with a private joke he asked Himani, "What? You're still here?" She bit her lip and followed her mother out, slamming the door.

The clearly uncomfortable lawyer got up, gathered his papers and excused himself. Sumit said, "Go man, go. I will need you soon, leave your visiting card here."

After he left, Sumit looked at Girdhari and said, "It seems I have to toe your line, Uncle."

"I am not your enemy, son. I know you are angry, you feel betrayed. I understand that, but please understand that no one is out to get you. All I am concerned with is Royal."

"I thank you." Sumit said gently.

Girdhari said, "Take care of your back, son." He and Vishnu left.

The smile left Sumit's face. He looked at Aditya and Mehak, "I need your support, both of your support. Give it to me unstintingly and I will make it worth your while."

Aditya looked deeply offended, "You can't buy me Sumit!"

Mehak laid a restraining hand on Aditya's shoulder, "I don't think he is talking about money Adi. I will lay down the terms, for both of us. Have you got it in you to meet them?"

He smiled. His sister understood him very well.

"Free me from Somnath. Support me and Adi those are my terms." Mehak stated flatly.

This time the smile on Sumit's face was genuine. He nodded.

"Himani is a fool of the worst kind, the kind that thinks it's smart. I want her maid and driver to report to me, can that be done?" he asked.

Mehak smiled and nodded. Sumit was more like their father than he thought. "It can be done. What else?"

"Adi, can your mother teach Vaishali the royal etiquette?" Sumit asked.

"She already has started. The bridal trousseau is being fixed by the same tailor who does her clothes."

He chuckled. Sejal auntie would try to show his mother down. "Thank heavens. Our mother's taste is awful!"

Sumit groaned. His back was in a bad shape. Mehak said, "Go and sleep, Sumit. We'll go."

He painfully went to his bedroom and lay down, mulling on some plans he did not want to share them, not yet. He lay down in bed, his painful back making sleep impossible. His mind kept reliving the moment the boulder came rushing down the hill. Who had tried to kill him? And why?

✦ ✦ ✦

12

The Chessmen Assemble

At seven in the morning, Sumit, supported by his driver and a servant, hobbled into the courtyard of the ashram. The salve and massage by the ashram healer had given him more relief than his chiropractor's medication had given him in years.

Martial arts classes were being conducted by Vaishali dressed in a Gi. He winced as she threw an opponent on the mat with a wild yell. Sid saw him as he walked to the dispensary, walked up and said, "Hey Jeej, you look horrible."

"Thank you," said Sumit with careful restraint as a folding cot was quickly set down in the shade of a safeda tree for him. "What are you doing here? No school?"

"It's Sunday. Your Girdhari uncle and Papa were to meet here. Ma and I came along. Vaish is taking class. Sejal Auntie is here too. "

He tried to stand up, "My uncle is here?"

A young man dressed in the ashram robes pushed him back on the cot, "Lie down on your stomach, Maharao ji."

Pushing his shirt up, he began massaging his back. Some of Vaishali's students gathered around him. Vaishali followed them and scolded the kids, "Is there a show going on here? Go away, shoo!" The children ran away giggling.

"How are you feeling?" she asked.

"Bad. What does my uncle want?" he asked.

"They are matching our birth charts and all that," said Vaishali.

Chandan came out of the Ayurvedic dispensary and scolded his assistant, "You should have taken the Maharao into the treatment room. Now go." The man left. "Couldn't sleep?"

"No," Sumit groaned.

"You store stress in your back. I would advise prayer and meditation," said Chandan.

Sumit laughed. Chandan smiled back, "I thought so. You're still an atheist."

"A realist," offered Sumit.

Chandan helped him up, saying, "You will never change Maharao ji. Now, sit up slowly. Then get up and walk around the courtyard for about fifteen minutes very slowly to loosen the muscles. Work out the anger and tension inside you. Start playing volleyball again."

He turned to go, but Sumit asked, "What is this rubbish about matching our horoscopes?"

"It is customary," Chandan replied.

"I don't believe in astrology," Sumit said.

Chandan said with a smile. "Come on, Maharao Sumit, stop being so negative. A positive attitude and less anger will help improve your back. Faith in God will help."

"Well I don't have that faith, and I find it very liberating," he said grumpily and got up from the bed, tucked in his shirt and hobbled towards the inner room where Girdhari and Shankar were sitting cross legged in front of the old priest who was studying the horoscopes.

Girdhari smiled at him and said pleasantly, "How wonderful to see you here. Mr. Bhatia and I are having both your horoscopes matched. We want to ensure that you will have all the happiness in life."

Whatever Sumit may have said died down unsaid in the face of such cheeriness. He turned and Vaishali put his arm around her shoulder and led him into the courtyard and they started walking slowly. She was tall, and came up to his shoulder. Walking with her was pleasant. He could feel his back muscles loosen. They walked around in a companionable silence. In a much softer tone, he asked, "So, if that old fraud says that we are incompatible, you'll back off?"

"You've been out of the country for too long. There are degrees of incompatibility, and bribing can make them all go away," she chimed.

He chuckled. "How much will that old fraud take?"

"Bribing Sant Anirudh is impossible. Chandan Pandit is easy. You do anything for those orphans of his, and he melts," offered the girl.

"So what does one have to do for his god-awful orphans?" he asked.

"Sejal Auntie and Chandan Pandit were discussing that some days ago. People donate wheat, rice and even dal. The ashram grows its vegetables. What they need is buffalos and cows for milk," she said.

Vaishali stopped and frowned. A tall girl, she could look over the ashram walls to spot two cars that came to a halt next to the gate. "Who is that? A boyfriend?" asked Sumit noticing her gaze.

She shook her head, "Oh that is Resham Shastri's car. For a moment, I thought his brother Puneet was driving it," she replied.

"And you do not like the poor unfortunate Puneet Shastri, judging by your tone?" Sumit observed, watching Somnath stepping out of Shastri's car and opening the door courteously for Devika. Himani and Rohtash stepped out of the other car.

"I threw him into the river once," she said tersely.

"Why?" he said turning his neck to look at her. Apparently his uncle had called the entire family to the ashram for the matching of horoscopes. But why were the ladies hobnobbing with the local politicians? They entered the courtyard. Sumit tried to ignore them.

"He is very cheap; he grabbed and tried to kiss me. So I pushed him into the river," Vaishali confessed, her cheeks red with embarrassment.

He laughed out loudly, "Wow! I better brush up my swimming skills."

Devika stopped, glanced at them, ignored them and walked into the Sant's room, holding her head high, her entire demeanor reeking of disapproval. "Why was I called?" she asked, in a loud imperious tone, easily audible in the courtyard.

Girdhari got up and shushed her, "We are getting the horoscopes matched."

A young priest standing next to the Sant said, "Please come into Santji's private courtyard. Santji will announce his findings there."

They were led into the private courtyard. Shankar Bhatia approached Sumit's mother and greeted her politely with folded hands. She ignored him. Vaishali noted the snub with pursed lips. Sumit said thoughtfully, "I've always believed that one should not get angry, but even. Will you marry me whatever the old fraud announces? You could settle scores."

Her angry eyes were fixed on the older woman, as she nodded firmly, "Yes I will."

Sumit nodded at Chandan Pandit, who approached them, and said, "I hear you need a couple of cows for your ashram?"

Chandan said, "The children need milk Maharao ji."

"Come on Chandan, avoid the Maharao bullshit," instructed Sumit.

He said, "Okay, but in company you shall always be Maharao, Sumit ji. I warn you though; I can't influence the Sant."

"You do have a system in your chart reading stuff where you can prescribe remedies don't you?" asked Sumit.

"The ashram needs a cow shed, two cows and two buffalos," Chandan Pandit said firmly, an understanding smile on his face.

Sumit smiled back, "You've grown smart."

"A goat too," Chandan added for good measure.

He nodded, "But of course. So we have an understanding?"

"Yes," replied the man of divinity.

"Then be ready for my next move," he said, gripping Vaishali's hand tightly.

Sant Anirudh came out, flinched in the sunshine and stood, taking his time. A couple of his boys set up a chair for him. Sumit's lips twitched. Having dated a lot of show girls, he knew all there was to know about stage presence. The old man may not have studied stage management, but practised it with innate flair.

Then Sant Anirudh announced, "This is a very auspicious hour, and I bring you good news. The Maharao has gone through a very bad phase of his life, thanks to Saturn. The dangers up to now have been emotional and financial. Now, unfortunately, with the retrograde Mercury, there is danger to his life."

"I don't believe in all this," Sumit said, but there was little conviction in his voice as he remembered the boulder hurtling down at them, and Vaishali pushing him out of the way.

"Nature, celestial bodies and the divine will continue to function whether we choose to believe in them or not. The good news is that your Venus is strong, which resonates with Vaishali's birth chart," declared Anirudh.

"What does that mean?" Girdhari asked.

"Vaishali not only brings him peace and stability. She protects his life. The match is good," said the holy man.

"Uncle, are you satisfied?" Sumit's voice was completely triumphant.

Girdhari asked, "What about the danger to his life?"

"I repeat, the girl's stars protect him against such dangers," came the reply.

"I am satisfied then," Girdhari said.

Sumit said softly, "Santji marry us, right now. After all, you said it is the auspicious hour."

Rani Devika said, "No! How can you? Your father died hardly a few weeks ago!"

A stunned Vaishali looked at her fiancé, whose eyes were dancing with unholy pleasure. "But why, mother? She protects me. Your saint said so. Unless, of course..."

Girdhari said, "Really Sumit, this is tasteless."

Vaishali saw the shock on her parents' faces and rushed to their side. Shankar protested, "We need time. We are not prepared for a wedding right now."

Rohtash said, "There is a renowned astrologer in Delhi. I'll consult him."

Himani said coldly, "Sumit, I just hope this is one of your tasteless jokes."

"No, I am serious." She looked at him disbelievingly. He pulled out his phone and dialed Mehak's number, "Hi, Mehak, do you have something in red that Vaishali can wear just now? She is wearing a Karate Kid outfit, and we can't get married with her in that."

The phone literally squawked. He removed it slightly from his ear and answered, "Yes, you heard right. At the ashram. Just hurry, Mehak. The Sant says it's the auspicious hour and all that. We can't miss that. I'll explain later. Please get something red for her."

Girdhari said, "Sumit, please consider. What will people say? You're putting the girl in a very awkward position."

Sumit turned to Vaishali, "I am sorry my dear, I know girls dream about their marriage and all that. I apologize for rushing you into it."

"Not me, I never dreamt about marriage. Never," she replied emphatically in perfect truth.

He laughed. "See uncle, she is special. I am not going to let her slip through my fingers."

Girdhari threw up his hands, "Very well then."

The men were deep in discussion and Vaishali looked at her mother, bewildered.

"Ma?" she said. Shrishti hugged her, "Vaishali, I...I don't know what to say. But remember, very few of us manage to make such a brilliant match. And it is happening in God's own house."

"Ma, he is a good man. He is rude and sarcastic, but I sense that he is good." Then she hugged her mother, "I am scared."

Shristi hugged her, breaking into sobs. "I am sorry; I know you are not ready. But what can we say about our destinies?" Vaishali hugged her, her own eyes wet. "Vaish, we will always be with you, remember that!"

Sejal entered the courtyard with regal grace. Devika flushed. Unlike Devika, who was dressed in a heavy white Benarasi silk sari with a gold border, which did not flatter her short dumpy figure, Sejal was dressed in a simple peach colored kurti and tights. Her hair was knotted into an elegant French knot at the nape of her neck. She outclassed every woman present.

She ignored everyone, walking up to Vaishali and Shrishti, "Vaishali? Mehak called and said you needed me."

Vaishali hugged her wordlessly. Sejal hugged her back and nodded at Shrishti, ushering them away with dexterity which was smooth and appeared natural. Once they reached the empty dining room of the ashram orphans, all three sat down.

"What do we do, Sejal Auntie?" Vaishali asked.

Sejal said, "Go with the flow, Vaishali. You can't fight it, it could have repercussions. My advice would be to go with the flow, but be smart."

Shrishti said, "What do you mean? Can my daughter be harmed?"

Vaishali said, "No Ma. He is a good man."

"Yes, he is good. I have known him since he was a small boy. He is a very affectionate boy, and has a strong sense of loyalty. But child, the haveli has its own politics. You need to set up your own line of defense, your team of loyalists. And as the new Rani, you will displace the old Rani. It is the natural order of things, but not necessarily pleasant."

Bala watched them not understanding what they spoke but could sense the distress. With trembling hands, she filled three glasses with water and brought them to the women.

Vaishali accepted the glass, noticing absently that her own hands shook. She looked at the girl's face and recalled the story of how she landed up in the ashram. One of the ashram boys had shared it with Sid. With effort, she smiled and said, "Thank you, what is your name?"

"Bala," the girl whispered.

"Thank you Bala. Ma, Sejal Auntie, some water?"

Shristhi took the proffered glass. Bala tried to slink away and Vaishali stopped her. "What is going on in the courtyard?"

"The prince wants the marriage to happen now. The Rani is screaming and crying. She always does that. She comes to the mandir daily to weep in front of Santji. If he is not there, she weeps in front of the Shiva idol."

Shrishti spotted Sid, "Siddharth..." she began but her voice broke and tears began to flow afresh. Vaishali slipped off her chair and put her head in her mother's lap, and Sid came and hugged them both.

Sejal said firmly, "Now is not the time to cry. You have to think clearly without emotions. Please control yourselves. I thought you were brave, Vaishali. What is this? You're getting married, not being jailed or something."

The voices in the courtyard grew louder and more aggressive. Shankar asked loudly, "Where are my wife and daughter?"

He rushed into the dining hall, along with Sumit and Girdhari. Sant Anirudh followed at a slower pace. Bala shrank back.

Vaishali stood up, took a deep breath and addressed them hesitantly, her eyes fixed on Girdhari, "I am not as old or wise as you all. Maybe someone may have a better idea. If the Maharao gets protected by marrying me, a small some kind of ceremony can be held now. Once the time is suitable, maybe, you know what I mean...I am sorry, I am not being clear."

Girdhari smiled and said, "Well done, child. Yes, this is acceptable."

"What is acceptable?" Sant Anirudh asked entering the dining area.

Girdhari folded his hands and said, "Santji, the bride agrees to a small informal ceremony right now."

Anirudh smiled and said, "Excellent. The ashram will make preparations in the yagna hall. Vaishali, this is Bala. She will help you get dressed. She is a good girl. I think you will find her capable."

Vaishali nodded; bit her lower lip nervously, "Thank you."

Chandan winced as he recalled the day, a long time ago when Santji had taken his eight month old sister from his arms and handed her to her foster parents. Steeling himself he added, "She is a good girl and has no home. I wish you could keep her with you in the haveli."

She stole a glance at Sumit and mumbled, "I don't know how the situation will be."

Sejal said softly, "Exactly! It would be useful to have someone totally loyal in such a situation."

Her eyes widened with comprehension and she nodded.

Sejal and Mehak helped her dress up in the red lehenga choli that Mehak had brought. "See! I guessed your height well. I wish I was as slim as you," Mehak said happily. Vaishali smiled. Mehak said, "Congratulations. I will be glad to have you as my sister-in-law."

Shrishti took off her gold bangles and earrings and said, "Wear them."

Vaishali wept, "No, Ma."

"Shh baby, we can't have you getting married without any jewelry."

She took off the simple tops Vaishali was wearing and replaced them with her heavier diamond studs and slipped her own chain around her neck. "Wear the bangles and stop crying. We need some make up and henna."

Bala came with a bowl of freshly ground henna paste, knelt down near Vaishali and started applying it on her palms. The design was simple but pretty. "Where did you learn to do this?" Vaishali asked her. "It is so pretty. But I will wash it off. I have no patience with this stuff."

She smiled shyly, "I know Didi. That is why I added some *katha*. You need to keep it on for just five minutes. I learnt it from some gypsies who stayed in my village."

Vaishali glanced at her mother and Sejal Banasur who were having a whispered conversation. She said in a low voice, "Bala, will you come with me to the haveli? I promise to keep you close to me and safe."

She nodded. "Didi I will be loyal to you to the last drop of my blood."

"No need to get dramatic. I will need you to help me settle down. In return, you will be kept safe and you will be paid."

Bala's eyes widened and she nodded. "Pack your clothes then. Are five minutes over? I need this gunk to be removed." Vaish waved her hands irritably. Bala smiled and said, "I'll bring some water and clean it."

Once that was done, the bride was declared ready. She was ushered back into the private courtyard. The ashram inmates had been busy at work. The place was festooned with marigold garlands and mango leaves, presumably bought from the vendors who sold these at the entrance of the temple to devotees. A mandap had been erected with bamboo poles, and the ashram boys were wrapping marigold garlands around the poles. Sant Anirudh had already started chanting the mantras. Everyone gathered in the courtyard turned to look at her as she entered, escorted by Mehak, Sejal and Bala. She faltered as it seemed to her in her overwrought state of mind that the entire Nausar had gathered in the courtyard. Then she realized that it was just Sumit's family, her family, Sejal and Aditya Banasur and Resham Shastri, his wife and his younger brother, Puneet.

Sumit was sitting cross legged in a dhoti and kurta which possibly belonged to Pratham in front of the *havan kund*. He came to his feet when Vaishali entered. "Sit down!" Sant Anirudh scolded him. He sat down again.

"I thought you fled," he said, as she came and sat down next to him.

She suppressed the flash of anger that rose in her. How could she have fled, and where to? Her family fortunes, her beloved brother's future were all linked to this marriage. "I am sorry I forced you. I'll make it up to you, I promise," he whispered. The look in his eyes reminded her of the expression she often saw in Sid's eyes, when he knew he'd done something inexcusable but begged for forgiveness.

She smiled, "If you don't, I'll make you," she whispered back, with more confidence than she was feeling.

Sant Anirudh scolded them, "These mantras are meant for you both. Will you pay attention?"

Sumit tried to maintain his composure but the reprimand reduced his bride to nervous giggles that brought a smile to his face, much to the displeasure of his mother and older sister.

"You stink of balm," she told him.

"And you smell of henna and Sejal Auntie's perfume," he shot back, slipping his hand into hers. "Don't be scared. I'll take care of you, I promise."

She smiled back. It meant more to her than the mantras the Sant chanted. After the ceremony was over, Vaishali's father said, "I would like to take my daughter home until a formal ceremony is held."

Aditya quickly came to Sumit's side, "You've got your way. Now, let her go man!" Sumit realized that he was clenching her hand so hard that it had red welts. He released her hand and smiled grimly, "Sorry for that. I am letting her go, for tonight. I will come for her tomorrow."

Then their attention was drawn to Bala who came with a small bundle and clutched Vaishali's hand.

"Who is that?" asked Shankar with surprise.

Vaishali said firmly, "My maid and companion." She asked Sumit, "May I keep her?"

Sid burst out incredulously, "Gosh Vaish, she is a person, not a puppy!"

Sumit laughed and nodded, "Yes, I meant to employ someone for you. Who vouches for her?"

Chandan said, "She is a good girl. She lives in the ashram but needs employment."

"Yes, you can keep her," Sumit said.

"Gosh, Jeej, you'll spoil Vaish horribly," Sid said with disgust, as his mother tried to hush him up. After hastily procured sweets were distributed, the assembled people left.

"What just happened?" Chandan wondered aloud.

The old Sant had a satisfied smile on his face. "I think we just witnessed the will of God."

Pratham and Chandan shared a look of acute resentment. The old saint was at it again, deciding what was best for others, based on some vague intuitive impulses only he could understand.

After the Marriage

Unlike Nausar, Banasur was a smaller province. In the olden days, most of its revenue came from the timber that grew in the vast jungles, and also from the river Nausar. In the recent days, certain invaluable medicinal plants had been discovered to be growing wild, which had given the small province a fresh lease of life. But it was, and would always remain the poor cousin to its richer neighbor, Nausar.

The erstwhile rulers of Banasur, Aditya and his mother Sejal drove to their haveli and parked in front of it. Sejal got out and gazed at her home. Unlike the grand haveli of Nausar, this structure needed more than a coat of paint. Walls were crumbling, drains were choked, seepage showing in damp patches in the structure. Sejal shrugged and walked towards the side door to the east, past what once was a pool where multicolored fish had frolicked. Now it was a mossy depression, choked with weeds. She rang the bell, asking him, "Are you spending the night here?"

"Yes," he said, following her into the few rooms they lived in and sat down on the couch, taking off his shoes. The rest of the haveli had not been opened for the past three decades. "I talked to Vishnu about purchasing this place and building some offices or a hotel. He said he would talk to his father. He was shocked; he asked why I wanted to make you homeless. I told him it was your idea. He did not believe me."

Sejal ordered the cook, "Two cups of tea."

She settled down on an easy chair, said, "So basically, he refused. I am not surprised. Vishnu is just like Girdhari, he does not have any spark in him. That sleazeball rang me again."

"Who? Chanchal Shastri?" asked Adi.

"Shh! Don't take names. It's too dangerous," his mother warned.

"Ma, the old man is dead. There is nothing to fear," Adi said, putting his arm around her. "Get over it."

She smiled tiredly, "I did not fear the old man, Adi. Let me caution you, though. Digvijay lives in Sumit; he is a younger and far more vicious version of his father. Today, it was like watching Digvijay in action."

Aditya studied his nails. "What did the sleazeball want?" he asked abruptly.

"Chanchal? He'll pay us a bit more. They want to go deeper into the forests. We'll get more now, to look away and keep our mouths shut. I agreed. Now I wish I hadn't. Sumit is too dangerous a man to cross."

"We need the money, Ma. This house needs a lot of repair," said Adi.

She looked away; she did not want to live here. But who asked a woman for her opinion anyway. She wanted it sold, the past erased. But he would never know that. To him it was his heritage, the royal seat of Banasur.

"What do you think about Sumit's marriage?" she asked instead.

"She is just a child, Ma. I feel sorry for her," replied Adi.

"I was younger than her, Aditya. Even your sisters were twelve and thirteen when they got married. It happens."

"I never thought of that. How did you face it all?" asked Adi.

"Your father was a good man. Your grandmother was mercifully short lived; she died a month after your father did," his mother recalled.

A car screeched noisily to a halt and the door opened noisily, slamming shut.

"Hello Mehak," Aditya said, without turning his head.

"Hi, I stopped at Royal One and got Chinese packed, and a huge black forest cake. Weddings make me hungry."

Aditya broke into a laugh. Mehak ordered the servant to go collect the packets from the car and sat down. "Someone should celebrate. My brother got married today. My mother and sister are going on as though he murdered someone or he was jailed or something!"

"Is that garlic chicken I smell?" Aditya asked.

"Yes, I also got egg fu yong and prawn fried rice."

They began eating when Sejal said, "I wonder if the bride and her family are eating today."

Mehak stopped eating and asked, "Why not? She just married the Maharao of Nausar. They would be celebrating!"

Aditya and Sejal exchanged glances but kept quiet. "Explain," Mehak said.

"The Nausars are not the easiest people to deal with, Mehak. Your brother just proved that. I would not be surprised if they are terrified."

Mehak nodded, as she picked up a prawn with her chopsticks and transferred it into her mouth and broke into a smile. "Brother Dearest will be too involved with his bride. She is quite a handful. You think he will be able to meet the board requirements in six months?"

Aditya smiled, "It will be entertaining to watch that playboy work, while his new bride demands attention."

Sejal smiled and took a piece of cake. They were underestimating Sumit Singh Nausar. Today, he reminded her strongly of his dead father.

"You both did well today, bonding with the new bride will help us a lot," Aditya said expansively. She smiled, how like a man! He thought the battle was won.

Mehak smiled, "She is likeable. Besides, I love doing things that irritate Ma and Himani."

Sejal stepped in, "Yes, she is likeable. She is also very young. Aditya, right now she is alone, she needs all the friends she can get. When does she move into the haveli?"

"Sumit would like to bring her to the haveli tomorrow," he said.

"Then you should go to her home tomorrow morning, and offer her your support. She is the wife of your foster brother and Chairman."

Mehak said, "I'll go with you."

"No, you accompany your mother. She was snubbed today in public. She will try and avenge herself tomorrow. Go soften the blow."

Mehak smiled and nodded. No wonder her father preferred Sejal to his own wife. She was wise and astute, besides being gorgeous.

✦

The next morning Vaishali woke up with a strange sense of not belonging in her own home. She stared at her face in the mirror, her mind chanting again and again, "I am married, I am married."

Her face looked just the same. She made a face and thought, "Well, what did I expect? I can't change overnight into a beauty like Pallavi Di."

Her mother's voice came from the living room and she went to her. Shrishti was sitting on the rug, the phone next to her. She had been ringing up relatives and packing her things into suitcases. "Your clothes," she said in a husky voice, wiping her nose, her eyes swollen and red. With a pang, Vaishali realized that her mother had wept through the night as she packed her trousseau.

"Ma, can't we delay my going?" she said as she hugged her mother.

"I tried to make your husband see that point of view, but he is firm. He is your husband. What can I say? First Pallavi, and now you...I have lost both my daughters within a month."

Vaishali burst into tears as she sat down next to her, hugging her. Bala peeped in from the kitchen, saw what was happening and came in. She sat down cross-legged and started folding the clothes and neatly stacking them. Sid walked in, in his pajamas rubbing his eyes. "God, stop behaving like tragedy queens. What if Vaish was married abroad?"

The doorbell rang. Sid went and ushered in Aditya. He took one look at the two women and grasped the situation. "You know, my mother had it tougher. My father died and six months later, both my sisters were married off and I was sent to the haveli."

"God! How did she cope?" asked Vaishali, horrified. Her mother and she were having a hard time, just thinking about it. His face softened, "She is special."

Sid said, "There, if Sejal Auntie could cope with it, you can do so too!"

Aditya said, "Sumit will be here in a couple of hours. His sisters and his mother are on their way."

Shrishti sprang to her feet, calling the whole family to help her clear the living room.

Vaishali joined Bala on the floor, picking up stacks of clothes and put them into the suitcases. She muttered, "When I talk to them, they look at me as though I have snot on my face."

Sid snorted with amusement. "So look at them as if they have dirt on their faces. It's not like you to bother about such stuff."

Aditya also pitched in and they quickly cleared the living room. Shrishti said, "Go dress up, Vaishali, and you too Sid." She rushed out to hurry her husband up. Vaishali nodded, but stopped to pick up the phone, which was ringing.

She was still on the phone, accepting an ecstatic and inquisitive cousin's congratulations when the ladies arrived.

Devika walked in and cast a disapproving glance at the living room, and then lowered herself into a couch, "I just wanted to see what the bride will be wearing for the formal function. After all there will be guests from all over the world."

Vaishali smiled sweetly and said, "Clothes."

Mehak said, "Oh come on Mother! Let's get it done. Vaishali, here is your *vidai* dress. Wear this right now. Sant ji has also sent some sacred thread and a charm that you are supposed to wear, for your safety. We will have a small pooja here and then take you with us."

The Maharani said distantly, "On the function, I have decided that you will wear a very nice set of priceless Burmese rubies done up with antique gold. I hope the jewels won't clash with whatever you wear on the function. The pride of Nausar depends on it."

Vaishali shot back, "Thank you for your concern. If they do, we can rebuild the pride of Nausar with some other outfit at some other occasion, can't we?"

Her mother intervened hastily, "Oh no, she will wear cream and gold. Vaishali, bring the new lehnga choli. The stones will go so well with it."

Vaishali dug her heels in, glaring at her mother-in-law, her eyes dark with anger.

Shrishti clucked her tongue and rushed in, bringing the cream and gold lehenga to the living room. Himani murmured, "But she is so dark. Is cream just the thing for her?" Vaishali stared at her with open hostility.

Sumit entered just in time to hear Himani's words and put his hand on Vaishali's shoulder. "Good morning Himani. Has your breakfast disagreed with you or is this your usual charm?"

Himani turned red and muttered, "I just wondered if she should wear something so light colored at the formal function."

"Really? Maybe we should not have such a function. I am against any sort of ostentation. Vaishali, should we have a function or would you like to go to Venice for a month or so? My mother and Himani have really stuffy guests most of the time."

Vaishali smiled, her temper subsiding. Mehak laughed, "Oh come on, Sumit. A formal function has to be held, you know that! Come on people behave. Sant ji will be here any moment for the pooja. Vaishali, go and change please. We can't have your vidai in your night clothes."

Vaishali looked down at her Tweety Bird pajamas and left the room. Shrishti ushered Sid away. Seeing that none of the Bhatias were in the living room, Sumit glared at his mother and Himani, "I warn you both. If you misbehave with her, if I notice any kind of mistreatment...I hope I am clear."

Shankar entered with Chandan, "Sant ji has gone to the haveli to prepare for receiving the bride. Chandan Pandit is here to conduct the send-off. Shall we begin?"

Chandan stood at the gate and chanted a few mantras for peace and prosperity. Vaishali was then ceremonially ushered into Sumit's car. Bala stopped for a moment next to the priest and then quietly sat down next to Vaishali and the car drove off.

Aditya noticed this wordless interaction and pointed it out to Mehak. By noon, after more rituals, Vaishali was ushered into a set of rooms in the west wing, an annexe of the haveli. "The family has dinner together mostly. Lunch and breakfast are served in your own rooms, Rani," the old servant told her respectfully.

She nodded and looked around. The floor was Italian marble and cold. The furniture belonged to ancient times, it was heavy and carved. She disliked it on sight. She wandered into the bedroom where a huge double bed stood in the centre. There were arm chairs and a small coffee table arranged near the window that overlooked a spacious balcony. A massive wall-to-wall cupboard stood against the other wall. She quickly went back to the sitting room. It opened into a small kitchenette, which was attached to a small room, modestly furnished with a bed and a chest of drawers. The living room had another door. She opened that and jumped back as she saw Sumit. He had thrown his shirt on a chair and standing bare-chested, talking on the phone. Sumit saw her, disconnected the call and said, "Have you checked up your rooms? Come let me show you." He walked into the sitting room and said, "This is your sitting room; there is a bedroom for you and a small room, which your maid can use. There is a small kitchen. I am not sure if the coffee machine and fridge are installed. Check that out. If the furniture is not to your taste, ask my sisters, no forget Himani, you can ask Mehak where she gets hers from. Her taste is better."

She nodded silently. He gave a tight smile and added, "My rooms are connected to yours through this door. If you need something, I will be here." He opened the door that led to his set of rooms, closing the door behind him, leaving her alone.

She sat down on the armchair, and looked around, feeling abandoned, lonely. Bala came in, followed by her things. Vaish smiled on seeing a familiar face. Her cellphone beeped. It was Sid, "Yo, Vaish, what's up?"

She grinned broadly as she made plans with her brother to meet him soon. She was not alone.

✦ ✦ ✦

13

The New Car

The next few days were rather lonely for Vaishali. It is not easy for a girl to be transplanted from her own home and family, and put into a huge building where people kept to themselves. Everyone in this house had a life, and after bringing her here, they just went right back to living it. Her life had just suffered a hiatus. She missed the easygoing atmosphere of her home; she missed the streets she had played cricket in. She even missed the shrill whistle of the pressure cooker that woke her up in the morning. Here, morning tea came to her bedroom with a polite knock.

She sat up in bed as Bala brought her tray in. "I'll go mad if this goes on," she muttered as she jumped out of bed and walked into the bathroom. She was bored and upset. Sumit was pacing up and down on the balcony she shared with him, talking on the phone. Grabbing her mug of tea she marched out into the balcony.

"We need to talk," she said ominously.

His eyebrows shot up. Not a stranger to female-speak, he knew this was a precursor to a fight. "I'll call you later," he told the person on the other side and gestured to the cane armchairs kept in the balcony.

She sat down and said bluntly, "I am bored, I can't stay here."

Bala quietly brought Vaishali's tray and put it on the table. "Get my tray too," Sumit said.

Bala jumped up in fear and scooted.

"What's biting her?" he asked surprised.

Unable to resist it, Vaishali said, "She finds you scary."

"Mad woman! Vaishali there is plenty to keep you occupied in the haveli. Ask my sisters, they are always busy. They can guide you."

Vaishali flushed at the unconsciously patronising tone in his voice. She said angrily, "No, I will not ask your sisters to keep me occupied. You are my husband. You brought me here and it is your job to watch out for me."

Her voice rose slightly and he looked at her coldly. "Madam, behave! Stop acting like an ill-bred and cheap vegetable saleswoman."

Angered beyond words, she got up and stomped off to her room and slammed the door shut. She kicked the couch in her temper, stubbed her bare toe and then sat down sulkily on it.

Bala stood for a while at the door, watching her and then crept up to her, "You are very brave, Didi. But that is not the right way to behave with your husband."

"No, Bala, I am not brave. I am very bored. Even this ancient T.V. does not work. Stupid place. I want to go out. I want to go back home."

"You are married, this is your home."

She scowled. This whole sacrifice-my-life-for-my-family thing was supposed to make her feel noble, not bore her out of her mind.

She stabbed her cheese sandwich with a knife visualizing it to be Pallavi's face. It was her older sister's fault she was here in this awful masauleoum. "So what am I supposed to do?"

"Be nice to your man. That is the only way to get what you want. *Rajkumari* Himani's maid Mamta says that her mistress feels that your man will be bored of you within a month and go away."

She stabbed the sandwich again. Sumit opened the door, "If you've finished killing your breakfast, get dressed. We have to be out in half an hour. Wear your jeans; not any of those godawful clothes you're wearing these days."

"You heard him? Get my jeans out, hurry!" she told Bala excitedly, her good mood restored. She was going out!

"Much better," he told her approvingly as she got into the car dressed in her jeans and tee shirt. "The desi look is not your kind of thing. You need better footwear and accessories though, but this will do for now. Do you know how to drive?"

"Yes, but I don't have much practice."

He drove them to the car dealer and showed her a Skoda Octavia. "Your car. Like it?"

Her face fell. "Thank you," she said politely.

He took her aside, "What's the matter?"

"I don't want to be rude. Please don't think I am ungrateful but it's not happening. It's such an old woman car."

"Which car, in your opinion, is the very happening car for you?" he asked, his eyes beginning to twinkle.

"Your car," she said.

Sumit drove a Porche Cayenne. "Vaishali," he began repressively. She pouted, looking at him apprehensively. He drew a deep breath. "Okay, let us forget this old woman's car. But you will allow me to choose the car you will drive until you are used to driving."

She nodded. At least with a car she would be able to get out of the mausoleum. They spent a pleasant morning purchasing a Renault Duster and then drove to Sid's school to pick him up in the new car. He was frankly envious, and that made her feel much better.

Sumit told Sid, "Call your mother and tell her that you'll be back after lunch. Let's eat at Royal One." He lunched there with Mehak and Aditya often. It was their favorite haunt. Delighted they both nodded. He laughed and drove into the porch of the hotel, "Go to the Chinese Room, I'll join you."

They sat down and Vaishali ordered two huge chocolate sundaes. After the waiter went, Sid asked, "Vaish, are you okay? Are you happy?"

She nodded. Right now she felt on the top of the world.

"I am glad. After you left Ma freaked out. She went batty you know, bawling so loud, it was scary. Papa scolded her. She said that you were a Devi and you sacrificed yourself for the family and for me."

She made a gagging sound. "That's a bit extreme."

"Did you?" he asked, flushing uncomfortably. "I'd hate it if you did that for me you know."

"Nah, I sacrificed myself for a Renault Duster and fancy lunches at Royal One," she said airily.

He smiled and gripped her hands, his eyes slightly wet.

"Dessert before lunch? That's a new one," Sumit said joining them and sitting down next to Vaishali.

"We have bad taste. Let go Sid, let me eat," Vaishali said with soft smile. Sid smiled back as he dropped her hands.

With an effort to speak in his normal tone, he said, "Jeej, she is an awful driver. She backed Papa's car into the front gate and drove on top of it. It was totally crushed!"

Sumit laughed, "When we get home, you shall meet Thapa. He taught us how to drive. Mehak was worse; she once drove on to the verge and then left her car hanging on it, two wheels off the road."

"I heard that! Vaishali, don't believe everything Sumit says, even if it's true," Mehak said as she drew a chair and sat down.

Vaishali blushed. Mehak was wearing a gray satin shirt along with well-tailored pants. A delicate chain with a diamond pendant emphasized her long elegant neck, and she wore discrete studs in her ears. She felt childish and inadequate.

Aditya sat down next to Mehak.

Sumit said, "I thought we'd see you here. What brought you today, *Foo Yung*?"

"*Har Gau*," Mehak replied. "The new Chinese cook is great. But of course, he will be sent to the Mumbai or Delhi branch. We may as well enjoy the fare for now."

"You must have been Chinese in some previous avatar Mehak," Aditya said. "Have you finished?"

"No, we haven't yet started. Apparently Vaishali and Sid like to have sundae as appetizers. I have yet to order," Sumit said.

"We saw your car on the way here. Someone rammed into it," Aditya said, as Mehak waved to a waiter.

"An accident? Is my driver okay?" Sumit asked.

Aditya said, "We stopped to check. A tempo rammed into your car, and the driver fled. Not much damage, the fender is damaged. What surprises me is that how could someone not see the car? I mean one had to be blind not to see it. It's a bloody truck!"

"What do you mean?" Sumit asked.

Mehak said, "It is broad daylight and impossible to miss something as huge as your Cayenne, Sumit. The new Superintendent of Police was at the spot. Nice man. He said he would come to meet you one of these days, you know, pay you respects."

Sumit frowned, "How bloody feudal. Mehak, is he invited for the function?"

"Of course," she said, toying with her chopsticks.

"Good!"

Lunch came and the talk turned general. After lunch, Sid insisted on taking a cab home and was quickly shot down. Adi said, "I'm going to Banasur and will drop you on my way."

Sumit drove Vaishali back home in her new car. She said formally, "Thank you very much for the car and for the nice day."

Sumit laughed. "Next time, don't behave like an irritable cat. Talk about whatever is bothering you like a rational human, okay?"

She blushed and nodded.

"Thapa will come tomorrow in the morning. He will be your driver and teacher, okay? And, please stay in the haveli until the function; it's just a couple of days away. I'll just go attend to some work. See you at dinner."

"Would you like to take my car?" she asked shyly.

He laughed, "Your car eh? Just as I thought. You'll do well in this family. No I've called a cab. Run along now."

She smiled and ran along, making a note in her mind to listen to Bala. The girl had pointed her in the right direction. Her staff was growing, now she had a maid, a driver and she was also the proud owner of a car. Maybe Sid was right, she was being spoiled, but she was having too much fun to complain.

As usual, she met no one as she walked up to her rooms. She sat down on the bed and turned on the ancient television, reliving the day. This marriage could work; she just had to understand the man.

Bala walked in ashen faced. "What happened?" Vaishali asked.

The girl was shivering with fear. "Didi, we are in a very dangerous place!"

"Huh? Dangerous? With all those guards and the huge walls?"

"The danger is inside these walls. In the kitchens, they say that Rajkumari Himani prays for your death, which is why that accident happened today."

"Sumit's car met with an accident, but we were in another car."

"Black magic!" She began to shiver.

As much as Vaishali wanted to sleep off the heavy lunch she sat up in her bed and took Bala's hand in hers. It was cold. "Bala, there is no such thing as black magic. What did you hear?"

"They say the Rani practices black magic. She curses people," Bala whispered.

"Shh, there is no such thing. Now, you will have to be with me at the function. We have to get you pretty clothes to wear. The tailor will be here this evening. I think a nice lehenga or a pretty salwar suit would be best for you. What do you think?"

Bala smiled, but the fear did not leave her face. Vaishali sighed, aware that blind faith in sorcery and black magic existed in the villages. She gently shooed her away, "Bala I want to sleep. I won't need you until the evening."

The girl nodded and went to her small room, perhaps too shaken by the gossip in the servants' hall. Vaishali dozed off, to be woken by a knock on the door. She waited for Bala to get the door but when she did not, she opened the door to find a small box in a blue wrapper outside on the mat. She picked it up and tore it open. It was a string of rudraksha beads interspersed with small beads of gold. Bala had crept behind her and she stared at it suspiciously, "Who sent it?"

"There is no name on the box or the wrapper," Vaishali said.

"Don't wear it, Didi." She backed away. "It may have a spell cast on it."

"Okay, cool it," Vaishali said, feeling a finger of superstitious fear touching her. "I won't wear it." She shoved it into a drawer along with its box and wrapper and Bala gave her a relieved smile.

"I'll get your tea," she said and rushed off.

Vaishali took out the box and examined it once more, but found no clue about the sender. She put it back and forgot all about it. The tailor had arrived with the fabric and she had better things to think about.

✦ ✦ ✦

14

Missed Targets

On the day of the function, the haveli was abuzz with activity. Close friends of the family had flown in from all around the world. Of course the arrangements, the menu and the guest list were the talk of the entire town. The shamianas erected in the lawns of the haveli were spectacular and intrepid young men had a field day climbing roofs of buildings and nearby trees to peer in. The security had their hands full, shooing them away.

Aditya walked into the lawns an hour before the function to admire the arrangements, and found Himani's husband, Rohtash, berating the housekeeper, "This is basic common sense! South facing entrances are inauspicious!"

Kishan the elderly housekeeper said abjectly, "Sorry Sir, I did not know."

"Get it changed, immediately," roared Rohtash.

Aditya rushed to the spot, "What's happened Rohtash ji?"

"The entrance of the shamiana faces south!" he complained. "This idiot allowed it."

Kishan protested, "This was never discussed."

"I should have come out earlier. But I had a bad feeling about the date and time that stupid *purohit* had selected. I should have come out and checked the shamiana earlier," Rohtash grumbled.

Aditya glanced at his watch surreptitiously; the guests would be arriving within an hour or so. He smoothly suggested, "We can't delay the timing of the rituals. Only you can help us Rohtash ji. Can you check your books for some way, some remedy for such a thing?"

"Yes, yes! I must go back to the books," he muttered, as he turned towards the haveli. He turned and said to the housekeeper, "If anything happens, I will hold you responsible."

Aditya shook his head and said in a low voice, "Kishan ji, you carry on." That had been a near thing, the last thing they needed was Rohtash spoiling the function by his superstitious ramblings.

He turned to the sound of a chuckle, and his eyes lit up at the sight of an old friend from college, Brian Underwood who laughed and stepped forward to shake his hand with an amused observation, "Ah! You don't believe in the danger of south facing entrances?" Aditya broke into a smile and shook his hand, "Oh hello Brian, when did you land?"

Brian grinned, "This morning. Then there was this long drive to Nausar, it rattled every bone in my body. How do you people manage it?"

Aditya smiled. He said, "I trust the flight was good."

"Yes. And how is His Royal Highness doing?" asked Brian.

"Very well. Have you met him yet? He is inside dressing up," said Adi.

"No, I checked into Royal One and slept as soon as I arrived," replied Brian.

"Has your wife come with you? Come, I'll take you to him," offered Aditya and they started walking towards the haveli.

"No, Melissa could not get away," answered Brian.

Sumit looked resplendent in a peacock blue ensemble, with a pink turban trimmed with peacock blue on his head.

"Whoa, Your Highness, you look truly royal and pagan," Brian laughed.

Sumit laughed and hugged him. "Good to see you here, Brian!" He then checked his reflection in the mirror. "Yeah, I look like a peacock, just before the mating ritual."

"No, you look like a figure from the medieval 'Raj'. By the way, is that a real sword you are sporting?"

"Behold my Excalibur, or whatever the Indian equivalent is," said Sumit brandishing the sword.

Aditya jumped out of the way, "Sumit, be careful with that thing. I better be off, Rohtash is acting up. The entrance of the shamiana is causing him a lot of alarm!"

"Yesterday it was the mutton I ate that freaked him out. As per him I had to remain meatless on the day of my wedding and for a week henceforth. If I listen to more drivel from him..."

"Not to worry. I sent him back to those tomes of astrology he reads," said Aditya, cheerfully as he shut the door.

"Leave now!" Sumit ordered the servants.

"Very medieval and very grand," said Brian mocking him. Sumit laughed sheepishly and removed his turban. "It is really good to see you, Brian. You help keeping me normal."

Brian smiled politely. Once the servants left, the smile left Sumit's face. "Well?"

Brian said, "The land is ours. Gautam is transporting the machinery. Nashik is the place right now! I had never thought of it, I always considered Panchkula."

Sumit smiled. "Panchkula will be ours soon. I tell you, this is going to be huge. I would like to live long and enjoy it."

Brian looked at him keenly. Sumit was not an alarmist. He asked, "Are you sure, Sumit?"

"As sure as I can be. Brian, I need some inputs, an unbiased view if you will."

He shrugged and said, "Get real. This is the job for the Scotland Yard or whatever its Indian equivalent is."

"Brian, stop thinking I am crazy," he said.

"You hated your old man. Why do you care?"

"I still hate him. I can even understand why someone wanted to kill him. But what if someone wants more than revenge? I am very attached to my own life and health. I want to enjoy the money and power."

Brian shook his head and asked, "Any likely suspects in your mind?"

"Of course! The whole race of humanity! My old man was a nasty piece of work. And in my family, well, let's begin with my uncle and his sons. With me out of the way, they can edge my sisters out and take over the whole gig. They benefit from my death now that the old man is not alive. Then there is Aditya."

"Hey no. He is not the sort."

"My father did his family a great wrong. He has always been very kind and affectionate towards me and my sister. He maybe harboring a grudge. One never knows."

"I always felt that you should have stayed in touch with them," Brian murmured but knew that his friend and partner had an implacable uncompromising side to his personality.

"I've been away too long," Sumit sighed. He wanted to tell him more, about the boulder that spooked him by charging towards him and Vaishali, the accident his car suffered. It actually confirmed his suspicion. Devious Singh was not the sort to die in an accident, he had been killed.

There was a loud sound of conches being blown and women ululating to announce the arrival of the bride. Brian jumped in alarm, "Blimey, what happened?"

Sumit laughed and said, "You wanted to witness pagan didn't you? Come watch the show!"

Together they went to the lawns. "The colors! The pomp! Mel will be so miffed she missed all this!" Brian said unstrapping his camera to take pictures as Sumit stepped forward.

Vaishali looked like the pagan princess, famously epitomized by painters of yore, dressed in an ivory cream silk lehenga whose skirt was embroidered with antique gold thread and red stones. It was teamed with a very bold choli. Her breasts were barely covered with ivory cream silk fabric. The rest of the choli constituted of ruby colored net. She wore the antique gold and Burmese ruby jewelry with it. The veil supposed to cover her modesty was artistically arranged to just cover her head, revealing more than it concealed. She stood near the entrance of the shamiana, flanked by her parents and brother, conversing with them. Rani Devika and Himani walked towards the entrance of the shamiana dressed in drab white of mourning. They may have desired to make a statement, but no one seemed to notice them. In fact no one had eyes for anyone but the new bride who looked sizzling hot and handled all the attention with seasoned flair of someone born to capture the limelight.

Sumit had eyes for no one but his bride. Brian saw the look on his face and shared a smile with Aditya who came to usher them in. So the pagan prince had met his match, and he was besotted with her.

Sant Anirudh stood on the stage, chanting some mantras. Sumit had flatly refused to go through the marriage ritual again, deeming it as unnecessary, leading to a lot of acrimony. Vaishali had sided with Girdhari and managed to get him to agree to a small token ceremony exchanging garlands and rings in front of an audience.

Rohtash was standing next to Shankar, talking earnestly. Sumit bit back a curse as he looked at his brother-in-law with irritation. He approached them. A young priest blew a conch to mark his entrance and led the couple to the stage.

He placed a hand under Vaishali's elbow and asked courteously, "Has my stupid brother-in-law been troubling you."

She flushed. Rohtash had been such a wet blanket. Choosing her words carefully, she answered, "No. He is worried about the entrance facing south. I think he was more cheerful when I pointed out that this means that people entering will be facing north, which should be auspicious."

He gave a bark of laughter and quickly converted it into a polite cough. "That should have shut him up."

Sant Anirudh looked at them impatiently. Sumit smiled and beckoned Brian and Aditya. They approached. Vaishali smiled at the men, and followed Sumit up the makeshift stairs to the stage, carefully balancing on her high heels, followed by Bala dressed in a cream and ruby colored sari, holding the silver salver, bearing the rings.

Brian positioned himself near the stage to take photos. The couple sat down on the fancy armchairs, exchanged the rings while Sant Anirudh chanted mantras. He then stepped back and left the stage. An attendant brought heavy floral garlands made of jasmine and roses. They stood up, faced the assembled guests with a smile, and picked up the garlands. The conches blared and the women ululated again. Brian winced taking a step back. He let the camera drop from his hands. It swung from the strap on his shoulder as he stared at the stage stunned. Vaishali, unsteady on her pencil heels, stumbled and fell into Sumit's arms and together they staggered against the flower bedecked makeshift back wall of the stage.

Bala, who had been standing next to Vaishali screamed, "*Didi, Goli! Goli chal gayi*!"

Brian rushed to the stage. He had been to plenty of hunts in England, and could have sworn that he had heard a muffled gunshot. The couple seemed unhurt. He and Aditya escorted them off the stage to a couch.

Aditya looked around, beckoned Kishan. "Call the tent man who was responsible for the stage."

Sumit protested, "Adi, relax man! It's my wedding function. Let us celebrate!"

Then he turned to Vaishali and asked solicitiously, "Are you okay my dear?"

She was grinning. "It was...interesting. The look on Aditya ji's face was hilarious."

He laughed and patted her cheek, "You are a brat. We shall deal famously with each other. Come let us meet the guests." He grandly offered his hand, which she took and they went to mingle with the assembled guests.

Resham Shastri, flanked by Puneet, his younger brother, and Somnath approached them. Resham said warmly, "Vaishali! I am so happy that the Maharao has chosen a girl from Nausar as his bride. Congratulations!"

Vaishali smiled formally and folded her hands into a namaste. "No no! Why the formality? After all, you are my sister," he said putting his hands on her shoulders. "You know my brother Puneet?"

"Yes, we studied together," she said.

Puneet looked uncomfortable. She smiled, "I have not changed so much Puneet, that you would not recognize me. You used to call me *Kaali Billi*, black cat."

"And what did you call him?" asked Somnath laughing uproariously.

"A fish," she said, the smile on her face broadening. "It's a long story," she said forestalling any questions, as someone else approached.

✦ ✦ ✦

15

The Bullet

An hour later, Sumit was called away. Vaishali sat down in relief, slipping off her pencil heels. Sid sat down next to her, looking sad. All through the evening he had stuck to her side like a lost puppy. "Hey, remember? You wanted Pallavi and me to hurry up and get married so that you could be lord and master. Well you got your wish!" she teased Sid, who tried to smile.

Aditya approached her along with his mother. She tried to come to her feet, but Sejal forestalled her. "Don't bother. Not used to pencil heels?"

"My feet hurt," she confessed.

"Wedge heels are a better option at such events. Nice dress. It's going to be the talk of the town. I think you will start a fashion," Sejal said.

"Thank you. Your tailor is a gem. You are very kind to me," said Vaishali.

Sejal's eyes narrowed slightly. Then she said, "Vaishali, a word of advice from someone who has had to deal with the

Nausars all her life. They think qualities like 'soft' and 'kind' are signs of weakness."

Sid said, "Jeej's older sister treats her like dirt, even the mother."

"Oh hush. It is nothing. I am plain looking and am not royal," she said with a shrug.

Sejal smiled. "Oh no! You are sensational. You have a good bone structure and the height and confidence. Don't let anyone convince you that you are not." Then smiling at some personal joke, she said, "I think you can be so 'royal' that you will outshine every woman in the haveli. If you want, I can send you a teacher, he taught my daughters certain royal graces."

"I can't thank you enough," said Vaishali.

"I'll have her call you," Sejal said. It would please her a lot if the new Rani completely outshone and dethroned Devika. Slowly the crowd thinned and they saw Resham approach them, "Excuse me, but have you seen Puneet?"

Vaishali shook her head. Sid said, "I saw him some time ago, with Somnath ji near the bar. Then they went out that way," pointing at the back of the shamiana, towards the makeshift kitchen. Resham went that way and they continued talking.

It was very late when Himani came to their table. She ignored Sejal completely and said abruptly to Vaishali, "You are wanted in the haveli Baithak."

Vaishali refused to get pushed. She said, "I will be there presently. Sejal Auntie, I loved talking to you. Can we meet again?"

"Sure, call me whenever you are free and we can spend some time together," said Sejal with a smile. "Will you still be teaching martial arts at the ashram?" she asked the girl.

"I hope so," said Vaishali.

"Excellent! Then we will keep meeting," Sejal replied.

Vaishali fished out her cellphone and took her own time saving Sejal's number. Then she wished Sejal goodnight as Himani waited on with growing impatience. Then Vaishali slipped on her strappy pencil heels and stood up. Himani said caustically, "Let me tell you that you are making the wrong sort of friends."

Vaishali snapped back, "I prefer associating with people who are well mannered and pleasant to talk to."

Himani muttered sourly, "Now I am babysitting his bratty wife."

Vaishali gritted her teeth angrily and followed Himani inside in complete silence. Sejal smiled broadly as she watched them leave, satisfied that the new bride was well able to withstand any attempts to suppress her.

Vaishali limped into the hall, helped by Sid. Her feet were raw, thanks to the footwear. She stopped at the entrance next to a huge chessman. Her parents, Sumit's family and some servants were talking in hushed voices, and paid no attention to her and Sid. She limped in slowly. The first voice she heard was that of Rohtash who was saying loudly to anyone who cared to listen, "I knew it. South facing entrances are inauspicious. I warned you."

Sid left her side and walked up to the table next to the swing. The silver salver that had been used to carry the rings to the function now contained a small piece of twisted metal. Vaishali followed him wondering what had caught his attention.

"Don't touch it!" Their father admonished them, "It is a bullet!"

That drew Vaishali closer. She stared at the flattened piece of metal with horrified fascination.

Aditya said, "Where is the housekeeper? Damn it, where is Kishan?"

"He's questioning the servants. They may have heard something or seen something."

The moment Kishan entered, Rohtash began berating the hapless man. Sumit said, "Oh cool it, Rohtash. This is a bullet; it came from someone's gun, not a bloody south facing entrance."

Sid chortled, "Cool!"

"Hush!" admonished Vaishali still fixated by the bullet.

She looked around. Brian was standing slightly apart from the rest of the people, closer to them. She asked him, "What happened?"

"I was right next to the stage, taking photos when I heard a bullet whiz past me towards the stage. It was around the time you tripped and fell along with the stage. After getting you both to the couch, Adi and I went back to check. This bullet was embedded in Sumit's chair."

Sant Anirudh's warning! She picked up the tray, and shook it slightly. The piece of flattened metal moved a bit.

Vishnu said, "I repeat, we must call the police."

Maharani Devika said angrily, "No! I have said this once, and I will say it again. We will not have any police snooping in our haveli. It has never happened and will not happen in my lifetime."

Kishan mumbled, "That girl screamed Goli, bullet."

"Which girl?" asked Sumit.

"*Choti* Rani's servant, she was on the stage."

"Bring her here."

Bala was brought to the hall trembling and wringing her hands "Please sahib. I did not see anything. I was looking at Didi, and then suddenly I heard the sound. I don't know anything else."

She was questioned exhaustively. Her eyes looked haunted and wildly flickered without looking. She wept and tried to answer, but it was impossible to make sense of what she said, she was so incoherent. Sumit finally said, "Yes yes, we know. You did not see anything. Shut up now. Think back very carefully, and if you remember anything you have not told us, tell us or the police when they ask questions."

She shut up, tears pouring down her face. The conversation veered back to the bullet. Vaishali placed the tray back on the table, strangely unmoved. Then she caught sight of her hands, surprised to see them trembling. She backed away and sat down heavily on a swing, with her hands under her, feeling exhausted and cold. Then the room blacked out.

Mehak cried, "Sumit, Vaishali!"

Sumit turned quickly and saw Vaishali slump in the swing and said quickly, "You, girl, attend to your Didi. Kishan get Madam's room ready."

Vaishali's parents and Sid quickly gathered around her. Shrishti called frantically, "Water! Vaishali, get up. Sid, did she eat anything?"

Vaishali was quickly shifted to an armchair, which was carried to her room, her family following her.

After a long time, the Baithak was empty except for Sumit who sat slumped on the swing lost in thought. He told the servant, "Turn the lights off and leave. I will go to my room soon."

He kept sitting living and reliving the moment he had been shot, swinging gently on the jhoola. He scowled, everything seemed dark and murky. Someone wanted him dead, but who was that person, and what was his or her motive?

He walked to the window and stared into the dark lawns. A light came on in one room at the far end of the haveli, from Aditya's set of rooms. In the light he could make out Mehak's form. She was walking with long strides towards Adi's rooms. He turned away, recalling the many times his father kept sitting here in the dark. He stared at one of the old man's portraits, and asked, "All right, what would your next step be?"

The portrait looked down on him, silently.

He had to move fast, make his own place at Royal. Everyone danced to Devious Singh's tunes; he had to have that kind of control.

He walked out of the Baithak to check up on Vaishali. She was sitting propped up with pillows, pale underneath the make up. Her mother was hovering over her anxiously.

"How are you?" he asked.

"I am fine," she said firmly. "I do not faint. I never faint. It must have been those stupid pencil heels. Or I must have been tired."

"Of course. Champs like you don't faint," he said straight faced.

She glared at him and his eyes twinkled as he tried to maintain a solemn look. She broke into a grin and said, "I am serious. I don't faint."

Shankar said, "I have been thinking, perhaps I should take her back home. She will be safe there."

"Everything happened in such a hurry. The gossips are saying all sorts of things. We want to take her back." Shrishti added.

"I am not a conventional man, so expect the unconventional from me. We were shot at and I aim to keep us safe. It is simpler for me to watch over her at the haveli. And madam, she was Vaishali Bhatia then. Now she is the Maharao's bride, she is Vaishali Singh Nausar. It is not the same," he said firmly.

"But you live in an apartment. Vaishali has told us that you go back every night to sleep in the apartment. My baby is here, alone." Shrishti was close to tears. Their fears were justified.

"Not anymore. I am shifting here," he said gently.

Her father shook his head and said, "No. I can't allow it."

Vaishali wondered what was bothering her parents. They had been in a great hurry to push her into marriage just a few weeks ago. Then the nickel dropped. She said, "He's feeling insecure about my future and my safety. Is that marriage we had legal?" she asked.

"Shush brat! You are recovering fast," Sumit said with a reluctant smile. "Mr. Bhatia, I intend to honor the marriage. My lawyers are preparing the necessary papers to get it registered in court. I would not have had this function if I were not serious. This is the word of the Maharao."

"You are rich and powerful people, Maharao. What if later you decide that our Vaishali does not suit you? Her life will be ruined," said her father.

Sumit clicked his tongue impatiently. "Do you want your daughter to live or do you want her dead? Someone tried to kill us, don't you get it?"

"Better dead than ruined," muttered her father.

Vaishali stared at her parent balefully. She sat up straighter on the pillows and declared, "I am not going back. I will stay here. But I have nothing to wear. And the television is old and there is no dish, I need a new TV with a dish. I hate the furniture. It's ancient and stuffy."

"Go shop then," Sumit said with a shrug. "Bill me for everything you want. It is settled then."

Sid said, "Vaish, I want to stay too."

"Don't be a pest. You have school," his sister said.

"It's Saturday today, Vaish. Jeej, please," he appealed to Sumit with the most engaging smile. "Can I stay for the weekend Jeej? I'll be good."

Sumit looked at the boy, hesitated and then said, "Sure. Now both of you go to sleep," he added, feeling like a stern teacher.

He ushered her parents out. Her mother came back, hugged her and said to Sid, "I'll send some clothes. If you need anything call. And Sidharth!" she said glaring at Sid, "Behave!"

Sumit knocked after ten minutes, the siblings were sitting in bed whispering excitedly. He said, "Good to know you're having fun. I have told the servants to send you some pajamas that belong to Shivam, and toothbrushes. And you can tell the maid if you need anything."

Reassured both siblings settled down, and then drifted off to sleep.

✦ ✦ ✦

16

A Nasty Surprise

The next day, the local SP's office had an unusual noon time visitor. The young Maharao, walked into the police station casually, and introduced himself, without any airs or fanfare. The SP Altaf Malik received his guest courteously. "Good morning Maharao ji. You did not have to come here. If you needed me, you could have sent a message, or called me."

Sumit shook hands with him, noticing the spare frame, intelligent eyes and the stubborn uncompromising jaw line of the policeman. He looked about mid-forty and had the dogged look of someone who enjoyed working against opposition. "Thank you Malik Sahib. I came to pay you a courtesy call."

"How kind of you," Malik murmured, taking in the younger man's appearance. He had heard reports about the Maharao's wild parties and slotted him as a spoilt heir to an immensely rich heritage. "It is unusual for a young man of your sort to pay a social call at a police station."

Sumit said, "I am thirty, SP Sahib, not a young man. I am here because I have reason to believe that my father's death was not natural."

"Really? Do you have proof?" asked Malik with careful politeness. The young man did not look subject to paranoia, but one could never tell.

Sumit said, "Not yet."

"Maharao ji, the accident happened in the morning in front of many witnesses. The truck has been located. We are trying to trace its owner. Apparently the truck was rented out often. The driver was from a nearby village. We will find him soon."

"You think I am being fanciful?" suggested Sumit.

Malik said carefully, "Perhaps the unexpected death of your father has shocked you?"

Sumit shook his head with a slight smile and said gently, "Perhaps." He was going to say something when his phone rang. "Where are you?" asked Aditya.

"I'm at the police station."

"What? We're coming over," said Aditya firmly.

Sumit smiled as he accepted a perfectly vile looking cup of tea and took a sip, suppressing a shudder. It was over boiled and had too much sugar. Courage comes in various forms, and for Sumit, drinking that tea was the greatest test of courage. He manfully sipped and he listened to the SP conversing animatedly with someone over the phone about the recent test match. So, the SP was a cricket fan. He made a mental note to know more about the SP. He looked too dynamic to be posted in a relatively quiet place like Nausar. The SP took a sip of his tea and smiled, "Sorry, sir. That was the forest officer. He missed watching yesterday's match. You must have missed it too, because of your wedding reception."

"I recorded it on my set-top box. I will see it tonight," grinned Sumit.

"Lucky you! I hear you were out hiking in the forests some days ago?" asked the sharp SP.

"Yes," Sumit said. So the SP was keeping tabs on his activities!

"Someone is illegally felling timber in large scales in the forests. Soon there will be no forest to walk in. The Forest Officer missed the match because of these timber thieves. They are very active in the area," he explained.

When Aditya landed up at the police station with Brian, Sumit and Malik were having a rather intense discussion about the merits and demerits of various forms of cricket. A true cricket lover, Malik was all for test cricket and Sumit preferred the one-day form. Both agreed that the Twenty-Twenty form was a travesty. "Maharao ji, you young people want everything fast. To savor a sport, you have to see it played in its authentic form," said the older man.

"My name is Sumit Singh. Please don't call me Maharao," said Sumit getting up. Aditya and Brian shook hands with the SP and they left. After the car turned towards the haveli, Aditya asked, "Why?"

"I just thought it was wise to know the local SP. After all, I did get shot at. Relax Adi, I did not tell him about it, not yet," said Sumit.

Brian said, "You know, I think you should have. It is unwise to keep secrets from the police."

Both Sumit and Aditya said firmly, "No!"

Sumit added, "Not yet at least. I need tea, the tea they drink in the police station is horrible."

"Your fault! You decided to sit and share a cup with policemen," said Aditya. "The haveli will give you a decent cup."

Meanwhile, at 3 p.m. Sid shook Vaishali awake. "Vaish wake up! Breakfast in bed for us!"

Vaishali sat up groggily, as Bala entered the bedroom with a trolley laden with food.

"Cool!" chortled Sid. "I love this life," he said, grabbing a plate.

Vaishali pushed him into the bathroom, "Don't be a slob. At least brush your teeth before eating. Bala, take the trolley into the sitting room."

They ate, showered, slipped into their jeans and ran out into the extensive lawns with Bala in tow. The shamiana and chairs from the last night's party had been removed, but the debris of the party was still strewn around the lawn. Sid ran to the spot where the stage had been and asked Bala, "Can you tell me where you were standing when the gunshot happened?"

The girl's face clouded, and she turned away, "I did not see anything."

"You know, you need to stop repeating things again and again. It gets boring," Vaishali said irritably. "You definitely heard something."

Bala hung her head down and replied sulkily, "Yes."

Vaishali pulled the reluctant girl to the spot, "Now stand exactly where you were standing last night."

Bala reluctantly took position.

"Yes, you were standing here. You had a tray in your hand. Where were you looking?" Vaishali asked.

"I was looking at you, Didi."

"So look where the stage was. And where was the foreigner Brian standing?" asked Vaishali.

Bala stepped forward to show her. "No, go back," instructed Vaishali.

Bala went back to her spot.

"Where did the sound come from?" she asked again.

"That side," she said pointing towards her left.

Vaishali walked and "And I was here, and then I fell," Vaishali said pretending to stumble.

The car stopped and Aditya, Sumit and Brian got out unnoticed by Vaishali or her maid.

Unaware of them and caught in her own enactment, Vaishali muttered to herself, "So, this means that the bullet came from there," she murmured as she walked towards the place the chairs had been placed. "The bullet passed you, and went to the chair over there. So, the man shooting should have stood somewhere there." She turned and looked towards a roof overlooking the lawn.

"Come on! What are you waiting for? Let's go and see," she yelled and ran in that direction.

Sumit stared at Vaishali scrambling up the wall like a monkey. He smacked his head, "My God! Doesn't she realize how dangerous this is?"

Sid and Bala caught up with Vaishali and started clambering up the wall, finding footholds easily in the ancient window ledges.

Brian broke into a laugh, "Your wife is a handful."

"Tell me about it," Sumit groaned as he lengthened his stride. Just then a scream rent the air. Alarmed, all three men broke into a jog, threw the door to the stairway open and took the stairs to the roof on a run. They were panting as they reached the roof to see a dead man lying sprawled against the small wall at the edge of the roof.

✦ ✦ ✦

17

The Corpse

"Oh God, the smell!" Brian complained.

The body was pale bluish and flies were buzzing around it. Vaishali was trying to calm a distraught Bala who was sitting on the floor rocking front and back as she said, "He's dead, he's killed, he's murdered."

"It is okay. He is just dead. Dead people can't harm you," Vaishali said in a trembling voice.

The girl kept rocking herself. "Breathe deeply and stand up. If you don't, I'll slap you," said Vaishali practically.

Faced with this no nonsense attitude, the girl controlled herself and stood up, chanting softly, "I did not see anything. I did not see anything."

"Was he lying like this?" asked Brian as he approached the corpse warily.

"No, his back was to us, he was facing the wall. I thought he was asleep and I shook him. He rolled over," Vaishali said shakily, not looking at the dead man.

"Who is he?" asked Adi. They stared blankly at the man's face; the head was at an unnatural angle. The neck was broken, and the throat was slit.

"I've never seen him ever," said Sumit staring at the face of the man.

Sid said in a scared whisper, "There is something shiny." They turned to see what he was pointing at. Vaishali started walking towards it.

"What is it?" asked Sumit in a goaded tone, "Oh no, you don't! Stop right there!"

"Something shiny," she said pointing at the spot.

"Stay back," warned Sumit as he and Brian approached the glinting object warily. Aditya restrained Sid from following them. It was a steel tray and held a used plate and glass.

Sumit took out his mobile and dialed a number, "SP Sahib, this is Sumit Singh Nausar. We met this morning. Can you come over to the haveli? We have a dead body here."

Then he paused and listened.

"Oh yes, it is definitely unnatural causes. His throat has been slit, and the neck is broken. Yes I will. Please hurry."

He looked down the parapet of the roof and yelled, "Thapa!"

The driver, a middle aged man with Nepalese features who was standing near the car looked up. Sumit ordered, "Bring three more men and stand guard around this place. Let no one enter or climb the stairs, no one, unless I say so."

"Follow me," he ordered the ashen faced trio. Bala stumbled. Vaishali supported the girl, and took Sid's hand in hers and together they followed Sumit. Aditya locked the door to the staircase and they left the driver and the other men to guard the stairway.

Shaken they entered the lobby of the main wing of the haveli. Himani who was lounging in the smaller hall, watching television, glanced at them and exclaimed in a shocked tone.

"Vaishali, why are you and your brother always covered with mud?"

"Summon Kishan," replied her brother coldly.

Bala moved towards the door. Sumit said, "No, you stay. You are never to leave your mistress alone. Never, you understand?"

She nodded, and came back to stand with Vaishali. Himani shrugged, "Such drama," she said snidely and picked up the intercom to convey the order. "What is wrong with you both? You look like refugees."

That brought Vaishali out of her shock. She snarled, "And you look over made up. You should fire your make up person. I am sure; I can help you find a better one."

Sumit smiled broadly, "Good for you, Vaish!"

Himani flushed deeply and got up to leave, saying, "I know when I am not wanted."

Sumit said, "Stay. I have called a meeting in the main hall."

"Really, when?"

"Now. Ring up Rohtash and call him here."

Aditya was already instructing the housekeeper to open the huge hall they called the Baithak, and switch on the lights. Sumit dialed a few numbers and walked into the Baithak.

Vaish and Sid followed. Bala tugged at Vaishali's hand and whispered, "Didi, I am feeling sick, can I go?"

"It will be over soon," she whispered back soothingly.

"I am scared of the police."

"Why should you be scared? The police only catches people who do something wrong." The maid was shivering and breaking into a cold sweat. Vaishali said, "Go. I will call you if we need you."

Bala fled. "What's she scared about?" asked Sid in a whisper.

"She's just a ninny," said his sister with a shrug, trying to suppress her own nausea. She had to appear brave. If she fainted again, her in-laws would consider her weak or worse, hysterical.

Sumit sat down on the swing and waited as everyone assembled. His uncle, aunt and Shivam were the first to come. Mehak came in next and took a seat, glancing curiously at Vaishali and Sid. Himani and Rohtash came in, followed by Devika who looked at everyone and took her time to fussily settle down on a couch, with her maid arranging a footstool for her to rest her feet on.

Once everyone had assembled, Sumit stood up and said, "My apologies for calling you all here at such a short notice. But this is an emergency. A body has been found on the roof of the East Annexe of the Haveli. I have called the police. They will soon be here to ask questions. I want you all to cooperate."

He looked at all his assembled relatives keenly and added, "Of course, no one leaves the city until the police investigation is complete."

Shivam was the first to break the stunned silence. "What if I have to go to Delhi or Lucknow or someplace?"

"I am sure you would not be so foolish. The police would suspect that you were running away because you were guilty," said Sumit with a smile.

Sid sniggered and Shivam flushed with embarrassment, as his father frowned at him.

Everyone began to talk at once. Maharani Devika asked angrily, "Why was I not consulted?"

Mehak asked, "Who is the dead person? How did the person die?"

Rohtash started chanting something that sounded like a mantra. Vishnu stood up and said in a loud voice, "Quiet everybody! Stop behaving like rowdies! Sumit is trying to say something. And you, Shivam! The next time I hear your voice in a meeting, you will be forbidden from attending them."

The voices stopped midstream. Sumit sneered, "Madam, I did not know that I had to take permission from you to report a dead body, my apologies."

Himani said angrily, "Sumit, how dare you mock mother!"

Sumit's reply was bitter, "Oh I dare! I dare a lot Himani. You would be wise not to push me."

Girdhari said, "Quiet! Sumit, you will apologize to your mother. Himani, may I remind you that Sumit is the Maharao and you will not challenge him. This is turning out to be a domestic squabble!"

Himani started protesting bitterly, "Sumit thinks too much of himself. He has been insulting me since the time he has come home."

She sounded like a peevish ten year old. Mehak started laughing, and quickly covered her mouth with her hand. Devika tried to soothe down her older daughter and the others started conversing again.

Sumit looked around at his dysfunctional family and wondered if one of them had anything to do with the shooting that had happened the night before, and if so, which one.

+ + +

18

S.P. Altaf Malik

Malik had just finished his evening tea and was looking forward to a half an hour game of cricket with his son, when he received Sumit's call. He cursed as he got off his cell phone. This was not good at all. Tonight, India was playing Australia, and he had been looking forward to watching it. He told his son, "Adil, can you call your *ammi*, please."

His wife came into the room. "I am going to the haveli, Nafisa. Don't wait for dinner."

She scowled.

"Oh, come on, woman, stop that. I know you will be happy. You can watch your serials," he said sourly. She always complained when there was a cricket match.

She tried to control her expression but a smile peeped through. "I will make some of your favorite kebabs," she offered.

"If you could cook up a cricket match when I come home it would be better," he said wistfully as he got into his police jeep and left for the haveli.

When he reached the lobby at the haveli, he could hear the noisy conference which was still going on in the main hall. He stopped the servant from announcing him, and opened the door slightly.

"Unbelievable. I still can't digest this. How did a body come to be on our roof?" demanded a male voice, he recognized it. It was Girdhari, the Maharao's uncle.

The young Maharao replied conversationally, "It generally happens when someone cuts a man's throat and leaves him on the roof." Malik smiled, the man was smooth!

The babble of voices that arose was cut off mid-sentence when Kishan opened the door wider and announced, "SP Sahib!"

The assembled people stopped talking and stared at him. Used to hostile glances, he strode forward and said, "Salaam Maharao ji."

"Call me Singh, Malik Sahib. Take a seat."

He remained standing, "I would first like to see the body. Has it been identified?"

Sumit got up and said, "No, apparently he is a stranger. Come, let me take you there."

"No Sir, that is not necessary. If someone can show me where the dead body is..."

Sumit nodded to Kishan who came forward. Malik left the room but lingered at the door. Mehak screamed at her brother, "You could have made the body disappear. Daddy would have got rid of it, burnt it or something."

"I won't do that, damn it, someone shot at me. Don't scream at me. If you disagree with my decisions, you can go back to your husband, Mehak. No one will stop you." Her brother was calm but the tone was menacing.

Malik frowned, someone shot at Sumit? That was news. He recalled the accident Sumit's car met with a few days ago. He nodded pleasantly to Kishan and said, "Let us go see the body."

The body smelt. Rigor Mortis had set in. Malik looked thoughtfully, "This is a local man. The features belong to this province. Who found him?"

"The young Rani, Maharao Sumit's bride," the old man said mopping his face with a hand towel. "Please Sahib, can I leave?" He was pale.

"No. Who is this man?"

"I don't know Sahib. I don't know how he got here. So many people came for the reception yesterday. This man! Sahib, this must be that one, the bullet...!"

"What bullet?" Malik asked casually. "Oh, the bullet fired at the Maharao?" He definitely needed to buy a fancy new set top box that would record the matches. He could foresee a lot of disruption of his peaceful life thanks to the new occupant of the haveli.

"Yes. Such a thing has never happened," Kishan said in a scandalized tone. He shuddered and muttered something about the deteriorating law and order condition.

"Did you see anyone?"

"No Sahib. The girl, the new Rani's maid, she heard the sound of the bullet shot and screamed."

Malik was examining the utensils lying on the roof. He asked conversationally, "Is this food from the party or did it come from outside."

"It is from the party Sahib," Kishan manfully tried to control his nausea.

"Thank you. Go now, man." Kishan fled, relieved. Malik examined the body as the police photographer he had brought along took pictures. After that, he went down as the body was bagged and removed.

In the baithak the fight continued. Girdhari said distastefully, "No one would have dared to attack us if my brother was alive."

Sumit smiled grimly and said, "Yes, our family is normally not at the receiving end."

Devika said icily, "I have had enough. You were always a rude and impertinent boy. How dare you imply such things about your own father?"

"Imply? I hadn't realized that I was so subtle," Sumit said quietly.

Himani quick to defend her mother said, "I won't have you insulting daddy, just because he is dead and can't stop you. I won't let you!"

Sumit scratched his chin, "I never refrained even when he was alive."

Devika said, "Quiet both of you. How can you fight like this in front of outsiders?"

Sumit smiled and said, "There are no outsiders here, Madam. Vaishali and Sid are already a part of the family, and Brian is like a brother to me."

Shivam whispered to Vishnu, "He insults us. Mother says that the girl is just a commoner, and she has brought nothing but trouble to the family. Now he calls a gora his brother."

Sid got up, incensed as he overheard this. "Shh! Don't react. Too many people around," whispered Vaishali. He sat down.

Brian shrugged his shoulders and said, "Sumit honors me. We are business partners and good friends for the last ten years."

"Really? That is interesting. What business?" asked Girdhari.

"We manufacture wines. You use our brand Coronet in your hotels too."

Vishnu said softly, "Wow! You are the Brian Underwood of Coronet?"

"Oh I am just a front, a twenty percent partner. It is basically Sumit's baby."

"You have been very secretive, Sumit," said Vishnu thoughtfully.

"I was waiting for the right time to inform you people. I think Brian can fill you up; he even has the copies of the balance sheets ready for such a discussion. I have to go meet the policeman," he said and left.

Brian explained, "I know it is a family matter, but the reason we kept it quiet was because Sumit felt his father would have issues."

"Oh yes, Uncle wanted everyone to toe his line. Uncle would have definitely had issues," Vishnu agreed. Girdhari and he shared a smile, recalling the many times Sumit put on a show to infuriate his father as a boy.

Mehak said thoughtfully, "They are good wines. So you have vineyards in France of course. Any place else?"

Shivam walked out of the baithak in a huff. He hated his uncle who always ridiculed him for being a sickly boy, considering him unmanly. This hatred had transferred naturally on his son.

Now, on his mother's insistence, he was allowed to attend family meetings, and he felt like a man. He wanted to be noticed, admired, and even loved. Instead...

He kicked a stone viciously, recalling his mother's pet grouse. "I wish Vishnu bhaiya was the Maharao. Ma also wishes that. Daddy is a fool, and Vishnu bhaiya is his sychophant," he muttered. Then he looked back at the haveli. "If Vishnu bhaiya was the Maharao, he would listen to Ma and get this place bulldozed and a new, shiny home built. Royalty should not live in such a ramshackle place."

He caught sight of Sumit and the SP in deep conversation near the East Annexe and crept towards them, intent on eavesdropping. He did not see Sid creep behind him, pick up a clod of mud and aim it at his back, and hurl it at him with all his strength. He fell down with a loud cry of fear. "I'm hit, I am going to die, I am going to die."

Sumit turned and rushed towards him. Vaishali reached him first, grabbed him by his sleeve and pulled him to his feet, brushing the mud away.

"What a coward! Get up, you stupid fool! It was just some mud. It did not even break your skin."

"You are a hooligan. You are worse than those cheap children who play cricket on the road. No princess of royal blood would throw stones at her husband's cousin."

"You royals do worse. Look at the Mughals. They killed their own fathers. If you had played cricket with street hooligans, you would have more sense than to badmouth your cousin's wife, that too within her earshot," she replied.

"I will tell Vishnu bhaiya. He should have been the Maharao. Your precious Sumit is not worth the mud on his shoes. He is just a characterless debauch."

"I am going to beat the shit out of this boy. Are you in, Sid?" growled Vaishali putting up her fists and taking an aggressive stance.

"Enough! I can fight my own fights," said Sumit vastly amused.

Shivam saw the smile on Sumit's face and said, with injured pride, "I am going to tell daddy. I hate you."

"Tell daddy what? That such a tall Rajput boy like you got beaten up by a girl?" Vaishali shot back.

He turned and ran away, more humiliated than he had even been in his nineteen years of existence. Vaishali and Sid tried to sidle away. "Vaishali, he is just an ill tempered sick boy. Try and make friends, not enemies. That goes for you too, Sid." Sumit said. They nodded, deeply embarrassed and slipped away.

Malik looked at them departing, and broke the uncomfortable silence, asking tactfully, "Who is the boy with your lady?"

"That is Sidharth, her brother. And the other one is Shivam, my cousin."

"I will take my leave today. I will be here tomorrow to question the staff and family," he folded his hands in a formal namaste and and climbed into the jeep. He had been lucky; he could still catch the cricket match.

"Hey, Malik, are you a betting man?" Sumit asked.

"Depends on what is being betted," Malik replied.

"Australia will win," Sumit smiled.

"Maharao, I can't match your stakes. But I think India will win."

He laughed. "Let's see," he said waving to him.

Charming fellow, but as poisonous as a viper, thought Malik as he drove away.

✦ ✦ ✦

19

Nightmare

Sid climbed into a couch in Vaishali's sitting room and said, "That was really bad luck. Next time we'll make sure Jeej is not around."

"No Sid, we behaved badly. What do you think Bala?" she asked her maid.

Bala smiled. "You know, you need to speak up, and smile. You look good when you smile," Vaishali observed.

Bala's smile became broader. "That's much better," Vaishali said approvinigly.

Devika's maid came and knocked on the door. Bala opened it, heard her out and quickly shut the door.

"Didi, the Rani wants to meet you," Bala said.

Vaishali got up and said, "Tell her to come after an hour. I have to change."

The message was duly conveyed. "Didi, I am scared. The Rani does black magic."

Vaishali snapped, "Oh shut up Bala. No one does black magic! Go and change, you're covered with muck from the roof. Sid, when I come back, you should be bathed and changed okay?"

Sid switched on the brand new wall mounted television, tuned into the cricket match and ignored his sister who scowled and went to take a shower.

An hour later, Vaishali was escorted to the old Rani's rooms. The huge sitting room was furnished in the British Raj style, and every available surface was decorated with elegant curios and knickknacks. The walls were covered with paintings, but not, she realized, a single one of the deceased Maharao's.

Devika entered, nodded to her and sat down on a rocking chair gracefully. Vaishali smiled back in response.

"I wished to thank you personally for saving my son's life," Devika said.

The girl smiled politely and said, "Thank you."

"I hear that he had a near accident when you went climbing some hills?" asked the queen.

"Yes, but that was not deliberate I think," she replied in surprise. "That was a huge boulder; it could have crushed us both."

"Sumit was a very rebellious boy; my husband indulged him a lot when he was young. He laughed at his little rebellions, his improper behavior..."

"What kind of rebellions?" Vaishali asked. She waited for the older lady to ask her to sit, when the invitation did not come, she drew a chair and sat down.

"He mocks the Gods; he flouts traditions, even as a boy, he never behaved like we wanted him to. I hope you will bring him back to traditions, to the belief."

"Madam, Sumit's father started the hotel business when it was considered unacceptable, did he not?"

Devika smiled slightly and bowed her head, acknowledging the reply. "This body, how did you know it was there?" she asked.

Vaishali noticed that the older lady was wearing a rudraksha string done up with gold beads around her wrist, that looked similar to the one that had been left outside her door a few days ago. She said, "Madam, I did not know. I just thought that if the bullet came from that direction, we could find something on the roof. I think it was the shooter. Someone fed him and then killed him."

Sumit's mother shuddered. "I am conducting a puja for Sumit's long life. The day you got married, Santji warned us about the danger to his life."

"That is so kind of you, Madam."

Devika murmured, more to herself than to Vaishali, "I never wanted much. The duty of a princess.... One was required to marry where the parents decided and be an obedient wife and a dutiful mother. Such things do not happen." Then she looked at Vaishali, with envy. Dressed in a red tee shirt, jeans and sneakers, her freshly shampooed hair a shining halo around her head, she looked young and vibrant. Unlike traditional brides, she did not wear a nine yard sari or cover her head.

It brought back bitter memories. Devika had been accused of being dull and boring by her husband, who had flaunted Sejal to her face, even brought Sejal's son into the haveli. With an effort she brought her mind back to the present. Vaishali was fidgeting in her chair. She smiled and said, "Young girls want to do so many things these days. I hear you want to work?"

"Yes Madam."

"Try and call me 'Ma' like the rest of my children, Vaishali. It would be better if you made a place for yourself first in the family. Working is so..." her mouth twisted disdainfully. Then she shrugged and said, "Maybe I am old fashioned."

Vaishali forced a smile on her face and rose from her chair. The lady smiled and said, "It was nice talking to you."

She smiled and replied, "Same here. May I leave now, Madam?" That overstuffed room made her claustrophobic. The whole haveli was stuck in a time warp; it made her long for fresh air, for those carefree evenings when she played street cricket or hockey with the colony kids. She stepped out of the main haveli and glanced towards the park where the party had been held a day before.

Who was the dead man?

Was he an invitee, someone she had been introduced to?

It was dark now, and she made her way to past the manicured lawns and neatly kept flower patches towards the west wing where her rooms were located. A tall figure wearing a hooded tee shirt and a sock on his face was waiting in shadows and pounced on her just as she came near the Easter lilies.

Bala screamed. Vaishali reacted immediately, landing a punch on her attacker's face and kicking him on his groin. Her attacker fell into the flower bed and Vaishali pinned him down with her knee, pulling the sock off his face.

"Shivam, you idiot!" Vaishali hissed in anger.

Turning to Bala, she snapped, "Hush! There is no need to squawk like that. We were just playing."

"You made me bleed!" Shivam whimpered as she got off him.

"Shut up and come with me, moron!" she whispered. "Do you want the whole haveli to start screeching at us?"

He tried to stand up, but he was trembling and unsteady on his feet. She grabbed him by his tee shirt and dragged him towards the side door of the west wing, and rushed him into her sitting room. Quickly shutting the door, she ordered a trembling Bala, "Get me a jug of cold water, cotton wool and some ice. And a first aid kit. Hurry!"

Bala did not move, she kept staring at Shivam.

"You're still here?" Vaishali snarled. The girl turned and flung the door open as she rushed to carry out the order. Vaishali dragged Shivam to the bathroom and said, "Wash your face."

"You hit me," he said in a small voice.

"What do you expect? You wore a mask and pounced on me," she retorted.

Sid laughed, "Ha! You expected Vaish to screech! Vaish is not a sissy, she's a sport!"

Vaishali wiped Shivam's bloody face with the sock he had used as a mask, and dragged him into the room. Bala entered, with an ice bucket and some dettol and cotton wool. Her hands were trembling. "Put it down, Bala. You'll spill," she ordered and took out an ice cube and applied it on his face.

"Owww!" he moaned.

"You really need to learn how to fight, before you try stunts like this. Haven't you learnt the basic tactics in school and college? First rule, protect your face," she said.

He mumbled something about correspondence courses. "I hated school. Those school boys were rough and they picked on me, just like you."

"*Oye* shut up. You called me a commoner, a hooligan, attacked me on my way here, and you say I picked on you? You know what? You have a seriously lame mind."

Sid asked, "No school? You must be lonely."

"I have febrile convulsions. Ma said school was unsafe. Those boys at school always beat me up."

"I wonder why?" taunted Vaishali, pushing him down on the couch and examining his face. "Your lip is cut, but nose and teeth are okay. The lip will swell up, but will be okay by morning."

He flushed, "I am sorry. It is just that if..."

"I know, you love your Vishnu bhaiya and wish that he was Maharao. You told us that. It won't happen, so deal with it." Vaishali said.

"Sumit Jeej is a regular sport. So why don't you become friends with him? We can be friends too. I have a lot of friends. I am never lonely." Sid added.

"You'll be my friend?" Shivam asked, holding the sock to his cut. Vaishali snatched it from his hand and handed him a wad of cotton wool.

"Sure," she said with a shrug as she handed the sock and a blood stained hand towel to Bala who paled as she took it.

Sid stared at him thoughtfully and replied, "I've had better friends, but then I have had worse friends too."

Shivam tried to smile and winced. Sid commented, "Oh come on, I hit Vaish on the face with a hockey stick and she did not complain much even though she could not see from one eye for two days."

"You did? She did not beat you?" Shivam asked.

"Of course she did!" he replied, with a shrug. Then he caught sight of Sumit at the bedroom door, "Oh hello Jeej. Are you spying on us?"

Shivam stood up, a pained expression on his face.

Sumit who was trying hard to control his laughter, let out a guffaw. "Yes I am. It has been informative and entertaining."

The three of them stared at him accusingly. "Oh don't look shocked. I was on my way to clean up before dinner. You three need not come. In fact it would be better if your mother did not see your face Shivam. I'll send dinner here."

"Join us Jeej," Sid invited him.

He grinned and said, "Some other time champ."

Then walked through the sitting room and opened the connecting door, "Vaish, a minute please."

She walked in and looked around, spotting a baseball bat. "Can I have that baseball bat?"

He suppressed a smile and nodded. She picked it up. He held her arm and gently traced a finger on the scratch she had acquired grappling with Shivam, "Put some medicine on this. You did well with Shivam."

She flushed and grinned happily, "You told me to make friends."

He patted her gently on her cheek and said, "You are quite something, you know that?"

She went back to her sitting room unaccountably happy. Shivam and Sid were sitting on the couch watching the match. She joined them. He was a storehouse of cricket trivia that awed Sid. When Sid learnt that Shivam had actually flown in the same plane as Harbhajan Singh, he treated Shivam with such reverence that Shivam melted completely.

Kamala came looking for her younger son after dinner and found him watching the match with Sid and Vaishali.

"What happened to your face?"

He shrugged, "We were trying Dhoni's shot. Don't scold us, Ma. Vaish Bhabhi already did. She even took away the baseball bat we were using as a cricket bat."

Kamala thawed towards Vaishali. "I hope he doesn't offend you. He is just a sick child."

"Oh no! He is just like Sid. I like him," Vaishali said.

"He has to have his medicine," she said glancing at the two boys cheering a boundary shot.

"Send me his medicines. I'll see to it that he takes it," Vaishali offered. The lady thanked her and left, with a smile, impressed by the new bride's good behavior and family values.

It was late in the night when Sid and Vaishali went to sleep, only to be woken up at around 3 a.m. by a blood curdling scream. Vaishali jumped out of bed and grabbed the baseball bat, and swung it, bringing down an ancient brass table lamp with a crash. Sid sat up mumbling something incomprehensible.

Muffled sobs came from the small room in the corner where the maid slept. With the baseball bat in her hand, Vaish opened the door, switching on the light. Bala was sitting on her bed, her head cradled on her knees, sobbing.

"What happened?" she asked, relaxing slightly.

"Didi he came in my sleep. He came with his throat cut," said Bala.

"Who?" Vaishali crept forward, still looking around for monsters in the small room.

"Bikram."

Vaishali froze. "Who's Bikram, the dead man?"

Bala spoke incoherently, "No. Yes. I met him once, with my husband."

"Are you married? Who is your husband?" asked Vaishali.

"He died," came the reply.

"Who? This Bikram. Yes I know," she said. "Stop crying. Dead people cannot harm us."

A movement in the adjoining terrace caught her attention. A shadowy figure was approaching the window. This was too much for the two girls who grabbed each other's hand, and started screaming at the top of their lungs.

Sid rushed to them and joined in the yelling.

They heard a muffled curse and then a click of a door opening and all three dove under the maid's bed. The door opened and someone flicked on the light switch. "What is happening here? Gosh child, get out. Come on, it's me!" said Sumit, kneeling down and peering under the bed. "Hurry up, my back hurts."

Vaishali wept, "There is someone on the terrace."

"It's just the guard. I had one placed over there."

The guard knocked the window pane, "Sahib I heard screaming."

Sumit stood up, "It is alright. Memsahib just got scared. What is the matter, girl?"

"I thought he was the dead man, Bikram."

"How do you know his name?" Sumit asked.

"I don't know him. Bala does."

Sid asked, "These girls woke me up. Is this Bikram a ghost?"

Bala let out a whimper from under the bed where she was still huddled up.

"You are not making sense," said Sumit giving Vaishali a little shake.

"Shut up, Sid. She knew the murdered man, she named him," she said pointing at the maid, who looked at them from under the bed and wailed, "I don't know anything."

Vaishali opened her mouth to protest, but Sumit said softly in English, "Don't speak."

Then he smiled gently and said, "It is alright, Bala. Come out now. No one saw or heard anything. It is just the police."

"Police?" Her eyes flicked from one face to another like a trapped animal's.

Vaishali hauled her out from under the bed clicking her tongue impatiently.

Sumit sat down on the tiny bed and asked, "You lived at the ashram, did you not? How did you get there? Who referred this girl to you, Vaishali?"

The girl backed away to the door.

"There is police on the terrace, there is police outside the door and the big sahib of the police will be here tomorrow morning. You can't run. You have to tell the truth. You want to tell me or the big police sahib?"

The girl started shaking and sweating profusely.

"You can't bully her like that!" said Vaishali angrily, hugging the girl.

"Oh yes I can. I want to know who tried to kill me and why."

"Sahib, please, not the police." Bala pleaded.

Sumit stared at her in silence. Completely intimidated, Bala fell to her knees, "I can't go back home. My father and brothers will kill me."

"We won't Bala. Just tell the Sahib everything," Vaishali assured her.

She turned away from Sumit and addressed Vaishali, "Didi, I am a widow. But I swear, I am not *punauti*. It was not my bad luck that brought the bullet to you. I was there at your wedding and nothing went wrong."

"What is punauti?" asked Sid. "Funny name."

"Shh, continue, girl," insisted Vaish, and to Sid, "Her name is Bala, punauti means jinxed, ill-omened."

"Quiet, the two of you," snapped Sumit. "Continue."

"I met Bikram the day I married him," began Bala.

"Who is this 'him', Bikram?" asked Sumit.

"No Sahib. My 'him' was Yashpal. He belonged to our village. We were forbidden to get married. He left the village and became a driver for a sahib in Nausar. One day he came with a lot of money and we ran away. He brought me here and we got married."

"Sounds too filmy to be true," said Sid.

"Of course not, it makes sense. So, he was a truck driver?" asked Sumit.

She nodded.

"How did he die?" Sumit asked again.

She clammed up and shook her head.

Sumit got up, stretched and said, "It is obvious she knows more. But she is not going to vomit it out this easily."

Turning to the hapless girl, he said, "Okay Bala, we will just go out for a drive, meet the police, just Memsahib, you, me and the driver."

"No sahib," she said and started weeping bitterly.

"Then speak," he demanded.

Then the entire story came out. Sumit said, "After they killed him what did they do to you?"

"A man took me to a room at the cremation ground and... and...then more of them came, I ran away. The priest, Chandan, he gave me his shawl and took me to the ashram."

Sumit sat there stony faced.

Vaishali started trembling, sat down next to the maid on the floor, hugging her as the implications of what she left unsaid sank in. "No wonder you got scared. Shivam's blood set you off, you poor thing." She asked Sumit, "Can we help her, please?"

"Bala do you remember where you hid the money?" Sumit asked.

"Yes sahib."

"Does anyone else know?"

"No, only Yashpal and I knew. We hid it together. That money is mine. Yashpal died for it, he died for me," she sobbed.

"Your precious Yashpal killed for it, Bala. He killed my father," observed Sumit coldly.

"I have no one, nothing. I just have that money sahib," pleaded Bala.

"Give sahib the money. I will make sure that we put something in the bank for you. I promise, Bala," said Vaishali softly.

"Vaishali, please!" he protested. Vaishali glared at him, while hovering protectively over Bala like an angry sparrow guarding its young. He capitulated. "Okay, fine. Yes, we will do that."

He rang up the driver he had given Vaishali, "Thapa, wake up, old man! We are going for a drive."

"Jeej, I am coming too," Sid declared, tugging his kurta.

"Oh God, I forgot you. Okay, all of you get dressed. Vaishali, get the girl to wear jeans and a tee shirt. She should look like a city girl. And hurry," Sumit said.

"Where are we going?" Sid asked.

"To get the money, of course! It is evidence," said Sumit.

"Right now? In the night?" Vaishali asked.

He looked energized and cheerful. "Why not?"

Thapa seemed unsurprised by Sumit's sudden plan, having been with him long enough to know his quirks. Sumit was ready in minutes, and he along with Sid went and got into the SUV and waited for the girls. When they came, Sumit nodded approvingly. Vaishali had covered both their heads with scarves and both of them had donned huge sunglasses. In jeans and a shirt, Bala looked unrecognizable.

Some hours later, Sumit, Thapa and an enthusiastic Sid dug the spot Bala pointed out in the abandoned field and took out the bag. It was almost dawn and the village was slowly getting out of slumber. Women started getting out of their homes to attend to the call of nature. The three men dusted the bag, handed it over to the girls and went behind some trees to relieve themselves.

Bala started panicking. "Didi, someone will see us. We must go."

"Hush. They will be here soon," Vaishali said, looking towards the trees.

"If my brothers see me, there will be trouble," said Bala.

"They won't recognize you." Vaishali said soothingly.

Bala looked unconvinced.

"Wear those glasses, cover your face with the scarf and close your eyes," advised Vaish, and she complied.

A couple of youths approached the car and peered inside curiously.

Vaishali whispered, "Don't move. Don't speak."

Sid was the first to finish. He walked back to the car and saw the boys peering at the girls, "Oye, what are you doing? Move!"

A cheeky village boy responded as insolently as Sid, "Who are you? Dacoits? Thieves? You're stealing something from the fields."

Sid backed away, calling in a loud voice, "Help, Jeej! Sumit Jeeja! Help me!"

"What are you doing here, city boy, tell me." The youth insolently swaggered up to the boy.

"Nothing, just taking a leak," he said, backing away.

"You have to pay for using the field," he declared.

"I don't have any money," Sid said, glancing towards the trees. Sumit and Thapa rushed towards them. That restored his confidence and he added boldly, "You are not a tax collector and there is no tax for peeing."

"Ho! Smartass eh? There is a tax now, because I say so," insisted the boy insolently.

Other youths gathered around them, losing interest in the girls.

Thapa said, "I have never heard so much rubbish in my life. There is no tax for peeing."

"How much?" asked Sumit.

"Five hundred rupees."

Thapa spluttered in indignation. Sumit deliberately took out his wallet. Then he said, "Now let me see, five hundred rupees for three men peeing. That should be minus two hundred for the manure we have given the field. That leaves us with three hundred."

"Five hundred," said the boy looking at the wallet eagerly.

"Three hundred," said Sumit solemnly showing him three hundred rupee notes.

"Oye take it!" said one of his friends.

He hesitated. "Don't be a fool! Take it," urged another.

He said, "Okay."

Sumit handed him the money and got into the car. "Drive, Thapa. Be fast old man!"

The driver needed no more urging. He pumped the accelerator and they drove off. "Humph! Tax for peeing, indeed," grumbled the driver. "*Ghor Kaliyug*!"

Sumit put his head into his hands, his shoulders shaking in merriment. He had not had so much fun for a long time.

"There! That was not so hard was it? We will go to the bank tomorrow and open an account for you and put money in it. No one came to know we were here. You are safe," he assured the maid.

He was very wrong. A couple of days later, four men came to the village and asked around. They came to know of a huge expensive car that drove into the village, where two men and a boy peed in the field. They also found out that the men were accompanied by girls who did not come out of the car.

A week later, a couple of policemen also came looking for a missing truck driver named Yashpal.

✦ ✦ ✦

20

The Two Rivals, Sejal Banasur and Devika Nausar

"Thapa let us drive through the hills, it is short and we'll get home in time to meet the policeman," Sumit instructed the driver.

The drive through the hills was scenic. As they crested the top, they could see the entire range of hills, with the river flowing through it. The sun was still low and the place looked like a picture postcard.

"I want to stop and take pictures. Can I?" Vaishali asked.

"Sure," Sumit said. Thapa stopped the car and they all got out to stretch their legs.

Sid said, "Chandan Pandit tells of a time when he was a boy and they walked through the hills to find the shivling."

"Yes, I've heard the story," Sumit said looking around. "My family is building a resort somewhere in these hills. The natural ambiance is good. It will be successful."

Vaishali, who had stepped away and was taking pictures on her smart phone, spotted what looked like a car, partially concealed by foliage. She went down on her knees, focussed and took a few pictures. Then she turned away and started taking pictures of patches of brown earth and rocks, mute testimony to the rampant felling of timber.

Back in the car, she went through the pictures and observed, "I don't think the new hotel will do well, in the current conditions."

"And why not?" Sumit asked.

She showed him the pictures she had taken. "The forests are going to disappear if this goes on, look."

He went through the pictures and frowned slightly, "Thapa, we need to take a detour man. Can you drive via Banasur. We have to go past Aditya's haveli."

"Sahib, the police man?"

"He can wait. We just need to check up if Sejal Auntie's car is at the haveli."

Thapa took a detour. Sejal's blue Audi was not there, but Mehak's Gypsy was parked in front of the haveli. They slowed down and then drove away, crossing Sejal's Audi on the highway that connected Banasur to Nausar.

Chairs were laid out in the front lawn of the main haveli and Altaf Malik along with his assistant Sinha were sitting on them. Sumit got out of the car and strolled towards them casually, "Hello SP Sahib."

Malik got up and said, "Salaam Maharao. We almost gave up on you. The Rani sent us a message that you had left in the night."

"Yes we had gone out."

"May I ask you where you had gone, sir?"

Sumit raised his brow and Malik hastily added, "Please don't get me wrong. In view of the fact that you were recently shot at, and a body has been recovered from the haveli, your safety and that of your wife's is our concern."

Sumit smiled, "But Mr. Malik, you suggested that I check out the jungles, so I took a tour."

"I did sir?"

"Yes, and the timber felling is rampant. My wife is deeply concerned."

Vaishali and Sid joined him and more chairs were brought to accommodate them.

"No, no. There is no timber felling in our jungles. Just what the villagers take for firewood," the policeman accompanying Malik said.

"My assistant, Sinha," Malik said.

Vaishali said angrily, "Do not blame the villagers. They just chop off branches for firewood. They do not fell whole trees. What we saw there was terrible. The soil is being eroded; think of the number of birds and animals that suffer because of the trees that are gone. Soon, the river will dry up."

"Ma'am is an environmentalist?" Malik asked mildly.

"Ma'am is a lot of things, as I am finding out. Do you need to question us right now? We would like to freshen up."

"Certainly Sir," said Malik standing up courteously. "We will question your sisters and the Rani till then."

Mehak sauntered into the lawn, "I have told the kitchen to send over some breakfast for you both. I'll join you after you have breakfasted. Hello, Sumit, had a good drive?"

"Good morning, Mehak. It was fun! We should do it together next time, drive convoy. Where's your car?"

Mehak brushed that aside with elan and nodded to Malik, "My brother-in-law Rohtash will join you in a few minutes."

Sumit nodded to Vaishali who got up and took Sid and Bala away. On her way she glanced back to see brother and sister walk towards the East Wing deep in conversation. A car parked in the driveway and Devika got out. A maid followed her, carrying a plate with marigold garlands, water from the river Ganga and other paraphernalia of worship. The old lady stopped, looked icily at the policemen sitting in the lawn and then swept past them, glancing at her son and daughter who were walking slowly towards the kitchen. She shuddered as the old lady walked into the main wing and the door closed.

Bala whispered, "She goes to the temple daily. Everyone from the ashram avoids her apart from Sant ji. They say..."

Vaishali glanced at Sid who was waving to Shivam and hushed the maid. "Shh Bala! Sid, our drive is secret. You can't tell anyone where we went."

He nodded. She prompted the maid, "You were saying Bala?"

"They say in the ashram that she performed very powerful yajnas which killed her husband."

Vaishali rolled her eyes. "Bala, I like you. I really do. And I think you've had really bad luck. But we will not be friends if you keep talking about stuff like black magic. Now go, freshen up and get me breakfast. I am starving."

Bala insisted, "They say that when the Maharao was alive, the Rani had a fight with the Rani of Banasur at the ashram. This old Rani threw some *bhasm,* ashes at the younger Rani and she fell down, bleeding from her nose. Her son, Aditya ji had to take her to the hospital."

Vaishali heard a balcony door open and looked up. Her mother-in-law was standing in the balcony, looking at Sumit and Mehak, her expression unreadable. She shuddered as superstitious dread crawled up her spine, and lengthened her stride. This place reminded her of the gothic romances Pallavi loved to read, complete with an ancient building, horrible furniture and melodrama! All it needed was hidden passageways and an ancestral curse!

✦

Sumit asked Mehak, "Why is your car at Banasur, Mehak?"

She shrugged, "Adi's car had battery problems so he took mine."

"So, he's at Banasur?"

"Adi shifted back there after daddy died. He spends most of his nights at Banasur." She asked angrily, "Are you spying on me?"

"No, we just happened to pass the old haveli at Banasur. Saw your car parked outside. That is indiscrete Mehak. If Somnath saw that, he would create problems. He is your husband."

"And you are not my keeper," she hissed angrily. "Keep your nose out of my affairs!"

"Women," he said throwing his hands up.

He walked to his rooms, stopping outside Vaishali's rooms. The door was ajar and some of the furniture was out in the passage.

"What happened?" he asked Sid who was sitting on some cushions in the passage watching the girls tug and push furniture.

"They have gone mad," Sid told him.

A brass floor lamp was pushed out of the door.

"Want me to talk to her?" Sumit asked.

"Nah! Bala is a scaredy poke. She gabbled something about black magic. It reminded them both of some rudraksha necklace they had shoved into a drawer on the day of the party. They can't find it and it's spooked them."

"How badly spooked?"

"Enough to change everything including the curtains. The furniture sucked anyway."

"So it did."

Vaishali came out with an armload of curios that she put on the floor. She straightened and said, "You said I could change the furniture."

"You can. But all of it, today itself?"

She flushed and muttered, "I can't live with all this for even a day."

"So don't. I'll ring up Kishan. He'll send some strong men to take out the furniture. Vaish, would it not be smarter if you clear it out, one room at a time?"

"Where will you sleep, Vaish?" Sid asked.

"On the floor, if I have to."

"No need for such sacrifice. I will be out for a few days. Use my rooms."

"They also have to be changed. Can I?"

"It's your home, Vaishali," he said gently.

She smiled happily and muttered, "Thanks."

"I'm sleepy, hungry and want to go back home. When Vaish and Pallavi di did this at home, everything became noisy and crazy. I am not going to hang out here," Sid said with conviction. "What are you going to do, Jeej?"

Sumit put an arm around him and smiled, "Run, of course. Get your things, we'll grab some breakfast on the way and then I'll drop you home."

✦ ✦ ✦

21

Malik's Investigations

A bullock cart creaked to a stop right near the Pracheen Mandir. Malik jumped off and said, "I don't understand these rich guys. They walked all this way, for fun?"

The forest officer Nehra said, "It is scenic and good cardio exercise."

Nehra unslung a camera and took a few pictures of birds taking flight, "The jungle bush quail! It is a stroke of luck to spot so many of them together. They are really shy."

Malik looked around, completely uninterested in the birds.

Nehra pointed uphill, "The spring is up ahead."

Malik followed him to the spring, Nehra looking around for more birds and was not disappointed as he spotted gray partridges and parrots. Some squirrels rushed up the safeda and pine trees, disturbed by them. Malik stopped where there was a track marked with crushed scrub and yellowed broken grass and raised his eyebrows.

"The boulder rolled this way," Nehra said.

"If it was an attempt to murder, it was terribly lame. If it was an attempt to scare, it succeeded," he replied, frowning as he saw his portly assistant Sinha climb up.

Sinha stopped to regain his breath and mopped his face with a huge handkerchief. "Sir, I spoke to some villagers. Lot of strangers have been spotted moving around in these parts these days."

"Sinha, visit all the nearby villages; find out where these strangers sleep, what do they do for food, if they are carrying arms, everything."

The man paled under his sweat. "Sir, but how? There are no roads."

Malik smiled sweetly, "Walk, Sinha. It is good cardio exercise."

"Yes Sir," the hapless man left. Malik smiled to himself. He had a hunch that Sinha, a local, was a little too chummy with the wrong sort of people, and was dragging his feet on the investigation. It would be good to have him out of his hair.

They walked uphill, to the place the boulder had originally been. There was a depression in the ground, a patch where grass had not grown.

"Moving the stone must have taken a lot of strength," Malik said.

"Someone said, 'Give me a lever I will move anything'" Nehra said.

"*Give me a place to stand and with a lever I will move the whole world*, Archemedis in the Doric speech of Syracruse," Malik said looking around for some sort of lever. The person who dislodged the boulder could have left it behind. He started kicking the grass with his shoe to search for some sort of clue.

"You give the whole police force a bad name, whoever knows of a cop who reads?" Nehra said. "So what is our playboy Maharao like?"

"Unlike any playboy I have met. He is fit, doesn't look like he does drugs. He's intelligent and a bit too cocky for his own good."

"And his bride? She is a local girl and was quite a terror in school. My daughters studied with her, and they are shocked that she managed to get such a good match."

Malik was now down on his knees, he had spotted something. He said, "Indeed!"

"They tell of a story from school when she threw Puneet Shastri, the MLA's son into the river for grabbing her. Then she and her friends made his life hell for three years at school, calling him fishy and making fish kisses wherever they saw him?"

"Fish kisses?" he asked incredulously.

"You know opening and closing their mouths like goldfishes do!"

Malik dug his fingers into the mud and pulled out something bright red, shaking his head, "Kids!"

"Yes," Nehra agreed with a laugh, bending down to see what Malik had found.

It was an MP3 Player. Malik brushed off the mud and switched it on. Strains of western music filled the quiet mountain air.

"The latest Nickleback album, my daughters are very fond of it," Nehra said. Malik slipped the player into his pocket without any comment.

They walked down to the bullock cart in companionable silence. Nehra took a shot of the parakeets that were perched on a wild Indian gooseberry tree, noisily lunching on some worms. Monkeys crossed their path and they stopped watching them scurry on to a safeda tree. This place was a wildlife lover's heaven.

"Your daughters are married?" Malik asked.

"Not yet. They want to study. I have two of them, and I don't have the money to meet with demands of grooms. Greedy people, it doesn't surprise me when I hear of ordinary government servants like us getting tempted to..." He did not finish the sentence. Malik pretended he had not heard his outburst.

"Invite me over for tea one of these days. I would like to meet your family," he said.

"Yes of course," Nehra said a little too enthusiastically to cover up for his indiscrete words. "Why don't you come over next week? My wife has gone to Pushkar with my daughters. They will be back by then."

"Thursday? I'll bring Nafisa and Adil with me, if Adil does not have any class test."

Nehra smiled and agreed.

Malik wanted to know more about the Maharao's bride. He had seen girls like her in the metros, aggressive and combative. Some of his batchmates had been like that too. Girls like the young Rani became IPS officers or social activists. They did not become brides in feudal families.

✦

The Shastri home was located in the centre of Banasur district. It had once been a small modest home, but politics had proved to be a lucrative business and changed the fortunes of the Shastri family. They now lived in a bungalow which was ostentatious. It was rumored that the architect who had built it was specially flown from Delhi. It looked like one of the nouveau riche homes built in Gurgaon or Noida.

Puneet's room was in the corner of the house, away from the rest of the family. He had been given this room because, his grandfather set great store by education. He wanted Puneet to study, and not be disturbed by the visitors that regularly came to the house. The seclusion suited Puneet who was an introvert. He was happy with his television, his playstation and the internet. He had a few friends and never opened up. Right now, he was sitting crosslegged on his bed, in his darkened room, a glass of Pepsi by his side. His breakfast lay neglected on the table. He was completely focussed on the television screen, the control of his PS3 in his hands.

Sharp knocks on his door disturbed his concentration. He grimaced and hit the pause button on his game of Assassin Creed 3, and asked, "What?"

"Puneet, open the door." It was Sarika, his brother's wife.

He opened the door and asked, "Yes Bhabhi?"

Sarika looked at him with irritation. "Really, you should be out with friends or with your brother at the Party office. What do you do sitting in that room the whole day? If your brother asks I am at the Nausar haveli."

"At the haveli? Why?"

"There is a small function for the expectant mother, the *godh bhari*. I am going there."

"Ha! That is why the hurry about the marriage! I always knew that girl was cheap!" said Puneet.

"Who?" She raised her brows.

"Vaishali, who else? So that is how she snagged the Maharao eh?"

His sister-in-law looked at him sternly, "Puneet, watch your tongue. The function is for Urmila, Vishnu's wife. Vaishali has been married for less than a month! The things this boy thinks!" She shook her head and walked away, saying, "In case your brother asks, I'll be back after lunch."

Puneet slammed the door shut, clenching his jaw in futile anger.

Vaishali Bhatia, he remembered clearly the first day she had joined school, short curly hair, dark skinned, white shiny teeth, in a brand new school uniform with a hanky pinned neatly to her pinafore.

It was the middle of the term. Apparently her parents wanted her to join an all-girls school, but that did not work out. He and his friends were already comfortable in the school and had started bullying the girls. Boys did that. He had called her Kaali Billi. Unlike other girls he and his friends teased, who either cried or complained to teachers or did both, she did neither. That afternoon, during lunch break, she had ambushed him and beat him up. He had gone to the teacher in tears. Everyone had laughed at him. So, he had waited for his revenge. He, along with some of his friends had waylaid her in the playground and beaten her up. She had fought back, biting and scratching. The games teacher had broken that fight up.

The matter should have ended there. Boys are boys. She should have understood that!

But that bitch had waited for months. One day, when the games teacher was absent, she had given him a thorough thrashing. He had screamed for help and she had beaten up his friends too. Sarthak, a close friend of his got a bloody nose and Rohan got a broken tooth. It had made her the most popular girl at school.

Once they grew up, he and his friends escalated their teasing games. They would waylay girls and kiss them. It was just a harmless sport. They expected the girls to cry or complain to teachers, maybe do both. They had kept away from Vaishali and her group. Who cared for that kaali billi? Vaishali Bhatia...

It was just a game! One day he had seen her alone near the river, it had been tempting. She was alone, unaware of his presence, defenceless. It had gone so wrong. Not only did she throw him into the river, but had even filmed him floundering in the water on her smartphone. The pictures surfaced on Facebook and videos on You Tube, with him trying desperately to breathe. The You Tube video was titled "Go kiss the Fishes." Kids started calling him Fishy. News reached his home and his grandfather had summoned him.

"So you think it is fun to molest schoolgirls?" he demanded.

"But other boys...I am not alone," said Puneet.

"You are not other boys; you are Puneet Shastri, Kewal Shastri's grandson!"

His brother was equally stern, "We are politicians, and image is everything. When I stand for elections, I do not want people to point at me and say, Oh that is Resham Shastri, Puneet's brother, you know that boy who forces himself on school girls!"

Now she was Vaishali Singh Nausar.

He switched off the television and went out. His brother's friend, Somnath Rajouria was sitting in the living room on a couch, reading the newspaper.

"Hello, Puneet," he said pleasantly.

"Hello," he said hesitantly. He had not seen Somnath ever since the function at the haveli. "I thought you would be at the haveli," Puneet asked.

"It's a women's thing," Somnath shrugged dismissively.

Puneet smiled politely, aware of the strained relationship between Somnath and his wife Mehak, the Maharao's daughter. No! That Maharao was dead. There was a new Maharao now, Vaishali Bhatia's husband!

"I was going to meet Chandan Pandit, some business. Would you like to come with me? We can take a cab." Somnath said.

He nodded, smiling shyly. Somnath, and Amol, his brother Resham's aide were the only people who understood him, and talked to him. Everyone else ignored him, thinking he was just a spoilt boy. "I'll pick up Amol on the way," Somnath said with a smile.

They stopped at the office, where SP Altaf Malik's jeep was parked.

"Let's drive away," Puneet said, color draining from his face.

Somnath said, "I don't think so. We should stay and find out what the police want."

Inside the office, Chanchal Shastri was sitting on the sofa, Resham to his left. On an armchair facing them, Malik sat an expression of rapt attention on his mild intellectual face. Amol sat passively on an office chair. Chanchal seemed delighted to have such an audience. He was holding forth expansively, "They are royal people, Malik Sahib. Their morals, their tastes..."

"Ahan?" said Malik. "But this is a democracy, there are no royals."

Chanchal laughed loudly, rubbed his belly and winked, "That was because of a woman's jealousy. Our prime minister, Indira Gandhi had a fight with Rani Gayatri Devi. She was jealous of her beauty, you see. She abolished the privy purses overnight. Women! Look what happens when they move out of kitchens and try to run countries."

Malik smiled politely. "You were telling us about the late Maharao," he said.

"He was a man with royal tastes, expensive cars, expensive homes, multiple wives. He was no longer king but insisted on running the whole of Nausar and Banasur like his own private kingdom."

"Banasur too?"

"His second wife comes from there. But then you people won't find it shocking, Islam allows three wives does it not?"

Malik's smile froze. He encountered this reaction often; many men were frankly envious of the prophet's edict for the believers. In his opinion, one wife was more than enough. He glanced at his watch, it was 6 p.m. His one and only wife would give him hell if he got late for dinner again. How did some people balance multiple wives?

Chanchal caught sight of Somnath and Puneet. Beckoning them, he introduced them to Malik. "Somnath, my son's friend and the present Maharao's brother-in-law, and this is Puneet, my younger son."

"I did not meet you at the haveli," Malik said. "I'm so pleased to meet you, Somnath ji, finally. You were at the function?"

"Of course. But I left early; young Puneet had too much to drink, so I brought him home."

"Ah, I see. Did you see anything out of the ordinary?" enquired the policeman.

"No, it was a regular party with the same old faces."

Malik drained his cup of tea, and took his leave with a polite salaam. On his way out, he picked up what looked like a pebble on the ground, and climbed the jeep. They maintained a studied silence until his jeep left. Chanchal said, "Nice chap, for a *mussalman*."

Resham admonished his father, "Grandfather says the man is dangerous. We have to be careful."

"Your grandfather sees Ravanas everywhere. Relax; the only Ravana of Nausar is dead."

✦

Malik sat down on a small armchair in his living room. Nafisa brought tea to find her husband spinning the rudraksha bead on the table absent mindedly as he sifted all the information he had gathered in the day.

Adil came and picked up the bead, "This is a three faced rudraksha bead."

"How do you know?"

"They teach us at school. Rudraksha are called tears of Shiva. The tree is an evergreen, which gives dark blue fruit, the color of *Neelkanth*. The berries dry up to get this color. They are used for meditation but are also used to control blood pressure and other ailments. Nausar has many rudraksha trees. Nausar also has sal and timber but now the forests are getting depleted. It has affected the ecology of the place. Many birds and animals are going extinct."

Malik looked at his son with pride, "Nafisa, our son is intelligent!"

"Humph, not really. He won't learn his school lessons. All he wants is to read about the forests and dinosaurs and things. They won't get him a job, math and science will. Adil, have you finished your homework?"

The boy turned away muttering, "Crime is being committed in Nausar's forests, crime against nature. As a police SP you should be looking after that. We soon won't have rudraksha, timber, parakeets, wild geese or even fish."

"Nehra would love him," Malik said wryly after his son left. "So would the new Rani of Nausar. My son does not think crime against humans is important."

"Save a dinosaur and you'll be his hero," Nafisa said, with a naughty smile on her face.

He laughed, tension leaving his body.

✦ ✦ ✦

22

The Legacy of Digvijay Singh

The corporate office of Royal Group of Hotels and Resorts was housed on the 12th, 13th and 14th floors of the flagship hotel Royal One. In the Director's office on the 14th floor, Vishnu was pacing around impatiently while his father sat looking out of the window. The gentle hills of Nausar were clearly visible. They had been lush green when the floor had been built. The view was not so green now, but that was not on the minds of Vishnu and Girdhari. The new Maharao was.

"Why does Sumit have to be so mysterious?" Vishnu threw up his hands in despair. He was trying Sumit's number but it was out of range.

Girdhari sighed, "Vishnu, he feels betrayed by his family. Perhaps he does not trust us and is trying to protect himself."

"Somnath is coming to stay here at the haveli tomorrow, for the EGM. I hope Mehak does not create problems." As Mehak's husband, he was a stakeholder in the hotels.

"Where is he staying right now?" asked Girdhari.

"Resham Shastri's place," Vishnu replied.

Girdhari sighed; he did not trust the Shastris. After his brother's death, they were getting bolder. He saw Sejal Banasur's distinctive blue car drive downhill and stop at the Shiv temple. "Has Sejal started taking interest in the forests? I see her car almost everyday in the hills."

"Why are you so interested in that woman? Now that uncle is dead we can discount her," Vishnu sneered.

Girdhari took off his specs, polished them. "Vishnu, stop listening to your mother and aunt, they are not deep thinkers. That woman ensured that we made brilliant matches for her daughters. She also made sure that her son enjoyed the same standard of living and education as you and Sumit did. Her son is currently the only person who enjoys the confidence of Sumit and Mehak."

"Sumit this, Sumit that, Sumit, Sumit, Sumit! Papa, you and uncle, both built this business together. If Sumit is not interested, we can buy him out. Why do we have to wait upon his highness's pleasures? Think about it."

Girdhari kept looking out of the window. Vishnu walked up to him and put an arm around his father's shoulders, "Papa, please consider. I am not behaving like Shivam. It is impacting the hotels. How long do I put off the bankers?"

"As long as it takes Vishnu," said Girdhari. Then he screamed out his frustration, "I hate his impudence, but his father has effectively forced him down our throats."

He began to cough, and Vishnu said, "Easy Papa, your blood pressure..."

Girdhari drank some water and then glared at his son, "Have you talked to that gora, Brian? Talk to him; get a feel of your cousin. He is just like Digvijay Bhai Sahib, but a more dangerous version. I warn you, do not make an enemy out of him. And Vishnu what are your wife's plans? Is she staying or will she return to her parental home?"

"Urmila will leave tomorrow."

"Order her to stay, make her cancel her plans. Do whatever it takes to persuade her. And get her to befriend the Maharao's young wife. Remember son, a man who can't control his own wife should not dream grand dreams of controlling an empire as big as Royal."

Vishnu looked out of the window without reacting, just the clenching of his jaw betraying his agitation. Urmila hated the haveli, and his mother and aunt. He did not look forward to telling her to stay. However, he had to admit his father was right. As a Rajput, he should be able to control his wife. He would talk to her.

Girdhari softened his rebuke, "He needs us as much as we need him, Vishnu. Haven't you noticed that he complied with each and every clause Bhai Sahib put in his will. He even got married. He needs us and Royal. And that little wife of his needs a friend at the haveli."

Vishnu nodded.

✦

Himani and Rohtash were sitting on their bed. Unlike the entire east wing which was assigned to Sumit, she had been given just two rooms. Daughters did not feature largely in the haveli's scheme of things, especially in matters of property. When Himani came back after her wedding, her father had assigned her two rooms in the south wing, close to the kitchen.

Now that she had children, one of those rooms was used as a nursery; the other was the couple's bedroom.

She had left the godh bhari ceremony early; her younger son was teething and needed her attention.

Rohtash who was babysitting the children, joined her once the boy fell asleep. Of course, the conversation veered to how Sumit's return would affect their plans and fortunes. Rohtash said, "Your father would not have allowed me to play an active role, my dear."

Himani winced as she recalled the scornful response from her father, "That husband of yours should open a jyotish shop. My hotels are not a joke. I won't have it. You have a percentage of the shares, by virtue of being my daughter. It is enough."

"But daddy," she had pleaded.

He had glared at her, "Is it my fate to be surrounded by daughters and their useless husbands? Weak, useless my children are! And your husbands? Parasites!"

Unlike Mehak who would have stormed out in anger, Himani had pleaded, begged but to no avail.

"I have talked to Sumit," she began tentatively.

"And?" he prompted.

"He listened to me patiently, but did not say anything."

"Himani maybe we should give up this idea. Your family does not want me in the business."

"But Rohtash, you wanted it so badly."

"Maybe it is not meant to be," he said with a resigned smile.

She tossed her head angrily and said, "No, I will not let you be humiliated and disappointed. I will talk to him once more."

He picked up a book and bowed his head in it to conceal a satisfied smile. His wife would fight for him. She always did.

✦

The function was over and the ladies were departing. Mehak smiled and whispered, "Prettily behaved, Vaishali. But you need to learn to not be so approachable. As the Rani you will have to be stuck up, you know!"

Vaishali flushed, "Mehak Di, I have known some of them for a long time, since I was a baby. How can I suddenly turn snooty?"

"Try. This behavior won't do. It's improper."

Vaishali scowled, she liked Mehak and wanted to fit in, but it was hard. Once they dispersed, she went back to her wing and walked into the terrace. Her new furniture still smelt of fresh varnish, which was overpowering. Bala, who was her shadow, followed her out. She whispered softly to her, "Oh Mehak memsahib is a fine one to talk about proper behavior. They gossip in the kitchen that she goes to meet Aditya sahib in the night."

"Really?" said Vaishali delighted. "What about her husband?"

"Arrey Didi, Mehak memsahib does not even talk to him. Aditya Sahib and Mehak memsahib are an item since they were small. When her marriage was fixed, she fought with her parents, but they forced her."

Vaishali had no compunction to listening to gossip. She sat down chummily on an armchair in the balcony, "Screw the royals and their stuffy ways. Bala tell me more."

"Aditya sahib's mother loves Mehak Di, and Mehak di spends most of her time in Banasur."

"And what about Himani memsahib and her mother?"

Bala glanced to the main wing. Devika was sitting out in the balcony, along with Himani. Himani's children played around them. She made a superstitious sign to ward off bad omens and turned away, "They spend a lot of time with swamis and gurujis. Every one is scared of them. I told you about the black magic but you do not believe me." Bala said with a shudder. "Didi don't eat or drink anything they serve."

Vaishali glanced towards her mother-in-law, and concealed a smile at the superstitious fear. "Okay. And what about Vishnu bhaiya?" she asked.

"Vishnu Sahib's wife hardly stays here. She just came for the function and will go back to her father's home. She did not even unpack her bags."

"I know that she is going back because she is going to have a baby," said Vaish.

"Yes Didi. She is scared of all the black magic here. That is why she wants to have her baby far away. She is afraid the old Rani will curse the baby. Shall I get your tea?"

Vaishali shook her head, "Some lemonade please."

Bala ran down. Vaishali started pacing up and down. She had no friend here. As a girl, she had always had her younger brother Sid, and her life. Bala was the only company she had. Her old friends seemed distant now. Not that she had much of an opportunity to meet them now.

Bala came back and said, "Didi, Vishnu Sahib is having a fight with his wife right now. He has forbidden her from going back to her father's. She is weeping. What if the old Rani does something that affects the baby?"

This was too much for Vaishali who said, "Bala, there is no such thing as black magic."

"There is Didi. The sarpanch of my village and the pujari and the temple warned us, they cursed us. We did not care and got married, and now Yashpal is dead."

Vaishali hugged the maid and said, "You miss him don't you?"

Bala nodded, and then said shyly, "Your man is here."

Vaishali got up and went to the edge of the balcony, which overlooked the driveway. Sumit was getting out of his car. She let out a sigh. Sumit was traveling a lot these days, Nashik, Panchkula and even France. Often he just slept in the apartment to get over his jetlag, and consequently spent very little time in the haveli. 'If this goes on, marriage will be a very lonely affair.' Vaishali thought.

Devika watched her daughter-in-law rush up to Sumit who ruffled her short hair affectionately and laughed at something she said. She made a face; Sumit treated the brat like a favorite lap dog. Mehak walked into the balcony and asked, "You called me here?"

Devika frowned at her younger daughter. "Himani tells me that you are still meeting that man."

"Yes, so?" she asked glaring at Himani. "By the way, his name is Aditya Banasur. He lived here all his life."

"You are a married woman now, Mehak. A yuvrani should know how to behave. Your father..."

"Is dead!" Mehak finished coldly. "Allow me to point out to you that the marriage was forced by you and daddy on me. It could never have worked."

"Your husband is coming here and will stay till the board meeting. You had better behave then, Mehak. We do not need a scandal."

Mehak turned away, fuming and walked away, slamming the balcony door.

Himani turned to her mother, "She has always been rash and impulsive," she complained.

Sounds of laughter wafted from the lawns where Sumit and Vaishali were talking. A cloud passed Devika's face. "Both my younger children have no class, no sense of dignity. How could our children have learnt anything better? Their father spent all his time with that woman!"

✦ ✦ ✦

23

Seduction

Vaishali looked around at her rooms with approval. She had banished all the bulky furniture and now the rooms looked spacious. She curled into the armchair and thought about all the dirt she had dug up on her marital family. So Sumit's father had a lifelong affair with Sejal Auntie. Unsurprising! She was so attractive, even at this age. She must have been a sizzling siren when she was young. Moreover, Sumit's mother was such a douche bag. A slight frown crossed her brow. It did not seem as though the family cared much for norms, considering Mehak's affair with Aditya. And her husband's own reputation for being a ladies man...

She shifted restlessly, and caught sight of Bala who was looking out of the window, "What are you looking at?"

She giggled, "Your husband is very handsome, Didi. And he is kind, he will make you happy."

Vaishali made a face. She feared that her man would please a lot of girls. Her phone rang. It was Sid. "Vaish, guess what? Papa has brought Pallavi di home. You were right about Raman."

"What do you mean?"

"Raman ditched her."

She laughed, "Serves the cat right."

He chuckled too, "They ran off to some place in Rajasthan, yes, Mount Abu. They spent some days together and then he ran away."

"Oh my God!" she giggled. It was wrong to laugh at her sister's plight, but she could not help feeling smug.

He chortled evilly, "The stupid girl kept waiting for him. She kept ringing him up and he kept promising to come back. Then the money almost ran out. One day his mother snatched the phone from him and told her to return home, he would not join her."

"And?" she prompted.

"You know what she said? She said that Raman could get lakhs and lakhs in dowry. Why should he marry a runaway?"

"How cheap! I always thought he was a spineless coward," Vaishali said disgusted. "How is Pallavi di taking it?"

"Arre, she is crying non-stop. But forget that! Here is the kicker. Ma is telling her that she is so beautiful; she would have made the best Rani ever. She's telling Pallavi di that it's not too late; the marriage is just in name. She says, 'Vaishali always wanted to study'. What are you going to do, Vaish?"

That brought her amusement to an end. She sat up abruptly and said, "'What? Ma is as silly as Pallavi Di."

Then she controlled herself and said, "Sid, I'll talk to you later. I have to go." She disconnected the call and threw the cellphone on the couch. No, she would not give up so meekly.

The ceremony had been held, twice. She was married to Sumit. She was Nausar's queen or crown princess. More importantly, she was the wife of the owner of Royal Hotels and Resorts.

She threw open the wardrobe and rummaged until she found the package that Sejal Auntie's dressmaker had insisted on her buying. It was a sheer olive colored nightgown, so fine that it took the contours of her body. "It is for your honeymoon, perfect for your height and figure," the boutique owner had said. She shook out the folds. Then she nervously straightened her hair. It was time to stake her claim on Sumit.

The family gathered every evening in the huge dining room, which could accommodate over fifty people to dine together. As usual, the housekeeper Kishan was hovering outside, waiting for the family to sit down, so that the food could be served. She smiled nervously and gathered her resolve, and walked up to Sumit and whispered, "I have to talk with you. Can we meet after dinner?"

"Sure. I'll come to the sitting room," he said. "Has the girl been troubling you? We can send her away and get someone else."

"No, she is okay. I'll come to your bedroom," Vaishali replied, and slipped away to sit down next to Shivam. She had forged a good relationship with him and found it easier to eat with him. Mehak joined them; Aditya who normally sat next to her was not here. Vaishali picked up a roti and toyed with it, with hardly any appetite. She was relieved that something was bothering Mehak who did not notice her restlessness. Shivam rushed through his food and got up muttering something about Delhi Daredevils vs Kolkatta Knightriders and left. Vaishali wanted to rush out after him, but forced herself to stay through dinner.

Finally dinner was done and she rushed back to her wing, showered and slipped on the nightgown, so that she did not change her mind. She checked her reflection in the mirror, she looked so naked! She sat down on the stool in front of the dressing table and closed her eyes. Bala stared at her round-eyed, picked up a hairbrush and ran it through her hair. Vaishali did her eyes up and then applied a wine colored lipstick. The maid looked at her with admiration, "You look like Bipasha Basu."

She smiled weakly and opened the connecting door slightly and stopped, slightly deflated. Sumit was not alone.

Himani was in his room, saying, "Why Sumit? He is a good man and he can handle the responsibility."

Sumit said patiently, "Himani, I am not looking after the hotels right now. Vishnu and Girdhari Uncle are. They make the decisions. Talk to them."

"You are a fool Sumit. Our father built Royal. He is the founder. You should take his place, otherwise our cousin and uncle will swallow our heritage. How can you sit and watch them do it?" her voice was rising.

"I cannot imagine Vishnu being so devious," he drawled.

"And I can't imagine daddy sitting in the sidelines while Girdhari Uncle and Vishnu run the show. Do you have the balls to take them on?" she retorted waspishly.

"I have it from my sources that Devious Singh did not want your Rohtash to be the food supplier for Royal."

She mumbled, "Why can't you call him daddy like all of us? He was old fashioned and possibly did not like sons-in-law involved in the family business. But you are progressive. At least consider."

"My answer is no. No, I won't agree; and no I won't interfere. Talk to Vishnu."

The door slammed so hard that Vaishali jumped. Himani's heels beat a furious retreat on the marble floor.

"She has gone Didi," said Bala, her eyes alive with excitement. Vaishali smiled back weakly telling herself not to panic and stepped into Sumit's rooms, closing the door behind her.

He was walking towards the door and stopped in his tracks as he stared at her. She gulped but willed herself to stand there unflinching.

"Are you sure?' he asked.

She nodded and took a tiny step forward looking him straight in his eyes.

"I won't step back," he warned.

She took a couple of steps forward, stumbling slightly as she stepped on the nightgown. He caught her with a groan, "Damn it girl, what game are you playing?"

Her lower lip trembled, she felt unsure, and close to tears. She looked up and he brought his mouth down on hers fiercely. She hung on to him tightly as a shiver ran through her body. His hands grabbed her hips and brought her closer, "I won't ask you again. If you want to back out, now's the time."

"I won't back out," she said, her breath coming in gasps.

He let her go and she stumbled, her knees weak with new sensations running through her body. Her moan of protest made him chuckle. "Easy, let's get rid of the clothes shall we?"

She stood and watched fascinated as he threw off his shirt and unbuckled his belt. She knew she should have turned her eyes away, but was unable to do so. He chuckled as he saw her staring raptly and said, "Come here."

She walked up to him, blushing deeply. He kicked his jeans away, and pulled off her nightgown, running his hands over her body. He kissed her collarbone, igniting her. She melted under his caresses, leaning against him, as he led her to the bed. She gasped, "I've never been...there has never been anyone."

"Shh, I know. You don't have to tell me that," he said, his rough hand between her legs. "Don't be scared. I will be gentle with you."

She groaned as his fingers moved into her wetness. "Look at me, Vaishali," he said, his intense tone breaking through the passionate haze in her mind.

She opened her eyes, her gaze meeting his passion filled eyes. "I said I won't step back and I won't. You are very young, but I warn you. I won't let you back out either. Ever. I keep what is mine, and you are mine."

She tried desperately to keep her mind focussed as his finger beat a crazy beat on her sensitive nub. "I am yours," she said huskily.

He laughed as he covered her body with his.

Once they were sated, she started giggling, "I get it. After the function, you kept away. You were running away from me. Why?"

He said, "You are so young, so... Oh damn it girl, go to sleep!"

She broke into infectious chuckles, "And what happened to your *I am no self-sacrificing fairytale hero.*"

He chuckled and then kissed her roughly on the mouth, "That is the only way to keep you shut I think!" She snuggled into him with a smile, resting her head on his chest, completely at peace.

Vishnu knocked Sumit's bedroom door early in the morning, but the two of them were oblivious to the sound. Then he ran into the sitting room and tried the connecting door, brushing past Bala. Pushing it open he said loudly, "Sumit, wake up man! Thank God you are here." The words died down in his mouth as he saw Vaishali sleeping in his arms and he backed away, saying abruptly, "Sorry. I am so sorry."

He went back into the sitting room and sat down on the couch.

Sumit sat up. Vaishali murmured something as she opened her eyes, looked at Sumit and blushed rosily. "You look beautiful," he said softly kissing her on her brow. "Vishnu is here, I have to meet him."

She nodded sleepily. He threw her a Real Madrid tee shirt, winked and went into the bathroom. He walked into the sitting room, belting his robe. "What is it, Vishnu?"

Vishnu said with a wooden expression, "SP Malik is here. There has been a gas leak in your apartment."

"An accident?" he asked.

"No, the police say the pipe was cut with a knife or a sharp edged object."

"My servants?"

"They are safe. A police patrol was in your area, they took your servants to hospital at once. I would not have come in if I had known...I am sorry to...I had to be sure you were safe."

Sumit put a hand on his shoulder, "Thank you for your concern, Vishnu."

He smiled as he saw Vaishali standing at the door clad in his tee shirt and shorts listening wide eyed. That expression of shock on her clean scrubbed face topped with tousled hair made her look like a school kid. He gave her a very soft smile and ruffled her hair, "Good morning Vaishali."

She mumbled, "It could have been you, what if you were sleeping at the flat? It could have been you!"

"But you saved me again, did you not?" said Sumit.

She did not smile back. He hugged her, "Cheer up! Where's that smile of yours?"

She gave a wan smile. He kissed her forehead and turned to Vishnu, "Where is Malik?"

Vishnu said, "In the main hall."

"Let us go meet him then."

Malik was studying the portraits in the hall. The late Maharao seemed to be fond of getting painted. He was standing in front of one, of him astride a horse, looking at the almost cruel face.

"Admiring the late Maharao, Malik Sahib?" said Sumit by way of greeting.

"You don't look very much like him," he said, with a salaam.

"Yes, it is said that I favor my mother. Come, sit."

Once they were seated, Malik said, "Sir, I had deputed policemen to patrol the area after the body was discovered at the haveli."

"I thank you, Malik. Did they see anything unusual?"

"I have called for the reports, but nothing out of the ordinary happened."

Sumit smiled and said, "And yet someone cut the gas pipe. I warned you Malik, but you did not take me seriously."

Malik flushed and said, "Sir, I don't like this. Nausar is a peaceful place. Do you have enemies, Sir?"

"Do I?" he asked softly.

Vishnu said angrily, "What sort of a question is that? You are responsible for the law and order situation, SP How did this happen?"

Malik welcomed the anger. That was understandable. He was uncomfortable with the small smile on Sumit's face. The man should have been raving and ranting. "Sir, it was unexpected. We only came to know when a servant came out vomiting."

"What if the servant had not come out? What if Sumit had been in the flat? There was a dead man on our roof. What is all this?" Vishnu said with belligerence.

"Hush Vishnu, you interrupt. The man was speaking," Sumit said quietly, staring at the man, his eyes cold as ice.

Malik came to his feet, staring at Sumit. Those eyes were as menacing as those in the late Maharao's portraits. It was not often that he had to reassess his opinions, but he had misjudged the man. He slowly lowered himself into his chair, "I will have a guard mounted round the clock for the haveli, and also your apartment, Sir."

Sumit snarled, "We do not need guards that simply take rounds of the area, man. We need security. I will be hiring private guards, with weapons. Also ensure that my in-law's place is guarded. If I have to pay, so be it. Just send me the bill."

Malik got up, and nodded to Sumit and Vishnu, and turned, almost running into Mehak and Himani.

Mehak said, "Thank heavens you spent your night here, Sumit! Shift back here!"

"What's the policeman doing here?" Himani asked. "Mother does not like them!"

"The police will stay, maybe even follow us around," announced Sumit.

Himani glanced at Mehak and said, "I have no objections to policemen following me around. But then I don't have anything to hide."

Malik pursed his lips, and walked away, filing this information in his mind. The young man had walked into his office to share his suspicion that his father was killed (something that seemed increasingly likely now). He had not mentioned that he had narrowly avoided death in the hills or mentioned the car accident. He had also not told him that he had missed being shot at his own reception. There was also the mysterious corpse.

His colleagues in Mumbai had been shocked when he had accepted the posting to Nausar. Nothing ever happened in Nausar, was the unanimous opinion. He flexed his shoulders that were tight with tension. So much for a quiet posting! The new Maharao was far too active.

A servant approached him, "Maharao ji wants you to wait for him." He nodded and walked towards the patch of roses in full bloom. Towards his left was the massive kitchen. How many people worked at the haveli? Could it be that someone was working for the Maharao's enemies? He needed a spy here.

The old Rani walked out of the main wing, a maid walking two steps behind her, carrying a plateful of flowers and other things for prayers. She was obviously going to the temple. The maid came up to him and said, "Rani ji wants you to make all this stop. She is extremely upset. The Maharao's name is being dragged into the mud with this scandal. It is in the news today."

He walked to the old lady and asked, "Do you have any suspicions, madam? Do you know if someone within the family or an outsider wants to harm your son?"

Somewhere a window slammed shut. Devika frowned, glanced towards the window and said, "If my husband were alive, no one would have the guts."

The car drew up and she sat in it, and it drove away.

He walked towards the window that had been slammed shut. It was a building close to the garage. A servant walked to it with a tray carrying a jug of lemonade and two glasses, and two plates covered with silver foil.

Breakfast for two...

He asked the servant, "Can you tell me who lives in that room?"

"Oh that is Aditya Sahib's room," said the servant. Malik nodded.

Sumit joined him, "I'd like to know what happened last night at my apartment, Malik Sahib. What do your men say?"

Malik nodded, he would have been very surprised if Sumit had not asked this. "Your apartment had visitors last night. A woman and three young men. They came in a red Santro Xing."

"Did your policeman get the registration number?"

Malik looked uncomfortable, "Sir, the *hawaldaar* thought she was one of your lady friends. He did not even check."

Sumit's eyes flashed with anger, but he said mildly, "Did this genius see anything at all or was he blind and dumb?"

"The woman wore something covering her head. She threw out a bunch of keys and these boys picked it up and ran into the lift. They wore monkey caps."

"And?"

"The lift stopped at your floor for ten minutes. It stayed at your floor for ten minutes, and then the boys came down and ran to the car which drove off."

Sumit asked, "And your men did not stop them?"

"For riding a lift in a building?"

Sumit looked away.

"Sir, it could have been some woman friend?"

He winked, "My lady friends do not pay for anything, Malik Sahib. If I want their company, I have to pay for their meals, clothes, transport and something extra. I doubt if any of them would kill a paying customer, it's really bad for business. And by the way, I pay really well."

"Have you considered that one of them maybe disappointed to learn about your marriage?"

He laughed. "My lady friends are not interested in marriage, for heaven's sake, Malik. It is the money, what you call it, commercial relationship that they like."

Malik nodded, and changed tactics, "Aditya Banasur is a close friend?"

"No, Mr. Malik, he is my brother." The tone was haughty and forbidding.

Malik said, "Your servants gave some sort of statement when they were being taken to the hospital. They knew of your practice of dining at the haveli, so they had dinner at the local dhaba, and were drunk when they came back."

"I see. And the car, did you get the registration number?" Sumit asked.

"The hawaldaar did not see it, it was removed, perhaps. Sumit Sir, are you aware that your father was driving a silver colored Santro when he met with his accident? He had not taken his driver or guard with him. I made enquiries and am not certain that he was visiting the club. He did not go there, even though he was the patron."

That disturbed Sumit's composure. He stared at the policeman, thoughts running wildly through his head. Then he ushered Malik to the police jeep, saying, "You and I need to have a talk Malik. There are things going on that I don't understand."

"Yes, today evening?" said Malik. "There are things that I don't understand either."

"Are you and your wife fond of Western music, Maharao?" he asked.

"I don't listen to music, Malik," said Sumit.

"Then this is not yours I take it?" he said, showing Sumit the MP3 Player.

"No, why do you ask?" asked Sumit.

"I found it near the Pracheen Mandir, right where the rock was before it was pushed down."

Sumit stood there, deep in thought until the police jeep finally drove out of the gate.

Vaishali watched the policeman get into the car. Her eyes followed Sumit as he walked slowly past the fleet of cars, deep in thought. She turned away, biting her lip. The Sant had said that there was danger to his life. Vaishali was not superstitious, or even religious. She taught the ashram boys martial arts because her mother could not find anything objectionable about her young daughter teaching something to ten year olds at the ashram.

She wondered if there was something the ashram people knew or saw. The more she considered this, the more plausible it seemed. She rang up the garage, "Send Thapa with my car. I am going out."

St. Agnes hospital was located near a roundabout in the town. The hospital was being cleaned thoroughly, as the staff expected that the young Yuvraj would visit. They were not the only people who were expecting him to visit the hospital. A truck stopped near the roundabout, and the driver settled down to wait. His instructions were clear, he was to wait for the Yuvraj's Cayenne, and once it came to the the roundabout, he had to act.

✦ ✦ ✦

24

Sumit's Move

Malik waited outside the haveli gates in the Gypsy. Sinha joined him, settling his obese frame in the back seat, and told his boss, "Even the servants have coolers in their rooms, you know. And did you see the generator plant? No power cuts for the royal family. I tell you those people live in style."

Malik sighed; he could not afford to buy an LCD television and a set top box to record matches. Some people have all the luck. "What do the servants say?" he asked aloud.

"You will find this interesting. Most of the servants don't know the young Maharao. Only one of them, the young Rani's driver does. But he refuses to talk about the family. At first, I thought it would be hard to get any information, but then I got talking to one of the girls in the kitchen. Apparently the Maharao's wife has taken an outsider as her personal maid, a new girl who is untrained. That has got her very jealous. It may not be much but she hinted at some secrets."

"Get her to tell you everything she knows." said Malik approvingly. Trust Sinha to get ladies to talk. Then he frowned. "Wasn't the maid the same girl who heard the gunshot at the wedding? Sinha, investigate the maid. Try to talk to her."

Just then a car went past them, carrying Vaishali and the maid. "Wonder where she is going. Damn the girl, she has not taken any security man with her. Follow her," said Malik.

The ashram was on the opposite side of the town. Vaishali wondered if the old Sant would answer her questions. Maybe Chandan Pandit would. He liked her because she paid attention to the small boys. She did not notice the car following them or the truck waiting near the hospital roundabout. The truck driver caught sight of Bala, and he rammed the truck right into the car and jumped out.

"Get that bastard who was driving the truck!" yelled Malik incensed. "Fucking unbelievable! Right under my nose, and that too, on the day India and Pakistan are playing the semi-final!"

He whipped out his cellphone and began yelling orders. His men, aided by passersby helped get the driver and the girls out of the car. An ambulance reached the spot and the injured people were taken to the hospital.

"Sahib, the truck driver," His driver said, bringing a slightly built man with pock marks on his face.

"Sahib it was an accident," the truck driver stammered.

Malik slapped him hard. "You take me for a fool?" He turned to Sinha, "Take him away and beat the truth out of him."

"I lost control Sahib," said the driver, almost collapsing in panic. He had acted on impulse, and had not expected the police to be around.

Sinha caught him by the collar and pulled him up. "You think we are fools? We saw you drive that damn truck into the car deliberately. Licence?"

He studied the licence and then asked, "Who are you working for? Who does the truck belong to?"

The man whimpered, his eyes flickering desperately around, looking in vain for some way to flee. Sinha brought the police jeep next to the man, who was handcuffed and then pushed into the jeep. Malik hitched a ride on a motorcycle passing by and reached the hospital.

✦

Sumit got into a cab minutes after his wife drove away. "Banasur," he told the cab driver briefly.

The cab driver Gul, a local, was an old acquaintance of the Maharao, who considered Sumit to be his best client. When Sumit was in town he stopped taking other passengers, and was generously rewarded for this 'exclusivity'. He glanced in the rearview mirror and correctly judged that his important client was not in the mood to converse. He drove in silence for a while, and then unable to keep shut, he said, "Sorry about your car, Maharao ji. But I hear the damage is not much."

Sumit grunted, of course everyone in Nausar knew everything that happened in the haveli. "Sejal Rani's home?" the cab driver asked, "Or the Shastri home?"

"Sejal Rani's haveli," he said.

"Today is Thursday and she goes to the ashram in the morning. She'll be back by twelve o'clock," said Gul.

Sumit checked his watch; it was just nine in the morning. "Take me to the ashram then, Gul."

The cab driver drove on to the Nausar Banasur highway, glancing time and again at his passenger.

"Speak," said Sumit after a while.

"I know it is not my place to speak about your family members Sahib," began the driver.

"Yes it isn't," Sumit snapped.

The man kept driving in silence. Sumit relented, "How long have we known each other Gul?"

"Ten years Sahib. You paid half the instalments on my taxi, Sahib. I am your well-wisher," said Gul.

"No. You are damn loyal to the source of the funds that's all. Now speak, damn you. I hate silent cab drivers."

"Sahib, take your wife and move out of Nausar. Riots are going to happen. Ask Sejal Rani to leave too, and your sister Rajkumari Mehak. These are bad times for Nausar."

"Explain," demanded Sumit.

"Sahib some evil people are instigating Hindu-Muslim riots," explained a worried Gul.

"Nonsense, riots do not happen in Nausar. Nothing happens in Nausar."

The man parked outside the ashram and killed the engine. "Yes Sahib. Of course you are right."

Sumit looked around; Sejal's car was not parked there. He said, "Since you know so much, do you know where Sejal Rani would be right now?"

He hesitated. Sumit clenched his jaw in frustration. What did the man know? Just then a young boy rushed out and said, "Maharao, please wait. Pratham Pandit wants to go with you to the hospital."

"What the...?"

Pratham came, along with a younger priest and got into the cab, without asking for permission. Sumit looked at him shocked. Pratham addressed the driver, "Hurry, take us to St. Agnes hospital."

Before Sumit could say anything, Gul asked, "What happened? Is someone hurt at the ashram?"

"No, Mian. Rani Vaishali and her maid met with an accident." Pratham said.

"What? When and where?" Sumit asked.

"I told you Nausar is dangerous these days Maharao ji," Gul said, quickly reversing the car. As they turned, Sejal's car drove past them, covered in dirt. It seemed as though the car had gone through slushy roads, the windscreen was splattered with mud. Sejal was driving, completely focussed on the road, the hood of her windcheater covering her entire face and body.

"These days, Sejal Rani is taking a lot of interest in the *shahtoot* and sal trees," Pratham said solemnly.

"Damn her, it's not safe." Sumit said, making a mental note to talk to Aditya about this. "Tell me what happened to my wife. And how did the ashram get to know about the accident before I did."

"The ashram is concerned about the girl, Maharao. We keep a watch on her."

"What girl? My wife?" Sumit said. Then he smacked his head, "Of course! The maid, Bala."

His phone rang. It was Malik. Sumit listened carefully and said shortly, "I'll be there in fifteen minutes. I am on my way."

A long time ago some missionaries had built a small hospital to their patron saint, St. Agnes. After independence it had been renamed as Nausar Government Hospital, and it grew larger, but was still known by its old name. The hospital was perpetually understaffed and was good for minor ailments, emergency stitches, snake bites etc. Any disease or ailment of a complicated nature was referred to specialists. The doctors manning the emergency were unprepared for their tryst with royalty.

Thapa berated them, "How can you put the Choti Rani on this bed? Get clean sheets! Who is the doctor?"

Vaishali, who was clinging to Bala, said in a shaky voice, "It is alright Thapa. Get your treatment done. Where is Dr. Arora? Tell him Vaishali Bhatia is here."

Then she sat down heavily on a stretcher, trying to soothe Bala who was clinging on to her, looking absolutely pale. Showing tremendous courage, Vaishali refused any treatment insisting that Thapa and Bala get attended to first. After Thapa got his stitches and Bala got her bruised arm attended to, she lay down asking again, "Where is Dr. Arora?"

Dr. Arora, who had known Vaishali since she was a little girl rushed in, "Hello Vaishali."

Vaishali grinned weakly and said, "Hello Doctor Uncle, this time it's not my fault. I wasn't driving."

The middle aged doctor grinned and put a thermometer into her mouth chiding her gently, "You are a princess now, little girl. Behave!"

Sumit walked in, his expression softening as Vaishali grinned at the doctor insisting, "I know I am a princess. I know the correct behavior and so I insisted that Thapa and Bala get treated first. Ouch!"

The doctor asked her, "Pain?"

"My neck," Vaishali replied. "No bones broken."

The doctor nodded at the nurse who helped her into the wheelchair. Thapa and Bala were taken away as well. "She is a healthy girl. She will recover fast, Maharao. I'll just have a few X-rays done and let you know in detail," the doctor told Sumit.

"You know me?" Sumit asked the doctor with surprise.

He smiled, "This is Nausar, everyone knows you. Though I must admit, I did not think that we would have you visiting us. Vaishali, her sister and brother have been our patients off and on. Now if you will excuse me," he started walking to the door.

"Doctor, if there is any problem, I will have her flown out of the town," Sumit said.

The doctor smiled, "Of course. But I anticipate nothing serious. She is conscious and unhurt. I will keep her under observation for the night and let her go tomorrow. Same goes for her maid. The driver, I suspect, has a dislocated shoulder. The X-rays will let us know more."

"My wife cannot spend the night here!" said Sumit.

The doctor glanced at some boys in their late teens who walked past the emergency ward slowly and said, "I agree. I would prefer that she did not, not without security. Now, if you will excuse me..."

Sumit nodded and the doctor left. Sumit looked thoughtfully at the boys, who looked slightly familiar. He had seen them somewhere. He walked out of the ward and stopped near Malik who was waiting around the premises to talk to him. Sumit said, "I have been in contact with a private security firm. Until I get my security in place, I need you to depute someone around her."

Malik nodded, "Around yourself too."

They moved away from the crowd of people who had recognized him. Sumit asked, "The driver of the truck?"

"He is in custody Sir. He is not speaking as yet."

"Make him speak. If your people don't know how to loosen tongues, hand him over to me. He attacked my wife, and I will not take this lying down," reprimanded Sumit.

Malik winced at the fury in his voice. "Sumit Sir, please don't get emotional. We will do our best."

Sumit put a hand on his shoulder and said, "Malik, I will ensure that you do not regret this. Go out of your way, put this on priority."

Malik sighed as Sumit walked away to his wife who was being wheeled out. Then he rang up his wife to inform her that he would be late again. He watched some young men walk out, climb into the Nausar Samaj Party car and drive off. He recognized Amol. Frowning slightly, he watched the car, quickly taking a photo with his mobile.

Vaishali settled down in her hospital bed and frowned at her husband who was looking around at the room with disapproval. "It's okay. I have stayed in St. Agnes once or twice. Dr. Arora is a good doctor. Stop being a snob."

He drew a chair and sat down next to her. "Vaish, this place is tacky, and it is not safe."

She moved painfully, her neck in a collar and took his hand in hers, "How are Bala and Thapa? Have you checked on your servants from the flat?"

He gripped her hand, "Thapa is taking this personally. He is very upset. Vaish, havent I told you to not take risks? Where were you going?"

"To the ashram first, then I wanted to check on your servants." He shook his head. "No, don't dismiss it. Someone tried to kill you. You expect me to take that lying down?" she said, her eyes flashing with anger.

He cupped her face in his hands and stared into her eyes, "Listen to me, girl. Right now, things are dangerous. Stay put at the haveli. Please, for my sake."

Her eyes widened as she caught sight of her parents entering the room and said, "If you kiss me, I'll obey you."

He chuckled softly, muttering, "Rogue," as he bent his head and complied.

"Ewww, stop it!" exclaimed Sid as he rushed in and hugged Sumit. "Vaish how can you have a real life accident without me? How mean!"

"Hey don't I get a hug?" she asked with a smile.

"Jeej has been hugging you. You don't need more," he said screwing up his nose.

"Hello Pallavi Di. How are you?" Vaishali said smiling, her hand gripping Sumit's possessively.

Pallavi smiled, her eyes straying towards their hands clasped tightly, and said, "Hi Vaish. Are you hurt badly? Hello Sumit Jija, I must warn you, she is a troublesome girl!"

'So this is Pallavi, an Indian version of Britney Spears, vapid and screechy.' Sumit thought to himself. He smiled and said, "Hello Pallavi. Vaish never gets into trouble. As a matter of fact, I do that, she saves me all the time."

Shrishti fussed anxiously, "Vaishali, how are you? What does the doctor say?"

"Oh some slight scratches," said Vaishali with a smile. Sumit sat down on the bed next to her, still holding her hand.

Shankar said, "You know, she will never complain, no matter how difficult the injury is."

"And she is ever so accident prone," murmured Pallavi. "In fact, thanks to her, we are familiar with St. Agnes and every private hospital in town."

Sumit glanced at his wife with amusement and dawning realization. The previous night and the demand for a kiss made sense to him now. She wanted to prove a point to her sister. He bent his head and whispered, "So that is why you wanted a kiss, brat?" She grinned sheepishly. He flicked a finger on her cheek and murmured, "You sly bitch! She is nothing compared to you." Then he got up and said to everyone, "I'll have to leave you all for some time. Champ, stay with your sister until I get back, okay?"

"Sure Jeej," said Sid.

"And you, stay in bed, okay Vaish?" he said dropping a light kiss on her head and moving out.

"I don't like these modern ways. Young people these days are so physical," grumbled her mother. "But then I guess he has stayed abroad all these years."

Vaishali lay down with a small satisfied smile on her face, and closed her eyes. "My head is aching and the doctor has told me not to talk too much," she said primly.

Shankar followed Sumit out. "Sumit ji, I said it earlier and you did not like it. But she would be safer at our home."

Sumit turned and snarled, "No, I won't permit it. She is my responsibility Bhatia Sahib. Her place is with me, whatever happens. I will not let you take her away."

Shankar gently put his hand on his shoulder, "I am her father, son. She is so full of life, our home has not been the same since she...I love her too... I... Just keep her safe, please."

He smiled tightly and looked ashamed at his outburst. Nodding slightly he hugged the older man, "I am sorry... Papa." He lowered his head and walked away. Shankar watched him depart with a lighter heart. Vaishali had done the impossible, she had won a place for herself in the Maharao's heart.

Sumit checked on Thapa and Bala and then walked out of the hospital deep in thought. Pratham was waiting outside for him. "How is she?" he askd Sumit.

"She is okay, slight scratches, that is all," said Sumit.

"Sumit ji, you are a rich man. For you one homeless girl does not matter. Chandan rescued her from very bad men and brought her to the ashram. He is worried about her."

Altaf Malik who had been silent spoke up, "The girl, Bala is safe. Why havent you people complained to the police about the bad men?"

"We are men of God, Maharao. The bad men are not our problem," said Pratham.

"Really? You think your precious God will protect you from them? Don't be silly Pratham. Anyway, the truck driver who attacked the car is in jail. Tell Chandan Pandit that," said Malik.

Malik stepped closer to them and added, "The man's name is Rawat. He is not telling us the reason he attacked the car yet. He will."

"We would like to meet Bala," Pratham said.

"We are not allowing any visitors, so I am sorry you can't meet her," Malik replied.

Pratham hesitated and then said, "We will be back, Maharao."

Both Sumit and Malik watched him leave. Malik said softly, "Maharao, Singh Sahib, many times people hide things from the police, for many different reasons. But then we are trained to dig out secrets. Actually we have little else to do. Escorting ministers and local dignitaries is such a boring job. So we dig out secrets. It is...interesting."

"I am not trying to hide things, man. If I had to hide things, I would not have called you," said Sumit.

"You informed me the very first time we met that your father was murdered. You still haven't told me why you think so. Then your wife discovers the body on the roof. I arrive the next day to investigate only to find that you took this driver, Thapa, your wife and her maid for a secret drive in the night. After your return, you start making many out of town trips. Your car meets with an accident, but no one is hurt. Today I had your maid investigated, and I find that this girl, a poor villager, barely fifteen, has opened a bank account, and has a large fixed deposit in her name. Sir, what is happening?"

"Malik Sahib, do you drink?" asked Sumit.

"Not on duty Sir."

"Well then, go off duty and join me at Royal for lunch. I have a proposal for you."

"No sir, no proposal. Just answers."

"I am a businessman. There is always a proposal."

Malik hesitated and then said, "Well okay, I will join you at Hotel Royal at 4 p.m."

Sumit shook hands with him and left.

Malik checked his watch. It was two in the afternoon. He drove to the residence of his good friend, Nehra, the Forest Officer to meet Nehra's daughters.

Nehra was surprised to see Malik at the door of his small government allotted bungalow at the edge of the town. He reluctantly asked his help, a local adivasi girl to bring out a few chairs in the garden. Malik sat down, politely refusing the offer of tea.

"I would like to talk to your daughters, Nehra."

He shifted uncomfortably in his chair, "They are just girls Malik. They would not know a thing!"

Malik smiled his mild smile and pushed his specs up his nose. "No doubt. But still..."

The two girls peered out of the window curiously. Nehra sighed and called them out. They came and said politely, "Namaste Uncle."

"Namaste. Sit down please. I want to talk to you about the new Rani of Nausar. You knew her?"

The girls sat down on the chairs demurely, their heads lowered. Their father drew his chair closer to the girls, protectively.

"Yes uncle," the older girl said.

"How well did you know her?"

"She was in our school, uncle. She was in her class," the older one said, pointing at the younger girl.

"Yes, Didi was one year ahead of us," the younger one said.

"How was she?"

"She was a good girl, uncle. She played sports."

"She was your friend?" Malik asked.

"All of us were friends, Uncle. We studied together."

This was going nowhere. He glanced at their father who was sitting protectively near the girls. The girls kept their eyes politely averted, focussing on the hedge of the little garden. The servant came out carrying glasses of water. He drank a glass of water, thanked them and left. There was a small quaint little market comprising small shacks, selling fresh vegetables, wild flowers and local handicrafts. He strolled to a small tea stall, bought a packet of cigarettes and lit one. Soon the girl who had studied with Vaishali came cycling furiously.

"Malik Uncle!" she said as she dismounted from the bicycle. He enviously noted that she was not out of breath. He threw away his cigarette and smiled, "Yes?"

"I am Sarika Nehra," she said.

"Yes Sarika?"

She was slim, short and bony like her father. She wore a kurti and tights, and a cap with its visor at the back like all young people. She said in a rush, removing her cap, "I dont know if any one would want to shoot the new Maharao. But many people would love to kill Vaishali. She was the sort!"

"Would you like a cold drink?" he asked her.

She nodded.

They went and sat down on the bench outside the tea stall. He bought two Pepsis and sat down opposite her. "What sort is Vaishali?"

"She is a fighter cock."

"A fighter cock?" Malik asked.

"She fights with everyone. Even boys are scared of her. She beat up some boys who used to follow her sister home, you know, tease her. She also beat up her younger brother's bullies.

We always thought she would become a feminist, a Morcha waali."

Malik sipped his cold drink. It was tepid. She giggled, "They called her kaali billi. Now she is Rani. Can you imagine?"

"Who called her kaali billi?" enquired Altaf.

"Oh every one did but not to her face. Who wants trouble? You know that MLA Shastri's son, Puneet? She beat him up so bad when we were small that he did *susu* in his pants."

"Why?" He did not want to hear kindergarten stories but he had paid for the cold drinks.

"He beat her and called her kaali billi on the first day she joined school. She joined karate classes that day. Then months later when she knew how to fight, she beat him and his friends up, alone. He did susu in his pants. He became a joke."

He took a huge gulp. "Wow, so this Puneet hates her?"

"So many boys hate her. She is dark and she thinks she is better than boys. Boys don't like girls who don't back away. But all of them have left town, all but Puneet and his two friends."

"So they are here, and they are jealous of her good fortune," he finished for her.

She nodded.

"Are they fond of music?" he asked bringing out the MP3 Player and switching it on.

"Everyone is Malik Uncle. Nickelback is so popular. Yes I would say they are fond of music."

"Thank you Sarika."

"Uncle, please don't tell my father I came to see you. He thinks I am just a baby, and have no sense," she said with a naughty grimace.

He smiled back. "I won't," he promised.

She left and he got into his police gypsy. He was late for his next meeting.

Sumit was sitting in the coffee shop of Royal One, waiting for Malik when the phone rang. It was Melissa. "Hi Sumit, Brian told me your wife met with an accident?"

"Yes Mel, but she is okay."

"She is just a baby, Sumit. She is completely wasted on a nut like you. The least you could have done was keep her safe!"

Sumit sighed. Women, in his opinion always played the high moral card. He said ruefully, "Believe me; I am kicking myself right now, Mel. I need your help."

"Why am I not surprised?" she said. "Already having marital problems?"

He inhaled deeply as the jibe went home. Then he smiled, "I love you too darling. But listen, this is something right up your alley. There is a young homeless waif, and I need to keep her safe. I need her to disappear for some time. Does your convent have a branch here at Nausar?"

"Is she Christian?" Melissa asked.

"Not yet. I would not want to make your job easy."

She hemmed and hawed. Then she said, "This can be difficult."

"I'll make a donation, a hefty one. Make it happen, Melissa. Someone is trying to kill the girl. Keep her alive, please."

"How old is she?"

"They all say they are nineteen or something. I don't think she is more than fourteen years old.

"Sumit, what is with you and young girls?" Melissa started.

"Gosh Mel! Nothing of that sort! She is just an important witness. I have to keep her safe."

"So you will brush your atheism aside and pay my convent?"

"I am a rationalist, you narrow minded Catholic!"

This banter could go on and on. Mel said, "I'll have to meet her. Besides I have this great desire to experience the life of royalty in Nausar, invite me to visit you."

"Done!"

She smiled, put the phone down and told her husband who was listening to the conversation, "Your precious Sumit has lost it. But we are going to be his royal highness' guests."

Malik reached the hotel half an hour late. He was led to a secluded alcove where Sumit was sitting, drinking beer.

"I'm sorry I am late. I was a bit busy," he said apologetically.

"Have you had lunch?" Sumit asked.

He shook his head. Lunch was ordered. Malik refused beer, settling with iced tea. Then his attention wandered to the huge screen. Irfan Pathan was bowling a blistering over. Sumit watched the man who stared at Irfan Pathan on the screen. Irfan got hit for a six on the last ball of the over. Malik clicked his tongue in disapproval and looked towards his host, who said sadly, "Yuvi would have performed better right now. The pitch conditions..."

"We will win, Sumit Sir. After all, it is Pakistan. How can we allow them to win at our home ground?"

"You want to win, Malik?" asked Sumit.

"Always," he said with a slight laugh as lunch came and was served. They talked of cricket through lunch and after the plates were cleared away Sumit said, "Put both my servants in a safe house lock up."

"Why?"

"I want them safe and out of the way."

"Sir, I can't put your wife's maid in the same cell as men. Besides, on what charges do I lock them up?"

"Not her maid and driver, man, the boys who work at my flat. No charges, pending charges, whatever. Get creative. You can do it Malik."

He hesitated, and Sumit pressed him further, "It is only for a few days. They will be safe this way."

"You are planning something," he said.

"I don't like being hunted. Yes I am."

"What? And why is the girl so important?"

"She was at the wrong place at the wrong time. She saw things."

"What things? I need answers if I am to help you Sumit Sir. And please don't do anything rash. Nausar does not have a top-notch police force. We were considered a safe district."

Sumit raised his beer mug and winked, "And I messed it up. Yes, you make a valid point. Malik sahib, she witnessed a murder. As yet you are not aware of this murder and are not investigating it, so can I request you to ignore it? Can you trace currency?"

"No, not unless it is marked. Don't believe movies about serial numbers and other fancy stuff. No one notices or cares about all that," said Altaf.

Sumit said, "I think I have to be frank with you. This girl had a husband, the truck driver who was paid to ram his truck into my father's car. He was supposed to disappear but he came back for more money. She witnessed his killing. I have the *supari* money with me. I wish it could be traced."

Malik took a hefty gulp of his iced tea, "Is it marked?"

Sumit shook his head. Malik said, "I see. It can't be. It is unmarked currency."

"Well Malik, I have given you some information." He looked at Malik expectantly.

"The Santro that visited your apartment building was driven by young kids. Those boys were drunk and looking for mischief. A woman threw them a bunch of keys, which fell near the lift."

"You've already told me that. And?" he asked.

"The guard remembers the key bunch; it's locally made, with rudraksh beads. The ashram people sell such key chains."

"You know the boys?" Sumit asked.

"I have a feeling your wife knows them."

There was silence as Malik started watching the match. Then he said thoughtfully, "I'll help you but on one condition. You allow me to question your maid and your wife. And of course agree to double your security. Two private guards and one police guard, round the clock for you and your wife."

Sumit grimaced. "One private guard each."

"Done," said Malik sweetly. Sumit looked at him surprised. Then he laughed. "That is what I call excellent negotiating skills."

"Sir, I am just a simple policeman."

"Topper in IPS exam 1980, good record, father killed by a Mumbai ganglord as punishment for getting too close, asked for posting to Nausar after that. You're hardly simple, Malik Sahib."

Malik drained his glass and stood up, saying, "Sumit Sir, be careful. You are young, arrogant and cocky. It has helped you in your business but this time the stakes are high, you are playing for your life. I can't promise the safety of your servants. If you arrange a place for them to stay, I will have it guarded. I can do that much."

"Thank you Malik."

He shrugged, "If anything happens to the unfortunate maid, it will be on your conscience. And remember, Sir, your bride has lived all her life in Nausar. She made a lot of friends in this place, but has made enemies too. Your brother, Aditya and his mother have been wandering around in the jungles. It is unsafe. Salaam."

Sumit finished his drink, staring at the television screen. He walked back to the hospital, deep in thought.

+ + +

25

The Night at St. Agnes

Sumit was glad to note that a policeman was sitting on a chair outside the door. It would serve as a deterrent.

"You get it," he heard Sid say insistently. "You're his wife. They will deliver too!"

"Just what are you planning?" he asked on entering the room.

They exchanged glances, and Sid said hesitantly, "Can we order pizza or something good from Royal One? Will they deliver? Vaish says lunch here was awful."

"Where are your parents?" asked Sumit.

"Ma's gone home. She wants to get us home cooked dinner and my pajamas. I am spending the night here. Papa is outside talking to Sejal Auntie and Mehak Di. They will allow them in after 6 p.m., visiting hours."

Sumit opened his wallet and took out some money. "Here, take this and go to my cab. I'll inform the driver. Go to the hotel and get whatever food you fancy."

Sid grinned and jumped off the chair, grabbed the money and left. "You're a sport Jeej!"

Sumit sat down in the chair he vacated, "Why were you going to the ashram, Vaish?"

She countered the question with, "Are you religious?"

"Not really."

"Me neither. I remember Santji saying there was a threat to your life. I don't think he had a vision or some bullshit like that. I think he knows something or saw something."

"Do you have enemies, Vaish?"

Her chin rose defensively, "Do you? Doesn't every one?"

"Yes. But bad enough to kill you?"

"Rubbish!"

"Okay Madam Cactus, calm down. I'm going out to meet Sejal Aunty and Mehak. You go to sleep."

She lay down, a frown on her face. Someone wanted to kill her? Why? For the first time in her life she felt scared. She wanted to go back to the haveli, it was safe. Or was it?

Sumit went out. Sejal, wearing an ice blue colored anarkali was sitting elegantly on the tacky plastic hospital chairs, her feet daintily crosslegged, clad in blue and silver mojaris. Mehak was sitting next to her in slim fit jeans and a gray silk shirt. Shankar, still in the crumpled safari he had rushed to the hospital in was standing next to them. They turned as he approached them. Shankar turned towards Sumit, anxiety on his face.

"She is just lying down." Sumit said, forestalling his anxious questions.

Shankar nodded and went to Vaishali's room. Sumit asked Sejal, "Aunty, please do not go into the jungles. It is unsafe."

Mehak and Sejal exchanged glances. Mehak laughed, "But why would Sejal aunty go into the forests? There is nothing there."

Sumit brushed that aside, "Shush, Mehak. I respect you a lot Aunty, and I am concerned about your safety. I am not interfering, I just want you safe."

"Thank you Sumit," Sejal said graciously.

He looked at her elegant attire and smiled, "Besides, the hooded windcheater does not suit you. I think we will be permitted in now. Shall we go in?"

They entered the room to find Vaishali sobbing her heart out with a very disturbed Shankar trying to soothe her.

"I don't want to stay here," she wailed as she saw Sumit walk in. "I want to go back home."

Shankar said, "Sure, I will get the discharge done. Then we can go back."

"No I don't want to go back there. I want to go to the haveli," she sobbed harder. "I don't feel safe here. I want Bala and I want to go back."

Mehak stepped forward but Sumit stopped her, "Vaish, listen to me. Stop crying. We will take you back home right now. But you have to stop crying. Do you understand?"

She nodded, her tears subsiding. "You will have to live with a guard all the time, okay?"

She nodded. "Why?" She wiped her face with the back of her hand. Sumit handed her a hanky and she made a ball of it and rubbed it on her face. Mehak gently prised it out of her hands and handed her a wet tissue.

"The police think it's necessary. I think I am going to get one each deputed to watch over both you ladies too."

Mehak gasped. "No!" she said firmly.

Sumit smiled at her and glanced at the frozen look on Sejal's face. Sejal quickly controlled her facial expression and said graciously, "Thank you Sumit."

Vaishali asked, "Can we go now?"

"No. I have to inform the SP and get the billing done. We'll leave after that."

It took two hours to complete all the formalities. By that time Sid had returned with packed dinner. He made no effort to hide his disappointment, "I got pizza and lots of chicken. I also got Momos. I thought we'd have a picnic."

Shankar took him aside and scolded him. Sumit came to his defense. "It's alright. We can take the food home. Shivam would love to eat the pizza with you. Can he come with us?"

Shankar frowned, "No, he can't."

Sid tugged at Sumit's sleeve and looked at him imploringly.

"Please Papa. It will cheer Vaishali up. He can go to school from the haveli. I will ensure that," requested Sumit.

"It's Dussehra break from tomorrow. No school!" Sid said with a huge grin. When Shankar scowled, Sid added, "Please Papa. Please. With Pallavi di back and all the drama..."

Mehak and Sejal exchanged glances. Sumit was grinning, looking barely older than Sid. His wife and brother-in-law had thawed him completely. Shankar relented and said, "Okay, just for a day."

"Gimme five!" Sumit grinned raising a hand. Sid chuckled, meeting his hand with his own, "You're a sport Jeej!"

✦ ✦ ✦

26

Political Machinations

Nausar, St. Anirudh's Ashram

Quite unaware of the fact that her younger daughter-in-law had met with an accident, a rather disturbed Devika was sitting facing Sant Anirudh on the ghat of River Nausar. The cool breeze that wafted from the river made the weather pleasant. Anirudh was sitting next to a rudraksha tree attempting to counsel the upset Rani. Further ahead on the ghat, Rohtash was sitting deep in discussion with some priests. His wife Himani was having an argument with Somnath and Resham while Puneet watched them quietly with a smirk.

Anirudh said, "The ways of the Almighty are mysterious. Your husband had certain preferences that were causing you pain. If you look at it in a detached way, he will not cause you any more pain."

Devika looked angrily at the Sant. "It is fine for you to say so, sitting here in this ashram. I lost my husband!"

"Rani, you got your wish!"

"Don't presume to know what I wished for! I wished for her death, her destruction!"

She glanced away recalling how Sumit had highhandedly conducted his marriage, just to snub her. She swallowed a painful lump and whispered a half formulated question, "You abetted my son is his foolishness?"

Anirudh just clicked his tongue.

She continued, "Sant ji, I am not overreacting. I am the most unfortunate woman of these times. My children should have been caring and supportive. I have endured enough."

"Daughter, do not look for validation outside, inner validation is all you need."

She stood up, shaking her head uncomprehendingly, all at once irritated with all the platitudes, turned and left. Himani ran after her.

Puneet watched her run off and smiled. His smile broadened as Resham and Somnath chuckled. Intrigue was not everyone's cup of tea. Somnath said, "Stop laughing Puneet. She is upset. She just wanted him scared, but you tried to kill everyone."

Resham said, "Ladies should not play games not suited for their emotional temperament. I sincerely hope she can master her emotions. More fun and games are in the offing."

Somnath chuckled and agreed, "Yes, more fun and games."

Chandan approached them, his eyes stony. Somnath said, "Chandan mian, how are you today? There will be two trucks coming this way. The ashram has to ignore them."

He nodded and walked away without glancing at them.

Resham said, "She is right. You went overboard Puneet. We have a bigger game to play. Don't screw that up."

"The environmentalists?" Somnath asked.

He nodded with a grin. "They are going to start their campaign tomorrow at the Royal site. I am sending NSP workers to campaign with them."

"Can I go and campaign too?" Puneet asked.

"Don't be silly, Puneet. We are not to campaign against Royal openly. After all, it is the biggest job provider in this state!" Resham laughed and added, "It is heaven sent, this environment angle. Environment is a national issue, no, it's an international one. We will create a huge noise in front of the Royal Health Resort site, up in the hills, and it will hit national news."

Somnath said, "Devious Singh would have destroyed us had he been alive."

"But he isn't, is he," Resham replied with a slow smile.

They started walking slowly to the gate, unaware that voices carry over water, and Rohtash and the priests had overheard them. Rohtash stared after them, his eyes wide with shock. His eyes whipped around to the priests, who looked away, pretending they had not heard the conversation. They got up and left with a perfunctory Namaste. He sat still as slow anger burnt in his stomach. He had endured a lot of humiliation from his in-laws for the sake of his wife. But that was the lot of a *Ghar Jamai*. He accepted that. Somnath was his co-brother, husband of his wife's younger sister. Not only was he plotting against his wife's family, he had dismissed him, walked past him as though he was an invisible speck of dirt. It bothered him; he was also a Rajput, a prince. Like all Rajputs he equated fear with respect. Somnath's dismissive behavior was intolerable. He went down the steps of the ghat and sat with his feet in the ice cold water, watching the rippling waves. His wife would not comment on his absence, as she would think he was immersed in his study and had forgotten lunch. He wanted to jump into the river, end his miserable existence. Then his Rajput pride kicked in. No, he would not end his life so ignominiously. A true warrior does not go down alone. He takes a few opponents down with him. He would fight – but how? It was evening when he slowly got up and made his way out of the ghat, hailed a cab to the haveli.

Private Meeting at the ashram an hour later

"You think we should tell the young Maharao?" Chandan asked the old Sant.

"Why should we?" asked the older priest, sipping his tea.

"After all, his mother helped us get this ashram. The young Maharao has given us a shed and the cows and buffalos."

The old Sant said, "Maybe we should."

Pratham interjected angrily, "Chandan, you are too emotional. Sant ji you know nothing at all about the world outside the ashram. If we tell the Maharao, he will be annoyed at us being privy to such matters. If the politician comes to know, he will destroy all that we have built."

"So we do nothing?" Chandan asked in horror.

"For now," Pratham said emphatically. The Sant's shoulder drooped in resignation.

Two days later, at Haveli, Nausar

A deeply upset Vishnu was watching the news on television. The environmental lobby had staged a protest at the site of the Royal Resort, which was being built 80 kms away from the city of Nausar. It was being enthusiastically supported by the Nausar Samaj Party. The political leaders had even arranged private bus services to transport the protestors to the site daily, and all the disaffected and unemployed youth of the state had joined the protest. Vishnu grimaced as he exchanged glances with his father as Resham made an emotive speech on how the rampant greed of corporates would deprive the residents of Nausar of fresh air and clean water.

Mr. Subramanium the Executive Director of the bank rang him up. Vishnu switched off the television and took the call. The banker was expressing his anxiety. "No, it is under control, Sir. Yes sir. Yes yes, I understand."

He put the phone down, and started walking around the study in agitation. "What did the man say?" Girdhari asked.

"He was in a meeting with the CMD of the bank. They want the situation resolved or they will call back the loan." Then he started ranting. "Bloodsuckers! When Uncle applied for the loan, they were happy to give it for nine percent. After Uncle's death, they raised the interest rate to twelve percent. Now they want to raise it further, and put yet another Director on board. What is the matter with them?"

"They don't trust us, Vishnu. They are scared now that your uncle is dead, they feel we won't be able to manage this empire," said his father grimly. "They would deal better with Sumit, but our Prince is not helping. He keeps disappearing without any information. Do you know where he is?"

"Last I heard he had gone to Nashik with Brian. Coronet is what he has created and he prefers that to Royal." Vishnu said morosely.

"Call him back. This is his place, his heritage. We have given him too much leeway. Damn it, the bankers will definitely prefer him to us."

"I did. He said he would be returning soon."

Girdhari dialed Sumit's number and asked, "Sumit, son, where are you? Oh that is good!" and he told Vishnu in an aside, "He is in Nausar."

Then he told Sumit, "Turn on your television and watch the news. After that, please ring me up."

He smiled with relief.

SP Residence, Nausar

Malik was watching the news on his brand new 38" LCD television, a gift he had recieved from the Maharao on Eid. He shook his head and rang up Sinha, "What is the situation like?"

"It is peaceful, just a regular political rally that is all."

"Another gypsy is on its way to relieve you. Let us hope it stays that way."

"It is not needed Sir. I will come back in the bus that the Nausar Samaj Party has organized."

Malik frowned a bit, but did not voice his objection. Local policemen often had their own preferences and as long as it did not disturb the law and order situation, it was wiser not to interfere.

The phone rang, it was Vishnu. "Yes Vishnu Sir."

"What is happening in Nausar, Malik Sahib? Never in our living memory has someone tried to spoil our name. We have given so much to this state, employment, progress. Why is your police force not doing anything?"

"Sir, if you are referring to the dharna at the Royal site, it is unfortunate. But the protestors are not breaking any law," he replied carefully.

"Oh really? They are creating disturbance. Stop them."

"Vishnu Sir, the Royal site is far away from the town. They are not disturbing peace and civilian life."

"You are useless Malik. So is your police force. Wear bangles and a sari, all of you!" he screamed and slammed the phone down.

Malik sighed. He did not like Sumit Singh's cousin. He settled down to wait and watch.

Suite 72, Royal One, Nausar

Melissa was explaining to Bala how her life in a convent would be, if she chose to go with her. Bala looked at her blankly, comprehending very little apart from the fact that she would be sent to some place away from Vaishali. Defensively, she turned her back on the white woman and her eyes wandered around, falling on the remnants of breakfast and then at the television. She jumped up as she saw a familiar face, a face that often gave her nightmares. She started babbling at top speed, and tried to make Melissa understand. "*Khooni*," she explained. Melissa stared uncomprehendingly. She pointed at a man leading some of the protesters and repeated, "Khooni!"

All Melissa could gather was that for some reason the girl was scared of the man she was pointing at. The girl looked at her and picked up a butter knife lying in the breakfast tray and jabbed it into her stomach. "Khooni!" she repeated.

Melissa numbly dialed Sumit's number. "Where are you?"

"We are at the pool, Mel."

"Both of you better come to the room now. I think we have found your murderer."

The men rushed back and settled down in front of the television waiting for the clip to be replayed. It was replayed after an hour. Bala pointed at a man standing exhorting his followers, and leading a chant, "Royal Hotel *Hai Hai*."

Bala stared at him and said, "He killed my husband. He shot him dead."

Sumit sighed and called Vishnu, "Vishnu, I am sorry. I know uncle wanted me back at the haveli. I'll try to be there for dinner. Call me if anything is needed."

He disconnected before Vishnu could protest.

"I want to go back to Didi; I won't go anywhere else. Sahib, please." pleaded Bala.

"Women! Your sex is perverse!" protested Sumit. "No, you have to go with the white memsahib. She will take you to Delhi and keep you safe."

Bala started bawling. "Okay okay, I will take you back to the haveli. Stop that whining!" he said throwing his hands up. "One condition. You have to tell everything to the police."

She sat down on the floor cross legged, her face averted. Melissa said, "Wow, Sumit, she is immune to your famous charm. I think the child is sulking!"

"Yeah yeah! Whatever. I have become respectable. I am a married man!"

Malik landed up at the suite with the footage. They played it and Bala pointed out Amol. "This man!" she said with a shudder.

"Are you sure?"

"Yes Sahib. This man made me a widow the day I got married. I will never forget his face for my whole life."

"Can you say this in a court of law? In front of a judge?" asked Malik.

She shuddered, but then Yashpal's last words, his outflung hand as he screamed 'No' to her when she was going to step out of the shadows flashed in front of her eyes. She gulped and nodded.

Malik turned to Sumit angrily, "You know what this means? This is Sarna, local muscle for the Shastris. He has political clout. How do you plan to keep this girl safe? By the time the case comes to court, she'll be dead!"

Sumit said softly, "This man is just a front. I have a feeling all of them, the gas pipe cutting, the killing of my father, the corpse on the roof, the young driver's death, they are all connected."

"And the Shastris are behind it? Oh come on Sumit Sir! You think they want to take over Royal? They are politicians not businessmen."

"Yeah, they seem to be the obvious villains, don't they? Too obvious," said Sumit, thoughtfully. Melissa was discussing something with Brian. Then she said, "The convent has ties with a children's hospital in Delhi. The girl needs therapy. She can be sent there for treatment."

"She has to be taken into remand, as a witness," Malik said flatly.

Sumit saw Bala's eyes, they were pools of terror. "Malik, I'll come to the police station tomorrow and file a complaint. Let us get the paperwork together. When the case gets to court I will get her there."

Malik grimaced. Then he said coldly, "You know why I dislike you rich people? You think you own the fucking law. As a material witness she cannot leave town that is final."

"Damn you, man!" snarled Sumit. Then he controlled himself and said, "Have it your way. You!" he said to Bala, "I'm sending you back to the haveli."

"I'll send her back with a police woman," assured Malik stiffly. "She'll be safe." He wanted to have a talk with this unlikely witness.

"Malik, hand her over to Vaishali, please. Don't scare her." Sumit said.

"Don't teach me my job, young man. I won't scare her," he replied disgruntedly, but then smiled when he saw genuine concern for the child in Sumit's face. "And Sumit Sir, take care of yourself and your wife."

Malik left with Bala and Sumit ran his hand through his hair. "Brian, are we ready now to take on Royal?"

"I have satisfied the bankers. There will be no trouble from their side. Coronet does own a sizable amount of Royal shares."

"Over sixty percent, if we combine the ones owned by me, Vaishali, you and Coronet," he said with a satisfied smile. Some had been inherited, Vaisahli would be given some, and over and above that, he had bought every single share that came up in the market, some in the name of Coronet. When his father had become curious, he had used other ways to buy them. At first he had entertained dreams of throwing his father out of Royal. Then later, when his anger had died down, he had still kept buying, it was his heritage. He said, "I'll announce it at dinner that we shall have that damn meeting of the Board next Monday. What the Board does not know is that once that comes through, there is going to be a major overhaul. I am going to purge the damn set up of my respected father."

At Banasur, Haveli

Mehak and Aditya entered the haveli dressed in sturdy denims, their shoes caked with mud. Mehak switched on the light to see Sejal sitting on the couch in the dark. She exchanged glances with Aditya.

"What happened, Ma?" Aditya asked her.

A sad smile flitted on her face and left. Hers was a strange and awkward position. She missed Digvijay but could not share her emotional state, or even mourn him openly. "Nothing. I was just thinking."

Both Aditya and Mehak took off their shoes in an awkward silence. Mehak smacked her head, "Damn it Adi, I forgot the food. Can you get the food, please?"

"We did not pick up any food," he said puzzled.

"I know we did not. I'm famished. Get something from the local place, anything. Even samosas will do. I'll make some tea. Have you had any lunch Sejal Auntie?"

He opened his mouth to protest and she glared at him. Grumbling audibly, he slipped into his slippers and left, slamming the door behind him. She heard the car start and walked into the small kitchen, placing the kettle on the gas, and said, "I miss him too. He was nasty, rude, a pain in the butt, but I miss him. He was...he was unique."

Sejal's heart welled up; tears fell down her face unchecked. She sobbed silently. Mehak glanced at her from the kitchen door, went back to the gas and sprinkled some cardamom powder in the water. The sobs intensified. Mehak stared at the water, and then switched off the gas. This called for something stronger. She poured two glasses of wine and grabbed a packet of crackers and some cream cheese wedges.

"Here," she said handing the older lady a glass of wine.

"So kind...so sorry," Sejal murmured accepting the glass of wine, and setting it on the table with trembling hands. She wiped her face with a tissue and said, "He was a strong man. He would have scorned my tears."

Mehak popped a cheese wedge into her mouth and nodded, "Yeah. That was his least endearing trait, but that was just the way he was."

"I wanted to forget him, wipe him off my mind..." Sejal said, taking a sip of the wine.

"Awww," Mehak said, surprised by the emotion. In her opinion, no one could love her father. He was a fairly unpleasant man. She held her tongue in check.

They sat in silence sipping wine and munching on cheese until Aditya returned. "I thought you ladies wanted to have tea," he said.

Sejal wiped her face with a tissue and smiled slightly, "You both have to confess to Sumit about the Shastri affair. It would be smart to do it before he finds out."

"What?" Aditya said.

"He will find out Adi. If you want, I'll tell him."

"He won't find out. His wife will keep him busy, I am sure of that!" Mehak said. "And soon it will be over."

"I know Vaishali. She is not the clingy sort. And I understand Sumit, he is like his father. If there is something a person wants to hide, he will go after it," said Sejal.

"Ma, we're doing nothing wrong," Aditya said impatiently. "We are just taking money to look away while the Shastris are cutting the forests."

"You are dealing...we are dealing with the Shastris. Digvijay would have killed us for that. He is already asking questions about our car being in the jungle. He'll find out."

"Damn it, why did he not sell the shares and go?" Mehak asked angrily.

Aditya smiled sadly, "Because he is like his father. Devious kicked him out, and that has to be avenged."

✦ ✦ ✦

27

Taking Charge

Sumit had driven to the forest and back. By the time he reached the haveli exhausted, he was not pleased to find Mehak and Aditya sitting by Vaishali's bed. He suppressed his annoyance. He was tired, wanted dinner and sleep. He had spent a long time with the forest officer Nehra and had found out things that did not please him. If the unrest continued unchecked, the mass deforestation of the area would be blamed on him and Royal. At heart he was feudal, and this was his territory, democracy be damned. These were his forests. Moreover, it was his resort that was coming up, and who were these environmentalists to object? They did not bother about the forests, but objected to the resort, which would give the state revenue.

He nodded to them and walked into his private bedroom for a shower and change. He came out fresher, to find them still sitting. Vaishali looked pale, as though she would fall asleep any moment.

"Not joining the others for dinner?" he asked.

"We had to talk to you," Aditya said.

He gestured to the sitting room and they accompanied him. Mehak babbled, "Vaishali has excellent taste. This room looks so large and airy now."

"It has been a long day for me, Mehak. Shut it and get to the point," Sumit said sitting down.

"We made a business deal with some people who dealt in timber, a long time ago." Aditya said.

"With our timber? My timber?"

Mehak nodded. "We needed the money."

He sat silently, "Who are these people and why are you telling me?"

"Daddy was old, he did not notice. It was okay at that time, safe. The felling was not so indiscriminate," Mehak answered. "No one expected you to come back and try to take over."

"Why this confession?"

"Sejal Aunty wants you to know. She sends a warning. The Shastris were small time timber thieves, but now timber mafia is getting involved. Sumit, these people are dangerous and will stop at nothing. We kept quiet and ten percent of the profit came to us."

He turned to Aditya, "Royal does not pay you enough Aditya?"

Aditya flushed, "What can Royal pay me? Can it give back my mother's life, her status? Could it give me back my province, bring my haveli back to what it was?"

"Leave, both of you. Go back to your thieving friends and tell them as long as Sumit Singh Nausar is alive, not one tree will be cut without my permission. And yes, tell them I can't be bought. Get out!"

"No!" Vaishali said from the door.

"Oh go back to bed, Vaish!" Sumit said coldly.

"I won't! Don't patronize me! She is your sister and he is your best friend. You can't do this!"

"Let it be Vaish," said Mehak getting up, and tossing her head. She looked pale and hurt.

"I won't let it be!" Vaish marched into the sitting room in her pajamas, a scrawny figure, her neck in a brace but her chin thrust forward, ready for combat. "You can't reject family like this. We can work this through. There must be some way."

"There is," said Aditya in a stilted tone. "If his highness wants to listen to a suggestion, there is."

Sumit looked at the three of them, Mehak with unshed tears in her eyes, trying hard to look unaffected, Adi pale and proud, his nose in the air, Vaish an angry tigress trying to protect her cubs.

"Sit down," Sumit said averting his face.

They looked at him, still angry.

"Sit down, damn you!"

Vaishali sat down; her knees were quaking, anyway. Mehak sat down next to her. Aditya hesitated. Sumit said, "Sorry Adi, I had a Rajput moment there. I do realize that if everything had been like the old times, those jungles were yours."

"Yours too, Sumit."

"I know. I've had one helluva day. Are you sitting down... please?"

Aditya sat down and both Mehak and Vaishali relaxed. "Damn you Sumit! You're unpredictable. Ma was right about you."

"What did she say about me?"

Aditya realized that this was not the time to compare Sumit with Digvijay and said, "Just that this would bother you but we had to come clean."

"The forest officer Nehra met me today and he has a gloomy vision of the future of the state. The state machinery is doing nothing to stop timber thieves. And they have the gall to blame Royal for damaging the ecology of the state!"

"Saksham sir says a lot of medicinal plants can be grown in Nausar. We have the soil and the climate for it. The river helps. The government gives grants, huge ones," Vaishali put in, hesitantly.

Sumit shook his head, "Repeat that."

She said, "Sorry. It's just that Saksham Sir was talking about it once."

"The guy who grows tussar silk? The one who was leading the hike to Pracheen Mandir?"

She nodded. "One does not grow tussar silk! It's not a plant."

"Whatever," he shrugged, dismissing it. "I'll be sending dinner for you here, Vaish. Stay in bed. After you both," he said opening the door and looking at Mehak and Aditya.

"Thanks Vaish," Mehak said. "That was brave."

Vaish smiled weakly, but was still trembling inward. Gosh, her husband had a cold and vicious side to him!

✦

Still fuming Sumit walked into the dining room. Somnath sneered, "Well, well, the Maharao has finally decided to join us. I thought we would have to wait forever for your highness to make an appearance."

Girdhari said, "Calm down Somnath. You know that his wife and servants have been attacked. Naturally he has been busy."

"So the Yuvraj finds servants and his bride more important than the EGM?" he said nastily. "Perhaps my respected father-in-law was right; he knew that the Yuvraj was incapable of running the business."

There was stunned silence and Vishnu quickly stepped into the breach, asking solicitiously, "How is Vaishali? Urmila wanted to meet her, but I asked her to wait. She needs her rest."

"Thanks for the concern Vishnu." Turning to Somnath Sumit yelled, "Hey you, you were saying something?"

Somnath flushed, the tone Sumit used was openly insulting.

Turning away from Somnath, Sumit walked to the head of the table, pausing to enquire about Shivam's health from his aunt. He turned, raised a brow to Somnath and said, "Continue please."

"I was saying that I don't like..."

"Kishan! Where are you, man?" Sumit called out, cutting Somnath off deliberately. He nodded to his uncle, and then drew his chair to sit down.

Kishan approached him, "Yes Maharao ji?"

"In future ensure that a chair is kept next to mine, for my wife."

Kishan nodded and scurried away.

"As I was saying..." Somnath said, his temper rising.

Mehak and Aditya, who had fallen behind, entered at this point, deep in conversation. Somnath flushed, his words dying as he took in the open camaraderie displayed by their body language. Aditya whispered something to Mehak who frowned but came and sat down next to Somnath and promptly started conversing with Vishnu who was sitting to her left.

"Oh you were saying something? Sorry but I find that you have no right to speak in matters of family or of Royal Hotels and Resorts, what so ever." Sumit said coldly.

Somnath could not handle this. He came to his feet and shouted, "As family member, board member and shareholder of Royal, I have a right! What right do you have? Have you done anything for Royal?"

"Shivam, how many shares do you have?" Sumit asked, with a drawl.

"Just two percent, Sumit bhaiya. When I am twenty one, Papa says I will be given more."

"Yes, you are just nineteen aren't you? Well, Somnath, Shivam has more stocks of Royal than you do. As per my calculations you have less than one per cent. As such, you have no position in the board. The EGM is to be held on Monday morning, and your presence won't be required."

"That is not true," he protested.

"I keep track. For the past few years your finances have not kept up with your lifestyle. In the last six years you have been selling stock. A drug dealer called Mahesh Bahl...remember how he refused to take some stock to settle your cocaine bill, and then changed his mind a week later? Then there is Binodini, a bar dancer, charming little thing but has a very shrewd head on her delicate shoulders. That man you bought the used BMW from, yes, Pathak. I have been buying them, and any other shares of Royal in the market, for the last ten years."

"I still have my wife's shares." Somnath blustered.

Mehak said, "No you don't. I gave my brother my shares."

He slapped her so hard across her face that she fell from her chair. Somnath bit out, "Whore!" and raised his hand again. Vishnu pulled her away as Aditya stepped between Somnath and Mehak, punching Somnath so hard that he staggered and fell, his head striking the fallen chair.

"You have fifteen minutes to get out of the haveli, and it would be in your interest to leave Nausar tonight, Somnath. If you want to live, that is," said Sumit coldly. He picked up his phone and dialed a number, "Starting now. Leave and do not return. My lawyers will be in touch with you for assault on my sister."

Somnath backed away from the hall, cursing loudly. There was a stunned silence. Then the entire room erupted in a babble of voices. Sumit walked away from his assembled family and spoke into his phone, "Gul, you recognize my brother-in-law Somnath?"

Gul answered and he said, "Good! He will just be leaving the haveli. Follow his car. Be very visible. He should know that he is being chased."

Gul, the cab driver who Sumit often employed rang up a few of his fellow cabbies and together they carried out the task with great enthusiasm, knowing that they would be paid generously.

Sumit took his seat and Vishnu walked up to him and clapped him on his shoulder, "Good going Sumit. By the way, how much of the stock do you own?"

Girdhari who was sitting close to the head of the table hugged him warmly. "I won't miss my brother. I can see he lives in you."

Sumit recoiled for a moment, and looked at the portrait of his father hanging on the wall, and broke into a harsh laugh. It was too ironical. Then he caught sight of mystified faces and controlled himself.

Devika started fussing, "Where is dinner? Why is it delayed?"

Kishan signalled the servants who brought in the food. Dinner was a noisy affair, with Girdhari and Vishnu openly rejoicing the way Sumit had treated Somnath. Vishnu lauded Aditya for coming to Mehak's defense. Even Rohtash joined in. The only solemn faces were those of Devika and Himani.

Himani kept staring at her plate, toying with her food. She sensed eyes boring into her and raised hers, meeting Sumit's gaze. She sprang to her feet muttering something incoherently about her children and left the room. Sumit watched her depart and then glanced at Mehak with an enquiring smile. Her eyes welled up with unshed tears and she mouthed, "Thank you."

✦

Despite Sumit's threat, Somnath drove straight to the Shastri residence at Banasur. He rang the door bell which was answered promptly by the servant who informed him that the family was having dinner. He expected to be invited to join them; he was a good friend of Resham's. To his surprise he was led to the small lobby and asked to wait. The lobby had some cane armchairs with cushions on them and a circular cane table, the kind manufactured in the Banasur cottage industry. He lowered himself into an armchair but was too agitated to sit still. Still seething with anger, he paced up and down while his mind kept playing and replaying the events. After twenty minutes, a small tray containing a bottle of whisky, soda, ice and nuts was placed on the cane table, and still no one came to join him. He poured himself a stiff drink and downed it. By his second drink, he came to believe that he had behaved like a gentleman, but the family had provoked him. Feeling much better, he poured himself another large one.

He did not want to go back to Rajoria. He was the youngest son, born to his father's third wife, a woman the rest of the family shunned as she was not a Rajput. His father had died within one month of marrying his mother who was thirty years his junior. As a young boy he had once heard servants gossiping about how the old man had been unable to stand the rigors of the nuptial bed, and died in a bid to prove his virility. Somnath had been born four months after his father's death. His oldest brother had been in his early forties then, and the head of the family. Theirs was a conservative family, and his brother ensured that his mother and he were given all the comforts of a home, but were kept away from power. When time came, he was married to a girl from a royal family, as befitted his status. Mehak had been somewhat of a shock to him, who had seen his mother as shy, submissive, always dressed in the widow's garb. Mehak had stayed with him for a week, just a week! At the first available opportunity, she had left. His brothers had laughed at him, so had his nephews who were of the same age as him.

He had come to Nausar and complained to his father-in-law. If a woman in his family had behaved like that, she would have been whipped. Instead his father-in-law had listened to his daughter's plea that she had to complete her studies. He had not seen the point of women studying – but his father-in-law had agreed to his daughter, even sent her to England to study. His wife was a rich woman and at first he had had hopes that the money would make life easier for him and his mother. But now, that seemed to be a pipe dream.

The bottle was almost over when Resham entered the room exclaiming, "Somnath! I am so sorry I could not meet you immediately. Some relatives had come for dinner. So tell me, what brings you back here? What news of the Royal Board meeting?"

Somnath's stomach rumbled at the thought of dinner, but he kept that thought down and said, "They insulted me and threw me out of the haveli."

Resham looked at him silently with raised brows and then asked, "Who did this? Why?"

"That son of a snake, Sumit! I am not a servant! I am Somnath Rajoria, a prince, and the husband of his sister Mehak! This insult will be avenged!"

Resham made soothing noises and kept his expression sympathetic as his grandfather's observation about Somnath rang in his ears, "He is a weak link, he can make noise, whine complain but do nothing more. The only thing he had going for him was his marriage to the Nausar family, and he could not make even that work."

"That bastard had the impertinence to tell me to get out of Nausar tonight if I wanted to live. Can you imagine that?"

"That is really bad! How horrible, of course this insult has to be avenged. But we can discuss that tomorrow. Tonight let's party!"

Somnath got up swaying slightly, and stumbled against the table. The whisky bottle fell. "Not in the mood!"

Resham smiled as he bent down to rescue the bottle, and poured the remainder into Somnath's glass "Maybe I can tempt you, my friend. There is this Russian tourist in town, blonde, she even has a red haired friend. They are staying at Royal. I met them at Sant ji's ashram."

Somnath shook his head. Resham said, "Has the Maharao scared you?"

Somnath laughed scornfully, "That idiot is not the Maharao. In Rajoria, we have a proper coronation ceremony. My mother-in-law suggested that it should be done, but he refused. So technically he is not king, why should I be scared?" His voice slurred and he swayed slightly as he stood up. He walked slowly and deliberately to the door, still carrying the glass.

✦

Sumit was half asleep when his phone rang, he checked the time, 3 a.m. It was Gul, his cab driver. He listened carefully and then said, "Don't let them see you, these men are dangerous."

He got up and slipped into his jeans. Vaishali murmured sleepily, "You'll be back won't you? Don't leave me alone."

"Yes," he said with a tight smile. "I'll be back."

"Don't leave me ever."

"Mush, my little brat?" he asked softly.

She flushed and said, "Must be the accident."

He had to laugh at that. "You know, keeping you safe is a full time job."

"Your job," she whispered, as he tucked her into bed. He walked out into the balcony and told the night guard that he was going out. He alerted Thapa who was asleep in a driver's room in the garage.

By the time he reversed his car, he saw Thapa carrying a blanket and pillow, spreading it near the front door of his wing. He drove out. It was 3:15 a.m.

✦ ✦ ✦

28

The Attempted Murder

Malik was deep in sleep when his phone rang. "Sumit Sir, what happened? Don't you ever sleep?" he whispered into the phone, as his wife turned her back on him, irritatedly.

Then he sat up, looking grim. "Okay, I will go there right now. I will also need the cab driver's statement, he is a witness."

Then he rang up Sinha who was on duty, "Take four armed policemen to Banasur jungles. I am on my way. I have news that Somnath Rajoria has been attacked."

It was 4 a.m. when policemen picked up a badly wounded Somnath from the jungle of Banasur. The man was barely alive and in no condition to make a statement. Sumit was standing next to Malik watching the proceedings.

"Before you came back to Nausar, this was a peaceful place," Malik observed, shaking his head dolefully.

"Don't blame me, you came here around the same time I did," quipped Sumit.

"Still," Malik said.

Sumit scratched his stubble "Before the old man died, people did not kill or wound my relatives."

"Why did you have your brother-in-law followed?" asked Malik.

"We had an argument and I threw him out of the haveli. I warned him to leave Nausar if he wanted to live. Then I told this cab driver to follow him, to scare him a bit."

"What is your name?" Malik asked the cab driver.

"Gul Shafiq Ali," he replied.

"What did you see?" asked Malik.

"The Sahib drove from the haveli. I followed him. He drove straight to the neta, Chanchal's home. Then after an hour, he left with Resham Sahib and his aide Amol. They went to Royal One. I parked outside hoping to get a customer. After two hours, Amol left with this Sahib. The Sahib could not walk, he was very drunk. I followed, but instead of taking the highway, they turned into the jungle. I turned off my headlights. This place is dangerous in the night, so many timber thieves."

He paused, collecting his thoughts.

"Speak," Malik said.

"The car stopped suddenly and this Sahib got out, cursing. Amol followed him out, they cursed each other. They were shouting. Amol called the Sahib *Nikhattu Ghar Jawai Madarchod*. (Jobless son-in-law living off his wife's family and mother-fucker). The Sahib slapped Amol. Amol knifed him and then others came to help Amol."

"You recognize them, these others?" questioned the policeman.

"No Sahib, it was too dark."

"Do not lie to the police. How do you know Amol?" pursued Malik.

"He comes from a village near mine, Sahib."

"Okay what happened then?"

"I called Sumit Sahib and hid."

"Report at 10 a.m. at the Thana. Till then use your head, remember all the faces you are pretending you did not recognize. Understand? And stay in town."

Sumit added, "Gul, drive back to the haveli. Do not go home. If it is known that you saw something, you'll be attacked or killed."

The man paled. "Sahib I am a poor cab driver. I am Muslim, and they will kill me. It is safer for us not to know them. My family will be in danger. Please Sahib."

"Don't be difficult Gul; you've gone on long trips lasting months! Tell your family you're going out of town. I'll make good use of your services and pay you too, rogue!" Sumit snapped.

The man left mumbling under his breath.

"I must say I like your style," observed Malik. "This Amol character is shady. He surfaces everywhere. The man your maid saw is Deepak Sarna, a friend of Amol's."

"That man Rawat? The truck driver, has he spoken?" Sumit asked.

Malik snorted bitterly, "He has turned religious. He keeps praying, chanting mantras and priests have started visiting him."

"Sant Anirudh's priests?"

"No sir, they are new faces."

Sumit showed him the broken string of rudraksha beads, "They call them tears of Siva. I found them in the flower bed, near the roof where we found the corpse. These beads turned up once again when my apartment was broken into. Why Malik?"

There was a silence as both the men were busy with their thoughts. Then they both stared speaking. Sumit laughed and said, "You first," as he glanced surreptiously at his watch.

Malik saw that and stood up. "I am sure you have more things to do Sumit Sir."

"Nothing at all. When I was younger, there was a small dhaba near the ashram. They made the most delicious *halwa, aloo* and *puri* for breakfast. I was thinking of breakfasting there. Care to join me?"

"Sumit Sir, has it occurred to you that someone was eager to act on your threat to your brother-in-law?"

"Yes," he said grimly.

Malik said, "All life is temporary, only death is permanent. The soul is immortal."

"What?" Sumit asked.

"The priest who visited the truck driver said that again and again."

"A threat?"

"I think so. He gave some gifts for the driver which we have confiscated."

Sumit said "Uhunh?"

"A *Bhagwad Geeta*, a prayer book and a rudhraksha string."

"These damn rudrakshas turn up everywhere!" Sumit grumbled. "Someone is drawing attention to the ashram. Too damn obvious!"

The phone rang and Sumit picked it up and listened. After the call, he raised an enquiring brow at Malik, "SP Sahib, are you trying to play games with me?"

"What do you mean?"

"How is it that there is a policeman at the haveli who wants to question me and my wife for an attack on my brother-in-law, at this unearthly hour?"

Malik checked his watch, it was 5:30 a.m., "What? Sir, I have not ordered any enquiry as yet."

"I am going back to the haveli," said Sumit.

"I am coming along Sir, if you don't mind," said Malik.

Malik gave some instructions to his people and climbed into Sumit's car and they drove back to the haveli. They parked in the garage and spotted Vaishali and Mehak dressed in pajamas, with shawls thrown on hastily. Mehak had covered her head and part of her face to conceal the bruise from Somnath's slap the night before. She was saying in a loud voice, "I am completely unconcerned about Mr. Somnath Rajoria's well being. He is a violent man; a wife beater. I think he must have done something that brought him to this condition. He deserves this."

"We have reports Madam, that your brother maybe involved in this attack," Sinha's voice was low but firm.

"Rubbish!" scoffed Vaishali. "My husband was in the haveli the whole night."

"Yes madam, I know you said that earlier madam," said Sinha, shifting uncomfortably.

"Sinha!" Malik whispered. "I had sent him to the hospital along with the ambulance. What's he doing here?"

"Let us watch. Perhaps we may learn more," said Sumit.

Mehak shifted in her chair and asked, "Where is Somnath?"

Sinha said in a sad tone, "I took him to the hospital, madam. He is lucky to be alive, he was knifed so brutally. Not a suitable sight for ladies." He shuddered dramatically.

"Oh, he is still alive? I hope he is in great pain, I want him to suffer," Mehak assured him with a grim smile. Sinha's expression froze and he mopped himself again with his hanky.

Vaishali said, "Please sit down inspector."

Mehak glared at her but she ignored it. "Thank you Madam," Sinha said, sitting down on a chair. Vaishali added, "I must say you people are so hardworking. You rescued Mehak Di's husband late last night and took him to the hospital. Then early this morning you have come here to ask questions."

"Thank you. A policeman is hardly ever appreciated."

"But I am a huge fan," she said earnestly while her sister-in-law gave a loud and disgusted snort. "Remember the movie Sarfarosh? In that policemen are given so much information by informants. Sinhaji, do you also have informants?"

"Yes madam," said Sinha completely thawed. He drew his chair closer and whispered loudly, "Our boss recieved a phone call in the night about the attack. Even my information comes from such sources."

"Well then ask your boss to get more information from the same person. If the man saw the attack, he saw the attackers too. Stop troubling us!" she said angrily, tossed her head and said, "Come Mehak Di, I think we have been disturbed enough by these men."

While Sinha watched open mouthed, both of them got up and walked into the house without a backward glance. Sumit smiled appreciatively. The ladies had conducted themselves wonderfully. Malik stepped forward and said, "Good morning, Sinha. I am happy to see you doing your duty so efficiently."

Sinha jumped out of his chair. A servant came with a tray containing two cups of tea and some biscuits. Malik took the tray and handed one cup to Sumit, saying, "It has been a long and sleepless night." Sinha looked sadly at the tea tray and kept standing there.

Sumit sat down and asked conversationally, "You did not answer my wife's question, Sinha. Did your informant not tell you who attacked Rajoria?"

"No sir," Sinha answered warily.

"Strange. The informant knew about our fight, my threat, and also about the attack, but not about the attackers? I find that hard to believe."

Sinha shifted uncomfortably from one foot to another. Then he muttered, "I will ask my informant again."

He turned to leave. Malik said, "Sinha, Sumit Sir gave me a ride. Please wait until I finish my tea. We shall go together."

"Yes sir, I take it I have to drop you home?" said Sinha.

"No, Sinha, we shall first go and inform Mr. Resham Shastri that his friend has been injured. He must be worried about his friend."

Sinha gulped and then nodded. "Yes sir."

"And I would like to meet Mr. Puneet Shastri too."

Sinha paled.

✦ ✦ ✦

29

Chanchal Shastri

Sumit watched the policemen leave, deep in thought. He had met Resham Shastri, the man was astute. His game was politics. He could take pot shots at Royal, to keep himself and his party in the news. That was more his style. Murder was messy. No, that man would not get his hands dirty.

He wished he had a cigarette. He had given up smoking a couple of years ago, but he needed one. He walked to the gate, hoping to bum one from any of the drivers there. Gul was regaling a rapt audience with the happenings of the night, "It was Sarna. The man is a *shaitan*. I saw him clearly. He is against all Muslims. He was leading those timber thieves. After Amol ran off, he and his men cut up Somnath like a goat."

Sumit stopped near the door, Sarna? Malik had mentioned the name. The drivers and guards were rapt in the story. Someone broke the silence, "Stop behaving like a new bride in the house Gul," someone protested. "Somnath was a fucking pain in the ass. I would have done the same for free," laughed another.

"What do you mean, Ramesh?" asked Gul.

"Like a new bride, the moment someone says something, she thinks the in-laws are against her, pah!"

The men laughed. A driver Sumit did not recognize said, "Ramesh ought to know. His wife calls him six times a day, complaining against her sisters-in-law, her mother-in-law, and her brothers-in-law. What is your phone bill like, Ramesh?"

"What do you mean by that?" Gul asked, not letting it go.

"No one cares about Hindus and Muslims. All people care about is money, enough to pay for food, clothes, school fees."

"And there are some who think that if all the Muslims go to Pakistan, there will be more for them," Gul said sourly.

Sumit decided to intervene before this became a fight. "Does anyone have a cigarette? And where is Thapa?"

Ramesh offered him an unfiltered cigarette, and said, "Thapa is not here Sahib."

Sumit said pleasantly, "I do not care if anyone is Muslim or Hindu, so keep it peaceful here okay."

They nodded. He moved out. The guards quickly straightened up, and looked alert. He took a puff and walked towards his annexe. Thapa was sleeping on the doorstep, his arm in a sprain bandage. He recalled guiltily that he had asked him to guard the annexe. "Go and sleep old man. Tell Gul to get my car ready. I will be going out after breakfast."

The man nodded, picked up his blanket and walked to the garage. Sumit walked to the chairs recently occupied by his wife and sister, and sat down. Unaccountably he recalled a statement Devious Singh was very fond of, "First put your own house in order." He shook his head; the place was getting to him. He was not fond of recalling his father's statements. His uncle, who was coming back from his morning walk came and joined him.

"Sumit, I hear Somnath was attacked?"

"Yes uncle, he was. I got the news last night and went with the police. He is badly hurt and is now in St. Agnes hospital."

"Well done, my boy." He stared at him in silence, making the younger man deeply uncomfortable. His eyes glistened with tears as he said, "I can die in peace now. My brother lives in you, my son. I have no worries now."

He walked away wiping a tear, leaving Sumit dumbfounded. Sumit followed him as he walked into the main haveli, caught sight of a portrait of his father, snarled at it and turned away to his own annexe which was mercifully free of his dead father's portraits.

He entered his bedroom and fell on the bed and passed out. When he woke up, he could hear Sid and Shivam laughing in the sitting room. He got up and rang up the kitchen for breakfast and joined them after a shower. Vaishali lay in bed, pale and listless. She was leafing through some old family albums. Sid and Shivam were sitting with her. "Hello boys," he said. "You know, the two of you should go hunting. The last time I went to Nashik, I got you air guns and pellets. Thapa has them. Run along and take them from Thapa."

"Woohoo," yelled Sid and Shivam took up the cheer and they both ran off.

"Thanks," said Vaishali gratefully. Her head was aching and she was grateful for the respite. "Mehak di rang up the doctors. Somnath ji is still in ICU. The doctors say he could die."

"Damn!" he scowled. He would have to rush to the hospital. His breakfast came and he started serving himself with a thoughtful frown.

"What are you thinking?" she asked.

He shrugged and ran his hands through his hair and said, "My uncle misses my father a lot."

"He idolized him, which is obvious. So does Vishnu bhaiya. They are scared, now that your father is dead."

"I was given the impression that my uncle was greedy. Damn it I am a fool!"

"Oh no, you are not!" she said indignantly. "Why are you sad?"

"Not sad, uncomfortable. My uncle looks for my father in me. It is..."

"What's wrong with that? Why complicate matters unnecessarily. Of course you are like him, so are your sisters. It is pure genetics. You look like him, all three of you. You and Mehak di look less like him than Himani Di. Look at this." she said and he went over to look at old photos. A slight smile tugged his mouth, Mehak was in pigtails and looked so skinny, and he had his face turned away from the camera. He always hated those formal family portraits. His mother always managed to get Aditya out of the frame.

"I look like my parents. On the day of our reception, after getting ready, I looked at myself in the mirror and I saw Pallavi Di," Vaishali gave a shudder. "Maybe I even behave like her or my mother sometimes."

He stared at her stunned and muttered "Out of the mouth of babes..."

"Huh?"

"Just something Melissa is fond of saying," he threw down a couple of cushions and settled down comfortably on the couch. He had to go and look up Somnath but it was pleasant to eat breakfast in this small sitting room with his wife.

"Ma says I am like my father, but I dont think so. She says mostly daughters take after their fathers," continued Vaish.

He stared at her for a moment, gave a tight smile, said, "Vaish, I am going to the hospital. Is Rohtash around? I would like him to accompany me."

Without waiting for her reply, he rang Rohtash up. In ten minutes he wolfed down his breakfast and left. Rohtash was waiting for him along with Himani. Once they had got into the car, Sumit began, "Rohtash, Himani tells me that you want a larger role in Royal Group?"

"Yes," he nodded glancing at his brother-in-law eagerly.

"I have a better plan," he said. "You are not a business man Rohtash. Your personality and intellect are not suited for the world of business. How would you like an independent role, free from Royal and free from all this?"

Rohtash, who, as a Ghar Jamai had endured a lot of humiliation from his father-in-law, eagerly asked, "What are you proposing?"

"A political career.... The assembly elections are in four months. Your brothers belong to the ruling party in politics, it will be a simple matter for you to obtain a party ticket. Start your campaigning. I will finance the expense. I suggest that you campaign in favor of economic development and jobs. They will be a hit with the residents of this state."

Rohtash turned in his seat to exchange glances with his wife sitting at the back, "Can I give you my decision till the evening?"

"If you agree, it would be important that the money and your links with Royal are not prominent. You hold some stocks of Royal don't you? I will buy them as a price for making you MLA." Sumit said.

"If we refuse?" said Himani thoughtfully.

"I can't keep hosting my sisters and their families forever, Himani. After all, I am a married man, and will soon have children of my own. I have their futures to plan."

Their eyes widened with comprehension. She slowly pursed her lips and nodded, and Rohtash said, "I agree."

Sumit nodded, his face impassive. "My man will get in touch with you with the papers which you will sign. Funds will be made available to you in stages. At first, I will give you some funds, as soon as you hand me the stocks. It will help set up your home. Once you get the ticket, I will give you more funds. Then we can review the amount you need for the campaign. I am also appointing you an experienced political manager. All the best."

They reached the hospital. Sumit parked the car, and Rohtash got out. Himani got up to follow him when Sumit said, "Just one minute, Himani." She stopped and looked at him, her apprehension plainly visible. He got out of the car and said, "I have vacated my apartment. Please pack and move in there. There is nothing to fear, I got the gas cylinders replaced with piped gas. There won't be any leakage."

She turned sheet white and tried to bluster, "What do you mean?"

"Keep him on track, sister. Otherwise you will find me very unforgiving," he said coldly. "He has to win."

Her eyes flashed with fury but she held her tongue.

"Your friendship with Resham Shastri and his family has to end. They are your competitors now. And your pleasant meetings in the ashram with Kewal Shastri's grandsons will not be right under the present circumstances. Am I clear?"

She was tempted for a moment to remind him that she was older than him. The thought crossed her mind and left. "Very wise of you, Himani." he said softly.

She turned and fled.

"Exactly," he said softly to himself. He parked the car and reached the ICU. Himani and Rohtash were trying to console Somnath's mother. Sumit raised his brows and Rohtash said, "The doctors are doing their best but will not say much."

Sumit spotted a group of young boys standing on one side. One of them was Puneet Shastri.

A nurse came rushing out of the ICU, Somnath's mother grabbed her arm, "What happened? How is he?" she asked in a quavering voice.

"Madam, let me go. I have to call the doctor," the nurse said pulling herself away. Sumit kept his eyes firmly on Puneet and dialed Malik's number. "Malik Sahib, I want to report an attempted murder. My brother-in-law was last seen in the company of one Amol, who I think was involved in the murderous attack on him."

The old lady overheard that, ran to the glass window of the ICU stare at the unmoving form lying on the hospital bed and then started wailing, but Sumit was looking at the boys. They paled and fled.

He followed them out and called, "Puneet?"

The boy turned and looked at him. Sumit smiled and said, "Give your brother Resham my regards. Tell him I want to meet him."

Puneet gulped and ran down the stairs. Sumit followed at a more sedate pace. To his surprise, Gul was waiting outside the hospital gate. "What are you doing here, Gul?"

"Sahib, I had gone to the police station."

"Ah yes." He handed him the car keys, "Go and get the car, it is in the parking."

Gul got the car and he climbed in. "Why are you so serious, Gul?"

"Sahib, do you believe in God?"

Sumit laughed. "What kind of question is this, Gul?" When the man did not respond with a smile he said, "Let us just say, God and I have an understanding. God keeps out of my business and I try to keep out of his way."

"The SP is Muslim."

"So is almost half of the world, Gul."

"There was a priest at the thana. He warned us of bad things. Allah and Ram are angry because something unpious has happened in Nausar."

Sumit bit back his initial reaction to scoff this. Instead he asked, "Amol and the Sarna fellow, are they from your village?"

"No sir, they are Hindu. Aligaon is a Muslim village," Gul's cold voice revealing his dislike for them. His next sentence confirmed that, "Amol likes to make friends with people from all around, know their secrets. He is a nasty fellow."

"Why? What did he do?"

"Long ago, when the shivling was dug out, Sant Anirudh gave away two babies to a land owner from Saksham Bhai's village. The girl was just eight months old; the boy was two years old. People say the girl was Muslim and the boy was Sikh."

"I am sure you have a point to make," Sumit said as Gul turned the car on to the Nausar–Banasur highway.

Gul relaxed. Like all cab drivers he was fond of talking, and an adept storyteller. "It was a long time ago, everyone had forgotten about it. Amol and Deepak Sarna started asking questions about the girl, her caste etc."

"Why?"

Gul shrugged, "The girl grew up in a rich house. Her father has cattle, and land right on the river ghat. He complained to the Khap who hunted Sarna down and gave him a thrashing. She is married now, in a town far away. She has babies, her own family. Why would he want to make trouble for her?"

Why indeed? Unless the rumor was correct and someone wanted to make trouble for the town...

"Take me to Saksham's place, Gul."

They drove past the ashram, towards the jungles. Sumit recalled the story of the priest who had come from the hills with small brahman boys and uncovered the huge shivling. A grateful and devout populace had donated freely to construct a grand temple and the ashram. The land for both had been donated by the royal families of Nausar and Banasur.

Gul brought the car to a halt near the small eatery Sumit remembered from the hike to Pracheen Mandir. It was closed. Sumit got out and looked around, taking the small well-trodden path leading into a thick grove of mulberry trees. A child was gathering mulberries in a small bamboo basket. She saw him, gasped and fled dropping the half filled basket on the ground. Sumit picked up the basket of mulberries and looked around, surprised. The place was deserted. Gul rushed up to him, "Sahib, let us go. It is not safe here."

"Why?"

"The canteen owner has asked us to leave. There will be trouble. Last night the *bahubali,* muscleman of the Nausar party was here. He threatened to burn down the village and the trees."

Sumit walked to the canteen. "Where is the canteen owner?"

"Joginder *Bauji*? He's at the ghat."

Sumit was a vineyard owner, and he recognized quality of soil. The soil here was alluvial and exceptionally rich in nutrients. He bent down and scooped some dirt and examined it. It reminded him of soil of some organic farms he had visited. The little girl peeped at him from behind a tree and hid when he smiled at her. He walked to the ghat, where the old owner of the canteen was sitting on the rough hewn and irregular stone steps.

"Where is Saksham, Bauji? I want to meet him."

"He will be back in a few hours Maharao," the old man said. There was no deference in his voice or his eyes. This was a proud man, who saw no reason to bow in front of people with fancy titles.

"So all of the young men have fled the village?" he taunted.

Joginder Bauji spat in contempt. "We do not need to flee from those neutered dogs. They will be back to fight, to protect our *Bhumi Devi.* We just needed to ferry the women and children out of the village, once they are safe, we can fight and die with pride."

"I saw a little girl still at the village," Sumit said softly.

"That is Panchi, my youngest son's girl. She loves the fields and trees. She will die here, but not go to the town. Her mother wept and pleaded but she would not go."

"Why?" The question was cryptic but the old man understood.

"We will die to protect our plants and animals Maharao. We will not allow those dogs to sell our Bhumi Devi for money. This was bound to happen. It was waiting to happen. Chappania's adopted girl was just an excuse."

"Can I help? How can I help? Shall I call the police?"

"Pah! The police whore for these netas, Maharao. So do other government officials. You talked with Nehra Sahib, did you not? You listened to his sorry tale. It is just *randi rona,* a whore's tears. He has two daughters to marry, so he will sell out for money. We will not, we have all we need. Our mother gives us all the riches we desire. We listen to her, we work with her, not against her, and our harvests are good. And we will die protecting her."

"Are you Bishnoi?" Sumit asked. He had read about the Bishnois who would fight the world to protect their trees and animals.

"Who is that?" the old man asked.

Sumit explained and he shrugged, "It is not a religion, Maharao. It is commonsense. If we abuse our own land, how will it give us food and water? It is not limited to this Bishnoi tribe you talk about. There are a lot of people who live with nature."

✦ ✦ ✦

30

Trapped!

Sid and Shivam were wandering around the grounds of the haveli. They had watched Vishnu leave for office along with Girdhari. Then Sumit had driven off with Himani and Rohtash. The last to leave had been Mehak, along with Aditya. Greatly emboldened by the fact that there was no one to stop them, Sid was cajoling Shivam to drive a car, "You can do it Shivam bhaiya. How hard can it be?"

"The elders don't let me drive," said Shivam firmly.

"Oh come on!" said Sid cajoling him. "After all they did get you driving lessons."

"But I don't have the key to any car," Shivam said, slightly relieved.

Sid said, "Stay here."

Before Shivam could protest, Sid stole into the drivers' area. Thapa was fast asleep, and two drivers were playing cards. The noise of the air cooler which was working drowned the sound of the door opening. Sid grabbed the nearest bunch of car keys and sneaked out. He ran back to Shivam swinging the key bunch on his fingers, "Now all we need to do is find out which car this belongs to, and we are set to go."

Shivam hesitated. "We'll get into trouble."

"Oh c'mon Shivam bhaiya, we'll be back before anyone knows."

"Let's have lunch and then go after my mother goes to sleep. We'll be back by tea."

"Done!" Sid said happily.

They rushed into the haveli into Shivam's room and demanded lunch. Shivam's mother smiled happily. She approved of Sid, and felt he was a good influence on her son.

After lunch, they rushed out, put their air guns on the back seat of the car, along with pellets and drove out of the haveli.

"If anyone asks, we are just going to get some ice cream," said Shivam.

"But you said we'd go to the jungle in Banasur," Sid protested.

"Yeah, but no one needs to know that," Shivam smiled.

"Wah bhaiya," Sid said, thumping his back. Shivam grinned in response but kept quiet, unsure as he was of driving on a busy road.

Vaishali was completely engrossed in a movie she was watching when the guard at the gate rang her up and informed her that Shivam and Sid had taken a car out of the haveli.

"Shivam was driving? Why did you not stop them?" she raged.

She groaned slightly, wore her neck brace and rushed down to the grounds.

Himani was standing in the driveway, overseeing the loading of her personal effects into a van, in a deep discussion on her cellphone.

"Did you see Shivam and my brother?" Vaishali asked.

Himani said, "I saw them drive out about fifteen minutes ago."

"You could have stopped them!" Vaishali said.

Himani looked at her with dislike. She spoke into the phone, "Hold on, Puneet," and then shrugged as she replied sourly, "Yes I could have. But then I am not a babysitter." She hated Sumit right now and easily transferred her dislike on Vaishali and her brother.

Vaishali lost her temper and slammed her fist on the van. "If anything happens to them, I will personally see to it that you suffer." Turning, she stormed away to the garage to get Thapa to drive her to town. Thapa and the guard tried to stall her. "I have the registration number of the car. Let me first find out where they went," the guard said.

"Find out on the way!" she said impatiently. She tried Sid's number which was switched off. That confirmed her suspicion, he was definitely upto some kind of mischief.

Thapa said, "Should we not inform the Maharao?"

She bit her lip and stamped her foot. "We can do that on the way."

The two men exchanged meaningful glances and obeyed her.

She was on the way when Shivam rang her up in a state of panic.

"Yes Shivam?"

"Vaishali Bhabhi," he squeaked, his voice sounding faint and far away.

"Where are you? Why did you not take a driver? What is happening?" she replied.

The line crackled and died down. She rang again but there was no signal. In a state of panic, she rang up Sumit.

Sumit was still at the village. She told him, "Shivam and Sid have taken a car and gone somewhere. I don't know what to do. I am not able to talk to them. I keep getting the recorded voice saying there's no signal. Shivam is driving!"

"What?"

"Sumit, they are driving on their own. What if they crash? They are just kids," she said, quite forgetting that Shivam was around her age.

"Relax Vaishali, I'll just check on them. Shall I come home?"

"Yes. And when you come back please ask your sister Himani why she did not stop them. She was busy chatting with Puneet Shastri when she saw them leave. She did not even try to stop them!" she said angrily.

Sumit grimaced, "Calm down Vaish. I'll check on them." He rang up Vishnu and told him, "The boys have gone out for a drive. Can you believe it? Shivam is driving! Does he have a licence?"

"Yes, but mother won't like this," said Vishnu with a laugh. "I am glad. Mother cossettes him, she is turning him into a sissy. They'll be back after their little adventure."

Sumit laughed and agreed. He returned to the discussion he was having with the old tea stall owner and Pratham. Chandan had helped ferry some of the villagers out by boat and was expected back soon.

✦

The boys were not in store for just a little adventure.

At about 4 p.m. they parked by the river. Sid wanted to drive in further, but Shivam managed to convince him to stay near the outskirts. At a distance they could see the *shikhara* or dome of the temple. Shivam did not want to appear cowardly in front of the younger boy, but the sight of the shikhara reassured him, made him feel that he was safe. Sid marched down a well trodden path calling, "Shivam bhaiya isn't this fun?"

Shivam grinned bravely and nodded, following him. They walked deeper into the jungle, taking care to keep near the path, looking for birds or animals to shoot at. They found none. Bored they let loose some pellets at trees. It was getting darker and they were planning to return when they spotted a small hut made of mud and bricks. Intrigued, they approached it. Outside, in its makeshift courtyard there was a hand pump with a couple of plastic buckets next to it. They were thirsty, so they pumped out some water and drank it. Then Sid pumped some water into a bucket and threw it on Shivam. Shivam laughed and retaliated. While they were doing that, the water washed away some of the mud that concealed a wooden trap door.

Shivam said, "Wonder what is underneath."

Sid, who had found the expedition rather tame uptil now, had become enthusiastic. "Let's find out."

Together they pulled up the trap door. The hinges of the trapdoor were well oiled and the trapdoor opened smoothly.

"Why cover the trap door with mud?" asked Sid surprised.

"Because they had to hide something?" wondered Shivam.

They peered down, there was a wooden staircase leading down. They heard a truck drive in and froze. Some men jumped off a truck talking. Without hesitation, both of them took the stairs, closing the trapdoor as they went down.

They used their cellphone light to look around. It was a large cave like structure, piled up with timber. They waited until the voices died down and then they tried to open the trap door. But whoever had come had found the trap door exposed and had locked it and they could not open it. It was then that Shivam had panicked and rung up Vaishali.

✦

Vaishali directed Thapa to take her to the market, the movie hall and all the haunts that Sid loved to frequent. She saw no sign of the boys, not even at the ice cream parlor. When she was turning back to go home, she ran into boys from Sid's class.

"Do you know where Siddharth is?" she asked them.

"I saw him with another boy, in a Scorpio on the highway. I waved but he did not see me."

Vaishali asked, "The Nausar–Banasur highway? Are you sure?"

"Yeah, they were driving very fast and did not see me."

She sat down in the car and called Sumit. "They have taken the highway, Shivam has the Scorpio. Sumit, I am scared now."

"The highway to Banasur? Why the hell have they gone to Banasur?" Sumit screamed. "Vaish, I am ringing up Malik. Don't worry about them."

He rang up Vishnu immediately, "Shivam and Sid have driven down to Banasur, and Shivam has the Scorpio. It's a busy highway. I am phoning Malik to send someone to check. Just message me the registration number of the car they've taken."

"Damn them! I better inform my father and mother," said Vishnu anxiously.

Vishnu picked up the phone to inform his father.

Malik assured Sumit, "Sumit Sir, don't worry. My men will find them before sunset."

Sumit said, "I'll go and look."

Malik refused. "Let the police do its job, Sumit Sir. You go home and reassure your family. Please go home, they need you."

✦

Sid was investigating the underground room they were in. He whispered, "My teacher says that timber felling in the Nausar region is illegal. I wonder if these people have permission to cut so many trees."

"Sid?" said Shivam in a small voice, sitting down on some logs of wood.

"Yes?" Sid asked, trying to look for an exit route.

"You think we will die here?"

"Rubbish," said Sid stoutly.

"I could. I am weak."

Sid had a robust constitution and had never worried about his own health. He snorted derisively.

"I think I will die," said Shivam.

Sid laughed at Shivam who was sitting; his head cradled in his arms, "Of what? We are not hurt. We are not starving and we are not ill."

"I am not carrying my medicines."

Sid considered this, "When do you have to take your medicines?"

"At night, after dinner..."

"So let's find a way to get out before that," said Sid practically. Shivam was beginning to scare him. He pointed at a sliver of light coming from somewhere high up and said, "Let us climb this pile of wood and try to reach it."

They started climbing up, when some logs fell down with a deafening clatter. Both the boys froze their hearts in their mouths. Shivam opened his mouth and Sid clapped his hand on it firmly. There was complete silence. Sid whispered in his ear, "Shivam bhaiya no! People who put this wood here are criminals. They will kill us."

"I am a prince of Nausar," said Shivam.

"You will be a dead prince of Nausar if we are found by these criminals. See, they have so much wood that they will burn us in here, maybe alive."

Shivam shut up, annoyed at the truth being pointed out by a much younger boy. He said, "Let's find a way out."

They discovered a narrow passage hidden behind a pile of wood. They crept towards in when they heard a door slam shut. Both of them ducked. Shivam unslung the airgun strapped on his shoulder and Sid, all his bravado fading, took cover behind the older boy.

The door at the end of the passage opened, and a male voice said gruffly, "Who is there?"

Another voice said, "Must be a cat or something. Here, kitty. Meow, meow."

The first voice laughed, "So you know Cat Language? Come let's go, there is nothing here."

The other man said, "Wait. We can't let a cat die here. It brings nine years of bad luck, you know."

The boys sat still, too scared to breathe. They heard footsteps drawing near, and Sid panicked, backing into a pile of wood that fell, trapping the boy. He let out a scream. The sound echoed in the still room. "I told you someone is here!" said the first voice and a torch light cut through the darkness.

The other voice said impatiently, "What are you doing? Come, we need to leave before people start coming here for the evening prayers."

"Lock this place up. We will bring more lights and search it later," ordered the first voice.

✦ ✦ ✦

31

Fire

Vishnu looked at the horrified expression on his mother's face and said, "They'll be fine. Boys tend to do such things mother."

Kamala shook her head, "The boy is sick. He should not be outside without any one responsible."

"Mother, he will be okay. It is just Banasur the boys have gone to. That is just an hour away," Vishnu said.

"He has febrile convulsions," she wept.

"He has not had them since he was seven, mother. Stop trying to protect him all his life. He is a Rajput, a prince. Don't you want him to grow up and be a man?"

Devika and Himani joined them. Devika asked, "What happened?"

"Didi, Shivam has taken out a car, and is driving. He has taken no one but Siddarth with him. Sumit's young brother-in-law is just fourteen."

"Yes, I saw them go," said Himani.

"And you let them? How could you?" demanded Kamala.

Himani shrugged indifferently. Devika looked shocked.

Girdhari said sternly, "You think you are very superior, don't you? Let me tell you, Sumit's bride shows more nobility than you. She is injured but is out since afternoon, looking for those boys. And one of them is your younger brother, your cousin."

"Vaishali is out?" asked Vishnu, alarmed. "She should not be."

"I checked up as soon as you called. She left around noontime. Thankfully she took Thapa with her," said Girdhari testily, his eyes sternly on the women assembled there. "I am not surprised she did not feel the need to talk to anyone at home."

Vishnu rang her up, "Where are you Vaishali Bhabhi?"

"I am on my way to Banasur. The boys have gone there."

"I know, Sumit told me. Come back home Bhabhi. Sumit will get the boys home safe."

"Yes I know. I rang Sumit up after I met some of Sid's friends who told me they had gone to Banasur. Just a minute, hold," she said and talked to her driver. "Vishnu bhaiya we have spotted the Scorpio, it is parked in the jungle slightly ahead of the ashram. I'll ring you back," she said and disconnected.

Vishnu said, "Hello, damn the girl, she has disconnected!"

Girdhari said anxiously, "I wanted to go to the hospital to check up on Somnath, but I think we better go to Banasur first, the jungles will be dangerous in the dark."

Kamala lunged at Himani and grabbed her shirt by the neck, "You allowed my son to go out into the jungle? Would you have done that if it was your son? If anything happens to him, I will never forgive you." She began to cry as her knees gave way.

Himani said feebly, "Sumit will make it okay. He will!"

Vishnu said to the family, "There are timber thieves and poachers in the area, not to mention wild animals. Someone attacked Somnath last night in those jungles. It is a dangerous place."

Girdhari was galvanized into action. "Do you have Thapa's number? Ring him up and find out what the position is. Someone get a car out, we have to go to Banasur. Ring up Sumit and tell him to meet us there."

✦

"So what do you grow around here apart from mulberry?" Sumit asked Joginder Bauji.

"We used to grow the usual, corn, rice etc. But then young people like Saksham and others learnt things in college. Now we grow medicinal plants for pharmaceuticals. They pay well. We also grow fruits for juice companies. They have strict quality checks but we manage. It is hard work, but money is easier now. Our young do not want to leave and go live in Delhi and other big towns."

"Have you considered growing grapes? The soil and weather is good for them."

"You will have to ask the younger people. I do not do plants. I fish. The river is good, and I like spending long hours alone in a boat."

Sumit smiled, "Most men who like to spend time alone in water are philosophers. If you don't mind, I would like to spend time fishing with you once this is over."

"Maharao, your father was a king, proud and money minded. I remember him. He did not think people like us were human. But you..."

"Me what?"

"You are a farmer, one of us. Don't let anyone tell you something else. I mean it."

Sumit stared at the river, as it flowed, busy, totally disassociated with the lives and aspirations of humans, touched beyond words. He tried to find words, but the lump in his throat made it hard. Finally he said gruffly, "Thanks, I mean it."

Joginder smiled back. Pratham came cycling down the ghat at a furious pace, stopped near them, his entire being bristling with outrage and dismounted, voice hard and bitter, "Joginder Bauji, the police dog did not want medicine or fruits. He came sniffing for information. Once he learnt that the village was empty, he left. The attack may happen any moment now."

Joginder said, "They will be back in another half hour Pratham."

"I hope. What are you doing here, Maharao Sumit? Go back to your haveli. It is safer."

"My brother-in-law got attacked today, Pratham..."

"I know!" His voice was grim. "Some kids from the village saw it happen."

"Who are these attackers?" Sumit asked meeting Pratham's fierce eyes squarely and then added, "Is it Resham Shastri?"

He hawked noisily and spat on the wet steps. "That one is a neta, he will never get his hands dirty. But he will profit from all kinds of things. The younger one is a guttersnipe. He loves filth. And your brother-in-law deserved what he got. God is just. Go now, I have said too much."

Sumit's cellphone rang, it was Thapa. "Sahib, Choti Rani is not listening to sense. She has run into the jungle."

Sumit cursed profusely and then said, "Go after her man. Wait, tell me where you are."

Thapa tried to explain and it sounded incomprehensible to Sumit. He said confusedly, "What is this *lakkad-kutiya*? and where is it?"

Pratham said, "I think I know what this means. Who is there?"

Sumit handed him the phone. Pratham talked to Thapa and nodded, "You switch on the headlights of your car and keep honking. We will be there."

Sumit asked, "Where is this place?"

"The lakkad-kutiya is a hideout of timber thieves in that area. It is not a safe place. You stay here, Maharao Sumit. Send Chandan and the others to help me, once they arrive. I will get your wife back."

"I'll come with you."

Pratham sneered, "No, your highness. Please stay here, stay safe. After all, I have grown up on your family's largesse. It's time I repaid some of it. Send Chandan."

He picked up his cycle and rode into the trees. Sumit got up, asking, "Do you have more cycles?"

"Check in the village. You'll find something," Joginder said. He pointed to the specks that had appeared in the water at a distance, "They will be here soon. Go with God. I will send the others."

Sumit walked through the mulberry grove and down the path, looking for a cycle. The little child beckoned him. He ignored her and grabbed a cycle. She followed him and tugged at his sleeve.

"What?" he asked impatiently.

She pointed at the direction of a tiny goat path, barely noticeable in the thick vegetation that grew around here. It was too uneven for anyone to ride a bike through. "It is shorter and faster," she told him.

"You better be right about that," he muttered, discarding the cycle and following her.

✦

Unaware of the danger, Vaishali ran into the jungle, and promptly lost her way. She stumbled through the jungle as indiscriminate firing started. She tripped on a root and backed into a tree, scared beyond words. It was late now, and the sun was setting. Somewhere close by, Sid and Shivam were lost in the jungle and they could get hurt. Getting up, she screamed, "Sid! Shivam!" Her throat dried up as she realized that she should not have. What if her voice brought the people who were shooting to her? Were they friends or enemies? She wished she had brought Thapa with her, instead of running into the jungle impulsively. She sat down heavily and started re-assessing the situation. Of course! Saksham's tussar silk farm was close by. She would find it and get help.

A gunshot rang next to her and got embedded in the trunk of a tree, dislodging a chip of wood, which hit her like a missile near her shoulder. She screamed involuntarily in pain and she ran headlong, deeper into the jungle, away from the noise. She stopped after a while, tired, her neck hurting despite of the brace, sat down and wept. After a while she stumbled forward, trying to find the river bank. She could orient herself with the help of the river.

Meanwhile Shivam was trying desperately to move the logs of wood which pinned Sid. The boy lay very still, causing Shivam to sweat in panic. "Wake up Sid. Open your eyes," he pleaded as he pulled away another log. Somewhere the trapdoor opened and he could hear the battle raging outside, but he ignored all that and concentrated on freeing the younger boy.

Sid moaned and stirred slightly. "Damn you, you scared me!" said Shivam roughly. "Help me move the wood."

Sid groaned, "Hurts."

Shivam looked around for something to use as a lever to prise the logs away when he saw small tongues of flame. He looked at them terrified, his mouth opening and shutting wordlessly, as the strong smell of kerosene hit him. He slapped Sid hard and said, "Get up, you fool. Get up or we will die."

Outside Malik and his small police force had surrounded the hut and were converging on it. An informant had informed him of various lakkad-kutiyas at random places in the jungle, where timber thieves stored wood. He had marked the places on the detailed map of Nausar, thinking that someday it may come useful. Nehra had never told him about them. It had shaken him that the haveli's Scorpio had been found close to one of them.

He rang up the forest officer, "Good evening Nehra. I am in your jungle and can smell timber burning. You think there could be a forest fire?"

"In this season? Not possible, Malik. It rained last night. Where are you?"

"Oh a local constable calls it lakkad kutiya or some such thing," he said pleasantly. "Not to worry, I am investigating."

There was a long pause, and then Nehra's voice said in a carefully bland tone, "Where is this lakkad-kutiya?"

"I don't really know, exactly. The smoke is getting thicker."

He disconnected, hoping Nehra would take his bait. His tiny bunch of policemen needed reinforcements and asking another department for help directly never worked. Inter-departmental politics sucked.

They were approaching the cottage warily when Pratham cycled past them at full speed, jumped off allowing it to clatter down on the forest floor and rushed to the cottage, unmindful of danger. He knelt in front of the trapdoor, pushing the stone someone had covered it with.

"What the...?" said Malik and ordered two men, "Go, help him."

"Help!" came a coughing cry from the basement, galvanizing the reluctant policemen. Malik quickly rang up the fire brigade.

A group of men came from behind the cottage, two of them riding horses and the rest on cycles and a bullock cart. He recognized Chandan's distinctive build, but the rest were strangers.

Pratham threw the trapdoor open and smoke billowed out of it. There was a lull in the firing as the attackers re-grouped, possibly to call their leader or plan a retreat.

Chandan jumped down the trap door. The firing resumed now, sporadically. The police constables backed off. Most of them were unarmed and were not paid enough to risk their lives.

Air rushed in through the open trapdoor and the fire blaze intensified.

✦ ✦ ✦

32

Rescue

Sejal Banasur was driving down the ghat when she heard gunfire. She parked her car and sat in it, scared that the firing was directed at her. She quickly slid the map on which she had been marking various roads and locations of the lakkad-kutiyas into the tear in the seat cover of the car. She planned to upload this on the internet, once she had enough funds to get away safely. What she was doing was risky, she knew it, but she banked on the fact that Chanchal Shastri was a fool, and that being a politician he would be unwilling to get his hands dirty.

The feelers had been sent time and again, even when Digvijay had been alive. But they had come in a round-about way. She had held out for a long time, until it had become clear that though the old man would finance her expenses, though he would foster her son and give her some pin money, he would not leave her with enough, should he die before her. Once that was clear, she had had a talk with Aditya. He had rightly pointed out; the timber thieves would go ahead and deplete the forests of trees with or without their tacit approval, so it made sense to agree. After all, once these forests were theirs.

She looked around and prudently switched off the headlights. The river flowed on unconcerned by the antics of the humans who thought they owned it or the land on which it flowed. She sat in the car debating what to do.

She had never dealt with the timber thieves directly. Aditya had talked to some middle man, who would come on the 4th of every month and hand them a cheque. Once Digvijay died, Chanchal Shastri came to meet her. It was then that she realized that he was behind the timber mafia in the state. The man was an idiot. Some people are born for intrigue; some learn it as they grow. Some think they are so smart, that they end up being very obvious. Chanchal Shastri was the third sort. He thought he was a master intriguer. At first, she was tempted to smile and let it pass. But then he said, "You must be lonely. How will you manage? I can help pass your nights."

Her lips tightened to a thin line as she recalled that crass offer. She had stood up and showed him the door. Aditya had laughed when she had told him about it. Really, growing up in Digvijay's haveli had made him more of a businessman and less of a royal. Mehak was a bad influence on him, too. She lowered the window of her car to let in fresh air. Mehak... she did not know if she liked her and approved of her as her son's wife, but was a realist. They would go ahead and marry whether she liked it or not, so she had to make the best of it.

She heard male laughter and Vaishali's angry reply, close by but indistinct. She took her gun out of the dashboard and got out of the car. What was Vaishali doing here? It was nearly sundown and the jungle area was dangerous.

Vaishali had walked through the jungle, orienting herself to the sound of the river. She was nearly at the bank when she heard Puneet say, "The night suits you, natural camouflage for the kaali billi." She looked around in the darkness, but could see no sign of him.

"Who else is with you, Puneet?" Vaishali asked.

"Why did you not leave town? You should have. Instead you married that man and settled here," he continued as he stepped towards her, along with his friends. The flames and wood smoke at a distance cast an eerie look to the entire area.

"What do you want, Puneet?" she asked.

"Revenge of course," he replied with a laugh. "You should have died when that stone rolled down at you. They say a cat has nine lives. I don't want to try nine times. So, here it is kaali billi, my best offer. You run, and we will catch you. The one who catches you gets to rape you first."

Sejal crept closer, age had dimmed her eyes, and she wanted to be sure she did not miss. A smile came on her face as she heard the scorn in Vaishali's voice, as she replied, "You were always a sleaze ball."

"And you are a whore, sold to the highest bidder."

A slight sound of movement, and then Vaishali's voice came, slightly closer "It was you who shot me and killed that man in the party?"

"That idiot was supposed to make you a widow on the day of your marriage. Well he's dead now, no loss to the world!"

A friend of Puneet said, "Come on Puneet, let's go. Someone will see us."

Sejal stepped forward, "Someone already has, and heard your confession too. Get behind me Vaishali."

"The royal whore has come to help you," Puneet said, laughing wildly as he lunged at Vaishali. Sejal took careful aim and shot at him. He fell down with a cry.

"Is he dead?" Vaishali whispered, shocked.

"No, just scratched. I am a sharp-shooter. I know what I am doing."

"I am dying. Help!" he screamed.

Vaishali slapped him, "Shut up, you oaf. You!" she pointed at his companions who were slinking off, "Take him home and get him something for his injury. Now!"

They fled leaving Puneet there. Vaishali smiled a grim smile, "Puneet, just like old times. Your buddies have run away. Now what do you have to say to that?"

Sumit said coldly, "I think he has a lot of talking to do, but not right now. Vaishali, are you okay? What's happened, Sejal Aunty?"

Vaishali was too overcome to say anything. She ran into his arms sobbing loudly, "You took your own time coming. Why?"

He hugged her, trying to console her. Taking advantage of their distraction, Puneet picked himself up painfully and limped into the darkness.

Once she had mastered her emotions, Vaishali turned, finding Puneet missing, she said, "Where is that asshole?"

Sejal said, "He left. I let him go. His car must be close by."

Vaishali said, "Thank you Sejal aunty."

"What are you doing here at this time?" Sejal asked.

So they told her. She said, "I hope they aren't trapped at the lakkad-kutiya nearby. That is where the firing is coming from."

"Give me directions, Sejal aunty and please take Vaish and go home. Vaish, I'll get them back safe. I promise."

She shook her head and rang up Aditya and told him, "Sid and Shivam are at the lakkad kutiya, the one near the mulberry farm. I think the thieves have set the basement on fire. You need to get there."

"Follow the smoke, Sumit. I'll take Vaishali back to the haveli."

Sumit looked around for the little girl who had led him here, but she was not there. Perhaps she had gone back to the village. He entered the jungle, finding his way to the fire. It was a short distance away, but there were too many bushes and trees, so he had to walk carefully through what should have been a five minute distance.

Malik was standing there, grim faced, barking orders at a completely mismatched force of forest officials, cops and villagers. Sumit said, "There is only one way this can work. We have to drive our cars right into that hut and then jump out."

Malik said, "We have just two jeeps, Sumit Sahib, and we can't risk our hawaldaars."

Aditya who had joined him nodded and rushed to his car, started it and drove it right next to the hut and using the car as a shield, he got out on the other side. The smoke from the basement was thick and choking. He crept close to it, recognizing Pratham who was already there, trying to peer in, his eyes watering. A hand reached out and both Pratham and Aditya grabbed it and pulled. Together they hauled Shivam out. He was coughing and choking. The boy raised his soot streaked face to him and pointed at the basement, "Sid and Chandan Pandit," he said between choking coughs.

Adi peered over the edge again and called, "Chandan? Where are you man?"

A loud noise of crashing wood shook the dirt floor and he cursed as he backed off. The smoke billowed out and he could smell the kerosene. For a few minutes which seemed like hours, there was no sound from the basement. A mud wall of the hut collapsed right near them. Pratham said roughly, "Get into the car, both of you."

Shivam opened his mouth to protest, when they heard a faint voice, "Help!"

Pratham yelled, "Chandan, I am here!"

"Pull the boy up carefully; he is hurt!" Chandan Pandit called back. Together Pratham and Aditya grabbed Sid and gently pulled him out. Then they helped Chandan out. The man's hands were badly charred. They climbed into the car, which was, by now pockmarked with bullets and drove out at top speed, not stopping until they reached behind the police cars.

Malik was rubbing his hands in glee as Nehra joined him. "And they told me in Mumbai nothing happens in Nausar!"

"Nothing did until you came," Nehra said sourly.

Malik said softly, "I often wondered why the Forest Department did nothing but moan about illegal felling. Unmarried daughters are a huge responsibility, aren't they?"

Nehra pretended not to hear as he barked orders, "You, use the hand pump, fill up water and pour it into the basement." He pointed at the villagers and said, "We need dirt, lots of mud. It will help stop the fire from spreading."

Malik turned away to check up on the boys and Chandan. Sumit was helping them into his uncle's car. He stopped

Malik, "They need medical treatment. I know you want their statements, you'll get them tomorrow."

He nodded, and stepped away to allow Girdhari to take the injured people away in his car. Chandan said, "S.P. Sahib, there is no one of ours trapped in there."

He started barking orders, "Has the route to the river been blocked? Good! Take aim and fire at the feet. No one should be allowed to run away."

Sumit and Vishnu walked away from the hut. At a distance, a crowd gathered watching the action. They went and joined them, and turned to look at the hut, it was in flames now, and Malik was barking orders into a megaphone. Most of the thieves had melted into the forest, but some had been injured and were unable to flee.

Sumit spotted Resham who was standing near his parked car looking anxiously in the direction of the hut. Sumit walked up to him, "The timber is all burnt Resham. It's a total loss."

"Be careful of your accusations Maharao, you can't prove a thing!"

"This is India, Resham. Nothing is ever proved conclusively, especially against our netas."

Resham smirked.

"But then, some things even the netas can't hide. Your younger brother carried out a poorly planned campaign against me and my wife. He is hurt. And worse, he has confessed. I suggest you carry out some housekeeping there and forget this for the time being..."

Resham scowled as he watched Sumit join Vishnu and got into his car and drove away.

He entered the living room to see his grandfather and father sitting looking worried as his wife raged and ranted.

"Why did she give him so much money?" she demanded shrilly.

"What is happening here?" he asked.

"I found this in Puneet's wardrobe!" she said pointing at wads of thousand rupee notes. "Go on, count them. They are about seven lakh rupees. He says Himani Puri from the haveli gave him this money. I want to know why."

Resham looked appalled, his worse fears realized, "Where is that idiot?"

Chanchal protested, "Oh come on, he is just a boy. I am sure that money was for something completely harmless and innocent."

"Shut up you fool!" said Keval Shastri. "Puneet was brought home by his friends. He has been shot and he will not say who did it and why. I have a bad feeling about this, Resham."

Muttering curses under his breath, Resham walked into Puneet's room. Puneet was asleep. He walked out and asked, "Where are his friends?"

Keval Shastri nodded in approval. The young man was astute. "I have already got one of them in the basement. The other one is being picked up. Come with me."

They got up and walked away to the office situated away from the main house. Resham locked the door behind them, and said, "The police have found one of the lakkad-kutiyas. There is fighting going on. The timber is burnt, completely."

Keval picked up a pen and spun it around on the table, then asked, "How bad?"

"Amol has been shot in the thigh. He could not flee. Sarna is dead."

"Send someone to pick up both their sons. They will live here."

Resham nodded. That would ensure Amol's loyalty and silence. Then Keval lowered himself slowly in his chair. He was getting old for this. Things never got better. Sometimes he felt that he kept running in one place to just keep going on. Perhaps it would have been better if he had turned down Digvijay's offer a long time ago to campaign against Paramjeet Banasur. But the man had been desperate, consumed with jealousy and very very persuasive. The money he had offered had been tempting too.

"Resham?"

"Yes *Daadu*?"

There was a slight knock on the door. Two young boys were ushered in, nervous and guilty, along with Puneet.

Resham opened his mouth and shut it as his grandfather frowned.

"Tell the truth, the complete truth."

Puneet stepped forward, his voice trembling, "She insulted me all through school. People forgot my name, I was known as Fishy, to some people I am still Fishy," his voice quavered with anger.

"What exactly did you do, and how many people know about it?" asked Keval coldly.

His confession left them stunned. Resham started raging and ranting, but Puneet's eye was fixed on his grandfather, who looked weary. Then Keval said, "Puneet, you have to leave the country, you understand? It is too dangerous for you to stay here anymore."

Puneet nodded and asked, "Daadu, my friends?"

"They will have to leave Nausar. I will be talking to both your parents. I will arrange for your admissions into colleges in Delhi or Bangalore under some quota or the other. If it ever comes to my ears that you talked about this..."

The boys trembled.

✦ ✦ ✦

33

Denouement

Sumit walked into his rooms to see Vaishali lying in bed, with Sejal and Mehak sitting on the bed around her. "How cozy," he remarked sinking into the couch.

"Sid?" Vaishali asked.

"He's fine. Girdhari Uncle has taken him to the hospital."

She looked anxious, tried to sit up, but Mehak restrained her. "You sleep. We'll wake you up and get you to talk to those two brats at the earliest."

Sejal got off the bed elegantly, adjusted her anarkali and walked into the sitting room, glancing at them. Such was the effect of her personality that both Sumit and Mehak followed her meekly and sat down on the sofa as she took the armchair.

"Sejal Auntie, why?" he asked. She smiled a sad smile, but did not reply. "Actually I should have asked Why now?" he persisted.

She looked away in silence.

"It set you free, did it not? The only thing I don't understand is the timing, why now? Please Sejal Auntie, I want to know."

"You can think what you want," she said with an elegant shrug. Sumit gripped her slim shoulders and said, "Aditya said that my father was going to the club. He never went to clubs. And the Nausar club is full of government servants, not exactly his cup of tea."

She nodded.

"He was coming to meet you wasn't he?"

"Yes, now can you please stop pinching me?" she said shrugging her shoulder away.

"After all these years...I know that you would have wanted to harm him many times. He really did you in. But why now?"

She turned and raised an impeccable brow, without any word.

"He treated Adi better than he treated me, Sejal Auntie." he persisted. "You know when I was younger; I wished you were my mother. Then Aditya and I would have been blood brothers."

She gave a soft wistful smile and patted his cheek. "You were always so loving and loyal." Then she added in a harder voice, "Think what you will Sumit."

"Leave her Sumit," said Mehak in a hard voice, she had a small pistol in her hand, and it was pointed at his chest.

"Oh my God, I suspected the wrong woman. Mehak, do you have a license for that thing."

"Sit down, Sumit." she said coldly.

"Mehak, put that gun down," said Sejal anxiously. "It is okay child. Where is Adi?"

Mehak continued, "You know why daddy brought Aditya home when we were kids? He was just a hostage, to ensure that his mother.... Yes he made Aditya Director Purchase, but that was to insult you, Sumit."

"Easy Mehak," he said warily. Like many Rajput princesses, she was a really good shot.

Sejal sat down on the armchair, her face in her hands. "Mehak who did you ring up to inform that our father was visiting Banasur?" Sumit asked.

"What? No one! I thought..."

He sat down wearily and said, "So, you were not behind Devious Singh's death? God, this is like a maze."

Mehak laughed harshly and said, "Oh my God! He deserved to die but I had no part to play in that."

"It was just the timber. That is all you people were doing!"

"They are our lands, were our lands. We were paid to look the other way, to allow the felling, that is all," said Sejal. "We did not do anything."

"Let me think this through. Resham Shastri wanted the timber, easy money to fund the expenses of the assembly elections. Perhaps the poaching was also something he was involved with. The protest at the Royal site was just misdirection. But then, someone informed a killer about the old man's early morning drive to Banasur...and got him killed."

"Mother went to the temple and prayed for Sejal Auntie's death. She kept howling in front of the idols each and every time daddy..." Mehak explained.

"And God bribed a poor foolish driver to run a truck through the old man's car? What rubbish!" Sumit said with a snort.

Sejal said slowly, "I heard she organized a yagna for my death. Yagnas are not performed alone. Other people sit and participate too."

"Let me guess, Himani and Rohtash must have attended it. Did Somnath attend it too?" Mehak asked. "He is very chummy with the Shastris."

Sumit said, "Mehak, just inform everyone to assemble in the baithak. We have to have a story ready for Malik. The man is too sharp by half. And where is my wife's maid?"

"I sent her to get something made for Vaishali. She's exhausted."

"Right. Stay here until I come back. And have the maid sleep next to Vaish."

Vaishali said, "Where are you going?"

"To meet Sant Anirudh and Malik, it has to be done right now. Adi is there too. I'll get him to the haveli."

Sejal nodded, "They know about this lakkad-kutiya. It is because of this one that Chandan Pandit keeps wandering around, even in the night. But they don't know about the others."

"You did, did you not? You informed Malik."

She nodded. "I could not allow the state to be destroyed. The duty of royalty."

"You were playing a dangerous game."

She laughed. "It was fun."

"You have to stay here until this blows over. We'll get your clothes tomorrow."

"Your mother..." said Sejal with a slight grimace.

"She need not bother you," said Sumit firmly. "Adi has his rooms there, you can stay with him. Or, if you accept my invitation, you can stay in my wing. It won't be for long."

He told Gul to take him to the temple and settled down in the back seat. Aditya rang him up, "Your brother-in-law has fractured his leg."

"My father-in-law is going to get on my case now," said Sumit ruefully. First Vaishali and then Sid, it seemed like proximity to him was proving dangerous for them. "Shivam is okay. Chandan had burns but nothing serious. I am dropping him back to the ashram," Aditya said.

"And?" asked Sumit, sensing that there was more.

"Sumit, Somnath is in a bad shape. I don't think he is going to survive. And his mother is bad mouthing you. She seems to think you got him attacked."

Sumit let out a deep sigh. "Explain it to her that we have witnesses and soon there will be confessions that prove otherwise, Adi. Damn the man! He will try to harm us even on his death bed."

The ashram was silent, even the customary lamps had not been lit. He entered and Pratham was sitting on the dispensary stairs. "Is it over?" he asked.

"I think so."

"I warned you Maharao."

"So you did Pratham."

"Chandan could have died."

"He saved my brothers. I would not let him die," Sumit said.

"You are not God, Maharao."

"God does not run this town, Maharao does," said Chandan as he limped up to the dispensary stairs and sat down.

"How are you Chandan?" Sumit asked.

"I was lucky. The boy was not. He was trapped under a lot of wood. For a moment there I thought he would burn alive."

"I thank you and offer you my help." Chandan looked at Sumit enquiringly, who added, "You are not brahman, are you?"

Chandan looked up, warily. Sant Anirudh, who was sitting in the shadows spoke, "No, he was not born a brahman, none of these three were. Those were times when the most important thing was to keep them safe and alive. I did what I had to, I kept them safe, all five of them."

Sumit looked at them wondering at the courage it must have taken. Anirudh added, sadly, "Amol knew, his home is near the home that adopted their siblings."

Pratham said roughly, "I am Sikh by birth, my name was Preet and Jassi, my younger brother was adopted by a really good family in the village. The same people adopted Azra, Chandan's sister."

Sumit started pacing up and down. No wonder they had kept shut about the timber. This could lead to riots! Then he said, "Sant ji, the world outside is harsh and cruel. It does not run the same way as you run your ashram. You will have to let him go!" Anirudh winced, and Sumit added, "For the sake of the ashram and those boys you are raising you will have to. Chandan, I seem to remember that you went to school."

"We are both qualified ayurvedic doctors," Pratham said. "Speak up man!"

Chandan looked up with trapped eyes, "I was not even six, you understand? I am a brahman since I was six."

"It won't matter if the truth comes out. You have to go away, far away. You seem like a sensible fellow, Pratham.

Make him understand. Meet me tomorrow. We are setting up a vineyard in Nashik. I will help you both set up an ayurvedic dispensary there."

At eleven, everyone started assembling in the Baithak, apart from Shivam and Sid who were at the hospital along with the Bhatias and Kamala who were spending the night attending to them.

The mood was weary and sombre. Sumit entered and there was sudden silence. Girdhari said, "Sumit, thank God the boys and you are safe."

Then he stopped and stared at Aditya who walked in with Sejal and Mehak. "Is it over?"

Sumit sat down wearily, "Perhaps it is. Siddharth nearly got killed. The doctors say that..."

Maharani Devika cut in, not concerned with Sid's safety, "So my suspicion was correct. She is behind all this!"

He shook his head and said, "No. First of all, I would like to publicly apologize to Sejal Auntie. I suspected at first that she was behind the Maharao's death. I was wrong, sorry."

He looked at Himani and his glance shifted to Mehak and then back to Himani, "It was a woman's act, to inform Devious Singh's enemies that he was going to Banasur; a woman's act, but not a very intelligent one. Sooner or later, someone would ask how Maharao's plan to meet his lady friend was leaked. But then you were not thinking, were you Madam? You were just consumed with jealousy, that even at this age, the Maharao chose to prefer her company not yours?"

"What? This is preposterous! I am a God fearing woman," snapped Devika indignantly.

"Yes. And your priests are your humble servants. You prayed, you wept, you performed yagnas and paid them huge sums of money, and you talked about how badly your husband treated you."

Himani said in a horrified tone, "No! It could not be Sant Anirudh. He is a saint! Besides what would he gain out of killing daddy?"

"Chanchal Shastri was his other faithful disciple and our father was a thorn in his flesh. It would be a simple matter for someone close to the Sant to leak out the whereabouts of Devious Singh to Shastri."

Maharani Devika was looking at Sejal and Aditya with acute dislike. "She must have told the Shastris. They are also from Banasur," she said.

"You know," said Sumit conversationally. "At one point in time I thought so, too. But then, the shooter at my engagement missed me. His dead body surfaced on our roof, perhaps punishment for missing me. The entire thing was too tacky. Aditya is very subtle and very efficient, and Sejal Auntie is classy. Nothing they do can be so crass."

"Why, thank you!" murmured Sejal faintly, as Adi choked.

Girdhari said, "I find it hard to believe that Sant Anirudh could do anything like this."

"But then the old man is perhaps sixty five or seventy years old. His assistants are younger." Vishnu said thoughtfully.

"Oh that they are," agreed Girdhari. "It must have been easy for Chanchal to subvert them."

Aditya said, "It must have been Resham. He always said that the old man was a snake and you were a panther."

"The man is a wildlife enthusiast," observed Sumit. "No wonder he wanted to raise environmental issues."

"Madam, have you met the Shastris outside the temple, ever?" he asked Devika.

She shook with rage, "How dare you?"

"Answer the question! You, Himani?"

Devika said "I have never met them alone. They are just politicians."

"Yes, and small time thieves. Himani answer the question!"

"I met Resham often, with Somnath and Puneet too..." she whispered.

"You fool!" Rohtash said.

"So what do you plan now?" asked Girdhari.

"Malik will be here in the morning to ask questions. The man is tenacious. It is not easy to pull wool over his eyes. We have to convince him that we had nothing to do with the Shastris."

Rohtash said, "But mother used to visit the Ashram daily. That is not possible. And then Himani..."

"I know. Madam, you will have to show anger, very great anger towards the Shastris. You shall accuse Somnath of leading your daughters astray, and putting your nephew and your daughter-in-law, Vaishali's brother in danger."

Rohtash said, "Black magic. Accuse Resham and Somnath of consulting tantrics, of using black magic to strike fear and destroy Nausar."

"Excellent idea, Rohtash. I told you that your skills lay not in business," said Sumit.

Maharani Devika nodded frostily and left the room. Girdhari and Himani went after her. Vishnu said softly, "She will be okay. She just does not like to be in the wrong."

He held out a hand to Aditya, "I don't presume to understand all that happened or why you were there, but I thank you for protecting my brother and Sidharth." They shook hands and he left along with Rohtash.

Sumit said, "My family has demanded and taken a lot from you, Aditya and Sejal Auntie. Can I make one more request? I want you to leave town at the earliest."

"I expected that," Aditya said stony faced.

"Coronet has a vinyard in Cote D Azure. It does not have a good administrator. We need someone we trust. Can you, Aditya?"

"I..."

"Of course you will take this hell cat with you," he nodded at his sister. Mehak smiled.

"Madam, I do not wish to uproot you at your age. But the Shastris will retaliate. It is not safe here."

Sejal gave a delighted laugh. "Uproot? Of course not. I hate this place. I think I'd like to go on a world cruise or something."

"It is settled then. I'll meet you at lunch tomorrow," he said folding his hands in a namaste, and walked to the door.

It was late in the night that it occurred to Vaishali. She sat up and shook Sumit, "That night in the apartment, who cut the gas pipe?"

"Depend upon it, some one must have prayed to dieties, and performed yagnas to hurt me. And the Gods must have decided to make the wish come true." Sumit replied cryptically. "Go to sleep now."

✦ ✦ ✦

34

An Unlikely Visitor

It was very early, about 7 a.m. when a tentative knock woke Sumit up. He got up and crept to the door to avoid disturbing Vaishali. The servant said, "Visitors for you Maharao."

He said, "Set some chairs in the garden and make them comfortable. Send them some tea."

He grinned in triumph. Yes things were falling into place.

He joined the Shastris in the garden in about half an hour. Chanchal Shastri had not come, but Keval Shastri had come along with Resham.

"Good morning," he said joining them.

"I had heard that you are an early riser, so we took a chance." Kewal Shastri said trying to rise from his chair. "No, please Sir, keep sitting," said Sumit courteously, as he sat down and poured a cup of tea.

Resham was sitting at the edge of his chair, looking extremely uncomfortable. Sumit concealed a smile.

Kewal Shastri said, "I deeply regret the events of the last few weeks. I have come to tell you that we are no longer supporting the protests at the Royal site."

Sumit smiled and asked, "The protest was giving us so much mileage. But I can understand that after the uncovering of illegal timber you would like to stay away from the limelight."

Resham said, "We were not involved. Just because you and that SP are friends you framed us."

"Really? I was not aware of that. But then if it's just a frame up, the statements of the timber thieves should correct such attempts so why worry?"

"I tell you we were framed. Why would we need to steal our own timber, it belongs to us, our state!"

"Indeed!" said Sumit, rocking his chair back and forth, a smile on his face.

Kewal kept quiet watching Sumit, as Resham tried to bluster. Then he smiled a wintery smile, "I should have taken out some time to meet you once you came back. I have a proposal for you, would you care to listen to it?"

"I have a deal for you, if you agree to it; I will listen to your proposal."

He laughed, "Like father, like son! What is your deal?"

"An eye for an eye. My father was killed; my brother-in-law brutally beaten within inches of his life, my young brother-in-law is in the hospital. I demand retribution. Amol and Deepak Sarna."

"Done, Deepak Sarna is dead," said Kewal. He had been expecting something of that sort. Resham spluttered in protest but held his tongue.

"There have been two attempts on my life, and one on my wife's. Should any more such attempts happen, I have witnesses, evidence to certain acts that may prove very embarrassing for your party Sir."

"I see. I will definitely pray for your safety."

"I thank you. My wife will be delighted to hear this. Prayers remind me, the Shiv Temple and Ashram. We have vested interest in keeping its reputation pristine pure, don't you agree?"

"I agree. My proposal is simple; we should be seen together as friends. It would do both our families good."

"I agree."

"Then we have an understanding. We will take our leave now." The old man got up and Resham quietly followed him out.

"One minute, Shastri Uncle," The old man turned and looked at him. He stood up and said, "Nausar has very little to offer to young men with excess energy and emotional unstability. I really think Puneet should study abroad. Cambridge would make a man of him." He shrugged and said, "It is just a suggestion."

Kewal Shastri looked at the grim eyes so much at variance with the smiling face. He said, "Puneet is already preparing for his trip to Australia. He wants to study at Melbourne."

"I am glad to hear that," he said softly.

Once the Shastris got into the car, Resham turned to his grandfather and burst out, "You agreed to everything he said. He is setting up Rohtash against us. You should have made him stop that."

"Shut up! He has evidence against you and your father. Chanchal is a fool, but even you underestimated this son of Digvijay's."

"He is bluffing!"

"Do you want to try and call his bluff?" the old man asked icily. Resham fell silent. "We are politicians, Resham. Unlike businessmen, we do not have to show results at the end of every financial year. We play a bigger game. Right now, we have to survive and regain credibility. We shall fight another day."

Resham nodded.

"Next time you plan something, discuss it with me and not your father, Resham. I have ambitions for you; you will be the Prime Minister one day. Don't mess it up by listening to Chanchal."

"Yes Grandfather." The younger man's eyes were full of dreams. Kewal looked out of the window, grim faced. Chanchal would have to be sidelined; he was too closely associated with Amol and Deepak, who would be announced as kingpins of this scam. Kewal Shastri did not intend these events to ruin his life's work.

✦ ✦ ✦

35

Board Meeting

The EGM was convened at 1100 hours at the board room of Royal One, the parent hotel of Royal Hotels and Resorts.

It was attended by the following:

Yuvraj Girdhari Singh, Finance Director.

Yuvraj Vishnu Singh, Additional Executive Director.

Yuvrani Mehak, Yuvrani Himani and Rohtash Singh, Members of the Board.

Aditya Singh Banasur, Director Purchase and Adhoc Member of the Board, acting as the Secretary.

The Bank was represented by its executive directors, Mr. S. Ramnath and Mr. Y.S. Subramaniam, who had specially flown over from Mumbai to attend the meeting.

Agenda

- The induction of Yuvraj Sumit Singh, Son of Late Maharao Digvijay Singh Nausar as Chairman of Royal Hotels and Resorts.

- The delay in the construction of the Resort in Hill Top, Nausar.

- The financial viability of the project and losses incurred putting the fiscal health of the group in duress.

- Any other matter to be put forward with the permission of the board.

Once the board was convened, Girdhari placed before the board the matter of Yuvraj Sumit Singh taking over as Chairman of the Board.

Vishnu seconded him. The rest of the board members voted for him, and the motion was passed.

Mr. Subramaniam said, "I express deepest condolences on the death of the late chairman on behalf of the Bank. I respected his business acumen a lot. I have certain apprehensions. First, the EGM has been delayed, and second, we know little about Mr. Sumit Singh personally. I have reservations. But the bank will not object to the appointment."

"Oh he is his father's son. You have nothing to fear. He will lead us to greater successes," said Girdhari proudly.

Sumit took a deep breath but kept his peace. The banker bowed his head to acknowledge this and said, "As for the Resort getting delayed. The bank is worried, Girdhari ji."

"As Chairman of the board, I assure you that the matter will be sorted out and the resort will be up in record time," Sumit spoke up.

"Maharao, may I ask how? The News Channels are telecasting the protest. Your shares are plummeting down."

"Not any more. Now that the Shastris have backed down, the protests are fizzling out."

Subramaniam shifted in his chair uncomfortably. His Chairman had been adamant. "Sir, I will have to raise the interest rate if the matter is not resolved within fifteen days."

"But of course."

"With the permission of the Board, I would like to place a matter for consideration," said Sumit.

"As acting Chairperson, I permit it," said Girdhari.

Sumit put his proposal in front of them. He had already thrashed it out with Brian."Coronet is an international wine brand. The balance sheets of Coronet have been placed before you all for your reference. Our market is huge, and we are doing well. I propose a merger of sorts. The details can be worked out to our mutual satisfaction, but it will require Mr. Brian Underwood to be member of the board. And I have a lot of employees in the UK and France who will be absorbed in the group."

Vishnu thought it over. The bankers whispered among themselves. They had seen it coming, but not this fast. Girdhari was stunned.

"It is logical," said Vishnu slowly. "But of course you would wish it. I cannot see any problem on paper, but it will require a lot of administrative work. My only reservation is on inducting Brian as a board member."

"We have studied the Coronet, Maharao. The bank approves, but we still place the proposal of our own man as a Director on the table," said Subramaniam.

Vishnu said carefully, "Sumit, why induct Brian as a Board Member of Royal? State your reasons please."

"Brian comes. That is non-negotiable. He is an excellent administrative man, and it would do us good to have an international face. If that is agreed to, Coronet agrees to pre-pay the two of Royal's smaller loans. If that is done, the bank has no reason to raise the interest rates."

"Those for the motion," Aditya moved hastily, pre-empting any protests.

Mehak moved for it, so did a chastened Himani, followed by Rohtash. After some hesitation, so did Vishnu. The bankers went into an intense discussion and then Mr. Subramaniam said. "We accept the board's decision for now. We will review the situation after the next financial quarter. It is the bank's desire to have a member on the board. A lot of our money is invested here, as such we would like to have voting rights."

"Certainly, the matter will be placed in front of the Board at the AGM," said Aditya pleasantly.

The bankers then rose and made a move. They had to catch a flight back.

Once they left, Girdhari voiced his doubts, "Never, even in those days when we had nothing but some crumbling property, have the bankers had so much power over us. And you want to give them more?"

Vishnu said, "Father, do you realize that merging the Coronet under the Royal flagship will have our shares sky rocket in the market. We will finally have an international presence! A seat on the board for Brian is a small price to pay."

"I have lived too long," Girdhari said with a slump of his shoulders. "My brother is dead and perhaps I should retire."

Sumit looked at him for a long moment. Girdhari was looking at Devious Singh's portrait with a wistful expression. He said in a soft tone, "Uncle, you are the anchor of Royal. We need you, your experience is invaluable. And no one has a better financial head than you."

"No son, the world is yours, not mine now," he said and got up to leave the room.

"Uncle, the resort that is coming up, alongside that, I am planning to set up a world class farm of medicinal herbs, the heritage of Nausar. Won't you stay on the board to watch it come up?"

Girdhari smiled, "I am retiring son. But this is an interesting project. I will not be on the board, but it seems like a great place for Kamala and me to spend the rest of our lives."

With that, he left the room.

Sumit looked at Vishnu and Aditya and asked, "What will mollify this old man? Should I step aside and make him Chairman?"

Aditya grinned and said, "No! He does not have any such ambitions."

"Then?"

Vishnu grinned, "A grandson from you would thaw him completely."

"Oh no! My wife will kill me! It's too early!" he said in horror.

They both laughed. "What? The great Sumit Singh is scared of his wife?" Vishnu teased him.

He first looked defiant and then sheepishly admitted, "Yes, I certainly am."

✦ ✦ ✦